AN ED BECKETT COMEDY MYSTERY

DEADFALL

B.J. BALFOUR

Ebook ISBN 979-8-9898502-4-2

Paperback ISBN 979-8-9898502-5-9

Cover by Adrijus Guscia

Gargoyle logo by Eucalyp

BOOKS BY BRUCE BALFOUR

<u>HISTORICAL NOVELS</u>

The River of Eternity (Book 1 of The Harem Conspiracy)

The House of Death (Book 2 of The Harem Conspiracy)

The Revenge of Sekhmet (Book 3 of The Harem Conspiracy) – coming

<u>SCIENCE FICTION NOVELS</u>

The Forge of Mars

The Digital Dead (sequel to *The Forge of Mars*)

Prometheus Road (Young Adult)

<u>THRILLER NOVELS</u>

Burning Season

<u>HUMOROUS MYSTERIES</u>

(as B.J. Balfour)

Deadfall

ONE

B etelgeuse is the brightest star in the constellation of Orion. It's a
bright red supergiant; a rare form of star that's billions of years old.
Nearing the end of its life, it's the largest type of star in the sky, and among
the brightest, which seems to say something about old age. When the end
comes, the star goes out with a bang as a supernova – a flashy event that
really shakes up the neighbors.

The glittering red light from Betelgeuse completed a five-hundred-year
journey to Southern California when it shot through a small telescope to
strike Ed Beckett in the eye. Ed was unharmed, but impressed by the stellar
performance.

When a dark shape blotted out the starlight, Beckett blinked and the
object dropped on past his field of view. He knew it wasn't a cloud; it was
moving too fast, and clouds usually don't plummet. Maybe an airplane,
but he hadn't seen any lights. Marine Corps Air Station El Toro was only a
few miles inland from Newport Beach, so it could have been a military jet.
Curious. Whatever it was, he forgot about it as he stood up straight and
tried to work the kinks out of his neck. He was only in his thirties, but an

hour of peering through the telescope on that warm September evening made him feel as if he had the neck of a much older man.

Beckett took a step back, then tensed up when something yelped and darted around his feet. Remembering Jose, the brown Chihuahua that lived there, he stumbled in his attempt to avoid stepping on the little dog, and managed to ram his big toe into a decorative lava rock boulder that bordered the garden.

Beckett screamed. Although brief, it was a complicated scream that expressed surprise, pain, and anger all at once – a work of art as screams go – and he focused its energy like a laser on Jose's head as he hopped around on one foot.

Undaunted by Beckett's performance, Jose pushed his food dish around in circles with his nose. The aluminum dish screeched like fingernails on a blackboard as Jose nudged it around on the rough concrete decking by the pool. The sound set Beckett's already frayed nerves on edge.

As the pain subsided, Beckett took a deep breath and plopped into the nylon webbing of a lawn chair that creaked under his weight. He gazed out over the still surface of the pool and massaged his foot as a breeze rustled through the bushes, attracting the little dog's attention. Jose's brain cell fired again, so he forgot about the food dish and scurried away to sniff out potential feline intruders in his domain.

The air smelled of chlorine and brine. A few hundred yards beyond the Mediterranean-style house, painted Navajo white with a red tile roof, waves boomed and hissed against the sandy beach – a relaxing sound that Beckett enjoyed. Offshore, the distant work lights of an oil platform shimmered like beacons over the black water. Palm trees whispered in the breeze. During the day, red hibiscus and purple passiflora blooms hovered over white lilies and bright pansies in a loud riot of color punctuated with chunks of black lava rock, but their colors were muted now under the calm blanket of night.

He'd enjoyed his little vacation, house-sitting for the Carvers, but they were due to come back from Europe in two days. The idea of returning to his cramped apartment in Fountain Valley depressed him; a recent earthquake had knocked most of his 7,408 neatly filed books from their shelves and he didn't have the energy to sort them in Dewey-sanctioned order.

A whistle got Beckett's attention. He glanced around, but couldn't identify the source. When the whistle got louder, he realized it was coming from overhead. He stood and squinted at the moonless sky, remembering the falling object he'd seen in the telescope. He saw nothing unusual at first – then a dim shape appeared. From the dark yard, it looked like a falling tree.

Beckett lurched backward.

The dark mass thundered into the pool and an enormous wave knocked him off his feet.

Feeling adrenaline surge through his body, the dripping Beckett sprinted to the back wall of the house, almost twisting his ankle on another lava rock. He flipped a switch and light bloomed in the deep end of the pool, filling the yard with a blue glow. Soft ovals of light played against the flowers, the wood fence, and the wall of the house, hyperactively rippling and mixing in complicated patterns. The water bubbled and sloshed, slapping against the sides of the pool and washing over the concrete deck.

Beckett sneaked up to the pool's edge. The water steamed, obscuring his view of a dark lump resting on the bottom. Whatever it was, it was hot. His flustered mind came up with odd possibilities: a meteorite, a big bird, a surfboard, a tire from a car accident he hadn't heard. Maybe a commercial jet lost an engine part on takeoff from John Wayne Airport?

A light snapped on in the second floor bedroom window of the neighboring house. The silhouette of a man appeared, framed by the window, no doubt attracted by the splash. When he saw Beckett standing by the pool dressed in blue jeans and a Hawaiian shirt, the man scratched his stomach, snorted, and lurched away from the window. Half-asleep, the man probably thought the noise had come from Beckett's loud shirt. The light went out.

Beckett returned his attention to the steaming mystery object, still resting on the bottom of the pool. The steam spread across the water like a protective curtain to keep the object hidden from view. To get a better look, Beckett would have to dive in and haul it out, assuming it wasn't too heavy. He crouched and felt the steaming water, ready to snatch his fingers back if it was too hot. But it wasn't.

Frowning, he stood up and took a step back from the pool's edge, stumbling when something crunched under his right shoe. Shading his eyes from the glare of the pool light, he looked down and saw what appeared to be two narrow white stones, each about an inch long, steaming on the wet concrete.

Thinking the stones might be part of the pool object, he decided to examine them under a better light. He tugged a white handkerchief out of his pants pocket and used it to pick up the stones so he wouldn't burn his hand. But it wasn't heat he felt through the cotton fabric – it was cold. Extreme cold. He walked across the yard and flipped the switch for the patio light. The sudden brightness made him squint.

The stones were smooth. They were both cracked at one end, so he decided it was one stone that broke in half when he stepped on it. As his eyes grew accustomed to the light, he could make out fine lines on the surfaces of the stones. Jiggling the handkerchief to move them around, his eyes widened.

One of the stones was tipped with a fingernail.

Beckett shuddered. The finger rolled off the handkerchief onto the edge of his right palm. Colder than an ice cube, it perversely stuck to his skin like a stumpy sixth finger.

He smacked his hand against the stucco wall of the house. Part of his new finger broke off, leaving a shorter stump attached to his hand. The burning sensation of the cold mixed with the stinging pain of hitting the rough stucco. He dropped the other finger segment and pulled the steaming finger stump off with the handkerchief, yelping as he took some of his own skin along with it.

He dropped the finger parts, then pressed the handkerchief against the oozing cut on his hand. He looked away, took some deep breaths to calm himself, and shuffled back toward the pool wondering how his peaceful evening had turned into a surreal nightmare.

The steam on the water's surface was thinner now, but the water still rippled. Sparkling shards of light jumped around on his clothes. Several dark shapes, surrounded by a red haze, were grouped together at the deep end of the pool. As he studied them, Beckett put the facts together, but the conclusion didn't make sense. If the finger fragment came from the object in the water, it might be a human body.

In several large pieces.

In the pool.

He shook his head in a futile attempt to clear the irrational thoughts from his brain. It wasn't possible. Cold corpses don't drop out of the sky into people's pools. Not in the wealthy enclaves of Newport Beach, anyway.

How was he going to explain this to the police?

Then he heard a crunching noise. Beckett turned around, expecting the worst, and saw Jose happily gulping down the finger fragments.

TWO

"**I**'d like to report a dead person in my swimming pool," Beckett said.

"Excuse me?" The woman on the other end of the phone had a young voice and a slight British accent.

"Dead body. Corpse. Call it what you want, it's sitting at the bottom of my swimming pool." Beckett couldn't keep the annoyance out of his voice. He was already having a bad evening and he didn't like bureaucrats. He perched on the edge of a bar stool and stared out through the sliding glass door at the rippling surface of the pool.

"This is the Police Business line."

"Dead people aren't police business? You want me to call the Fire Department?"

"You're supposed to call 911 with an emergency."

"The emergency's over. The corpse is already dead."

"Do you need an ambulance?"

"That's up to you. I'm new at this."

"You should really call 911. We don't tape the conversations on this line and I can't trace your call."

"You don't need to trace the call. I'll be more than happy to give you my location."

She sighed as Beckett gave her the address on Ocean Front Drive.

"And who is the deceased, Mr. Beckett?"

"Beats me. We've never met."

There was a slight pause on the other end of the line. "Are you reporting an accidental drowning or a homicide?"

"I think he was dead before he hit the water. I don't know. There are body parts all over the yard."

"Is this a joke?"

"If it is, it's not a very good one."

Beckett could only hear muffled words after that. Then a different female voice, speaking in a tone she probably used with small children, came on the line. "Wait there. We're sending someone over."

"Neither of us is going anywhere." Since she obviously thought he was a nut case, he wondered whether they were sending the police or a psychiatrist with a net.

They swarmed over the back yard like maggots on a road kill. Cops in uniform, plainclothes cops, paramedics, an ambulance crew waiting by the pool with a stretcher, evidence technicians, and a photographer. They were all wearing booties and latex gloves. Bright work lights illuminated the scene, with occasional assistance from the spotlight of a circling police helicopter. Two neighbors watched the action from a second-story window. The house on the opposite side of the yard, owned by a reclusive film actress, remained dark. While two uniformed officers kept their eyes on Beckett, he stood by the telescope and kept his eyes on the pink water of the pool, pausing only to sip at the glass of tequila in his hand to calm his nerves. He felt numb, but it was more from the nightmarish quality of the evening rather than the alcohol.

A storm of bubbles broke the surface, followed by a man's head. A cop with black scuba gear and heavy gloves brought steaming body parts up from the bottom of the pool in a net bag and placed them in a neat pile on the concrete decking. A spooky white fog roiled around the pile before slowly dispersing in the air. Each time the diver appeared, a thin man in a rumpled brown suit frowned at the misty pile, made a note on his clipboard, then tapped his pen against his head. Beckett wondered if the man cared about getting blood on his brown shoes. Most of the body pieces were too small for Beckett to identify at a distance, but he didn't feel any urge to move in for a closer inspection. The pieces looked firm and damp, just starting to ooze blood. He could imagine how delighted the Carvers would be to return home and find a huge bloodstain by the pool; God knew what else they were going to find in the bushes.

"Mr. Beckett?" It sounded like a rumbling volcano had spoken his name.

He turned to see a blood-red tie staring him in the face – some kind of cop humor, no doubt. Behind the tie lay a stiff white shirt, framed by the lapels of a dark blue suit. At a height of six foot three, Beckett rarely found himself at eye-level with a tie, and wondered if the tequila had altered his perceptions. His gaze followed the tie upward until he saw a face a few inches above his own head. The man was in his forties, black, bald, and looked familiar, although Beckett couldn't recall meeting him before. He had to be over seven feet tall, and that brought up the obvious basketball question in Beckett's mind – the same question people had asked him in high school when they noticed his height – but he prided himself on not thinking about people as stereotypes, so he didn't comment on the detective's stature.

"I'm Detective Daniels. Moses Daniels."

"Of course. I mean, hello."

Beckett had a slight feeling of vertigo, as if he were looking up at a skyscraper from street level. He took a step back so he wouldn't lose his balance, then offered his hand. Daniels ignored the hand while he looked over Beckett's head at the pile of body parts. The flash on the photographer's camera kept going off, making shadows jump all over the yard.

"Can I get you a drink, Mr. Daniels?"

"No, thanks. I don't drink."

"Have we met before?"

"I doubt it."

Beckett frowned, trying to remember. "You look familiar."

"I used to play basketball. A lot of people recognize me from the old days."

"Yeah. Maybe that's it," Beckett said, thinking about stereotypes again. He had little interest in sports, but it was possible he'd seen Daniels on television.

Daniels looked down and locked his eyes on Beckett's face. They were hard brown eyes, tinged with bloodshot red malice and suspicion. "Has anyone read you your rights, Mr. Beckett?"

"Yes, but I don't understand why."

"For your own protection. Do you wish to have a lawyer present while I question you?"

"I don't think that'll be necessary," he said, swatting a mosquito on his arm. When he took his hand away, a red splotch with legs sticking out of it marked the bug's resting place. Death followed him everywhere tonight.

"Okay, let's hear your story. What happened here?"

"I found a body in my pool."

"Your pool? The name on the mailbox says Carver."

"Friends of mine. They're letting me use their place while they're in Europe."

"You say you *found* the body. You're sure you didn't put it in the pool yourself?"

"No."

"You're not sure?"

"I didn't put it there."

Daniels eyed the glass in Beckett's hand. "How much have you had to drink this evening?"

"I don't know. A couple of ounces? I'm not much of a drinker, but these are special circumstances."

"I bet they are. So you don't make a habit of this sort of thing?"

"What sort of thing?"

"Killing people. This is your first one?"

Beckett paused for a moment to make sure he was following the conversation correctly. "You think I murdered that guy?"

"The man's body is in pieces, Mr. Beckett. I hardly think it was a suicide."

"I never said it was."

"Then you admit you killed him?"

"No!"

"Things will go easier for you if you confess. Then we can all go home and get some sleep. Except you, of course, since you'll be in jail."

"I'm not confessing to anything! I didn't do it!"

Daniels raised one eyebrow. "Calm down, Mr. Beckett. We can conduct this interview in handcuffs if necessary."

Beckett angrily exhaled and finished his glass of tequila in one gulp. Daniels watched his every move, evaluating and filing for later reference. Beckett understood how a bug under a microscope must feel.

"You keep referring to the deceased, assuming there's only one, as *he*. How do you know it's a man?"

"I'm not sure. I just assumed. I guess the hairy finger tipped me off."

"Hairy finger? You certainly have sharp eyes."

"It was stuck to my hand. I'd show it to you, but the dog ate it," he said, waving his arm in the general direction of the house.

"The dog ate it."

Beckett shook his head. "Never mind. It's a long story."

"I've got time," Daniels said, folding his arms. "And I like a good story."

He outlined his first experience with the frozen body part, then showed Daniels the wound on the side of his right hand while he told him about Jose, the hungry Chihuahua.

"You shouldn't have disturbed the evidence," Daniels pointed out.

"Trust me, I was much more disturbed by the evidence than it was by me."

Daniels glanced over to check on the diver's progress. "It must have taken you a long time to cut the body into so many pieces."

Beckett sighed. The questions were annoying, but he felt more confident when Daniels wasn't looking at him. "Power tools. They're great time savers."

"Then you're ready to confess?"

"No."

Daniels swiveled his eyes back around to bore into Beckett's head. "Ah, you're a clever one, I'll give you that."

An angry response formed in Beckett's mind, but he decided to drop it.

"Now, then," said Daniels, "what time did you discover the body?"

"Just after midnight."

"Were you alone?"

"Yes. I was out here using the telescope for an hour or so before I got a kink in my neck, then the dog tripped me with his food dish and I sat down by the pool. The lights were off back here, but I looked up at the sky when I heard a whistling noise. Then that guy took a swan dive into the pool." He wasn't sure why he'd mentioned the dog dish, but too late now.

Daniels looked up at the sky, then at Beckett, then at the neighboring houses, then back to Beckett. "Where did he come from?"

"I told you. He just fell out of the sky." Beckett was glad Daniels hadn't asked about the food dish. He hadn't planned to mention it; he just blurted it out without thinking.

Daniels exchanged looks with one of the uniformed cops standing nearby. The uniform shrugged. "Fell out of the sky."

"At first, I didn't know what it was. The splash soaked my clothes."

"I noticed."

"Then I turned on the pool light and the water was steaming."

"Steaming?" Daniels exchanged another look with the uniformed cop.

"Yeah."

Daniels frowned. As he answered the detective's questions, Beckett could hear himself shaping up as an insane axe-murderer in Daniels's mind. Beckett had a hard time believing his own story.

"Tell me, was the victim all in one piece when he dove into the pool?"

"I don't know. This may sound a little farfetched, but I'm starting to think he broke up when he hit the water. He was moving pretty fast, and I think he was frozen."

"I thought you said the water was steaming?"

Beckett nodded. "That's how cold he was."

"You'll excuse me for being somewhat skeptical, but I've been a cop for almost ten years now and I've never heard of a case where someone exploded on contact with water."

Beckett shrugged. "I admit it's a bit unusual."

"I think *impossible* is the word that describes it best."

"Like I said, Mr. Daniels, he was moving pretty fast."

Daniels squinted up at the sky again. "Possibility of a mid-air collision, I suppose. Or an explosion. Did you hear anything before your guest dropped in?"

"Just the whistling."

"He was whistling a tune?"

"No, it was more like the whistling of air past a fast-moving object."

Daniels locked his gaze on Beckett's eyes, holding them there as securely as a pair of handcuffs. "You have an interesting way of phrasing things, Mr. Beckett. What do you do for a living?"

That was a tough question. "A lot of things."

"Pick one. I'll let you know if it's the wrong answer."

"You might call me a consultant. And a science writer."

"A lot of unemployed people call themselves consultants, Mr. Beckett. Could you be more specific?"

"Well, recently I've been writing a lot of science articles for magazines. I also just finished a big software project for an aerospace company in Huntington Beach, and I have a small business in San Francisco that builds educational software for universities. Earlier this year, I worked on an archaeological excavation in Newport Beach and wrote a book about it."

Daniels just stared at him for a moment before responding. "Sounds like you get around."

"My parents used to say I couldn't hold a job." Actually, his parents had never said that, but Beckett liked to say they did whenever he thought he sounded pompous. Due, in part, to a sizeable trust fund his parents had established for his education, Beckett had managed to avoid reality and maintain his status as a professional student until he was thirty, when the money finally ran out. Then he'd embarked on a flurry of consulting and writing jobs out of a sense of panic.

Daniels looked thoughtful. "Now that I think about it, your name does sound familiar. Are you *Doctor* Beckett?"

"Well, I have a PhD, but I think *Doctor* sounds too formal. Besides, I hate explaining at parties that I'm not qualified to diagnose moles or perform surgery."

"I understand," Daniels nodded. "I keep having to explain that I'm really a cop and I don't play basketball any more."

Daniels seemed lost in thought. Beckett glanced at the pool, where the brown suit continued to measure body parts and make notes on his clipboard. He wondered if the interview would ever end. The breeze from the ocean felt chilly.

"Now I remember," Daniels rumbled. "You were the guy they interviewed on KOCE last month. It was that crime show, right?"

Beckett cleared his throat and looked at the ground. "Umm, *Orange County Crime Watch*. Yeah, that was me."

Daniels didn't seem happy. "I thought so. You aren't very popular with the Newport Beach police right now, Dr. Beckett."

"Yeah, well, I hope meeting me isn't going to affect your handling of this case."

"Me? Of course not. But you'd better keep your head down when you're around this many cops, Doctor. Some of them aren't as level-headed as I am, and you really made us look bad. We had to reopen cold cases that had been closed for six years. You know how much overtime it takes to handle that many cases? And we've got lawyers breathing down our necks to get their clients released from prison."

"I'll keep that in mind," Beckett said, continuing to stare at his feet. A person exposes one little police cover-up on television, and this is what happens. Talk about bad timing.

"By the way," said Daniels, "you're under arrest."

Beckett turned his shocked gaze on the detective's face. "You can't be serious."

"Give me one good reason why I shouldn't arrest you."

"Here's one – I didn't kill anybody!"

"That remains to be seen. All I have is your word that you didn't do it."

Beckett didn't have time to reply. A short man with black hair strolled up beside Daniels. Most of the Newport detectives he'd seen were well-dressed and this man was no exception. He wore a tailored brown suit and a matching silk tie. In tow behind the short detective was Beckett's paunchy next-door neighbor, the middle-aged man he'd seen in the window after his drop-in guest arrived. One of the cops must have noticed him watching while the body parts were recovered. The neighbor's eyes darted around with interest as he shuffled along in his terrycloth bathrobe, scratching his scalp through the thin brown hair he'd combed across his head to cover his bald spot.

Daniels turned to face the short detective. "Find something, Ortega?"

Ortega indicated the neighbor. "This is Mr. Fittipaldi. He lives next door and he's got an interesting story to tell."

Fittipaldi's eyes widened and he pointed at Beckett. "That's the man, officer! He's the one who did it! I saw it clear as day!"

Daniels glanced at Beckett before turning his full attention to Fittipaldi. "Exactly what did you see him do, sir?"

Fittipaldi jabbed a thumb over his shoulder toward the pool. "I saw him toss that dead guy in the pool! Yes, sir, he did it right in front of me!"

"Now, wait a minute – " Beckett began.

Daniels raised his hand for silence. "You'll have your chance to reply, Doctor. Mr. Fittipaldi has the floor right now."

Beckett sighed and looked up at the sky while Fittipaldi continued. Morons, he thought. He was dealing with morons.

"Damnedest thing I ever saw," Fittipaldi said, waving his arms. He was a man who liked to express himself. "He acted like no one would even notice. Yes, sir. But I keep my window open at night, just in case anything bad happens outside. That's right. I didn't used to do that, but some punk kid broke all the windows in my car one night and I didn't even hear it. Ever since then, I keep my window open. Yes, sir."

Ortega nodded impatiently. "I think we've got the picture, Mr. Fittipal-di. Your window was open. Tell us what got your attention."

Fittipaldi frowned, deep in concentration, as if he wanted to get every detail exactly right. Beckett could see he enjoyed his big moment in the spotlight.

"Well, sir, I heard a scream followed by a big splash. Thought it was a wave crashing against the house at first. We get that, now and then, when there's a storm offshore and the waves get real big. The surfers love it. Nearly took my house away one year. Yes, sir. Anyway, I heard this splash, so I jumped out of bed. My wife, that's Beatrice, she slept right through it, scream and all. Anyway, like I was saying, I got up and looked out the window. Yes, sir."

Fittipaldi paused to enhance the drama. He looked around to make sure everyone was paying attention.

"Go on," Daniels prompted.

Fittipaldi, shaking with emotion, pointed an incriminating finger at Beckett. "I looked out and saw this guy, dressed like he is now, soaking wet, standing right at the edge of the pool!"

"You got a good look at him?" Daniels asked.

"Yes, sir! The pool light was on."

Beckett snorted. "It was all over by the time you looked out the window. I saw you."

Fittipaldi turned his angry bloodshot eyes on Beckett. "You calling me a liar?"

"In a word – *yes*," Beckett said with a nod.

Fittipaldi took a threatening step toward Beckett, but Ortega grabbed him and held him in place. For a small guy, Ortega seemed pretty strong. Daniels waited for Fittipaldi to stop sputtering and calm down.

"About what time did you see all this, Mr. Fittipaldi?"

"I don't know. Around midnight, I guess."

Daniels raised an eyebrow. "You're not sure?"

Fittipaldi seemed to have trouble talking with his arms restrained. "I was asleep! I know it was after ten, because that's when I go to bed. Can I have my arms back, please?"

"As long as you're a good boy," growled Ortega, releasing him.

Daniels folded his arms. "Your wife never woke up?"

Sweating, Fittipaldi rubbed his neck. "Not until you guys got here."

"So you saw Dr. Beckett throw the deceased into the pool. Was he struggling?"

"Er, no, the dead guy wasn't. Not that I recall. He must have been unconscious."

Beckett thought he detected skepticism in Daniels's expression.

"Other than the scream, did you hear any voices, like an argument, before you heard the splash?"

"No, I don't think so," said Fittipaldi, scratching his head. "I was asleep, like I said."

Daniels nodded and glanced at Beckett before impaling Fittipaldi again with his eyes. "Okay, just one more question. How come you didn't call the police when you saw this man being murdered?"

Fittipaldi wiped the sweat from his forehead with the back of his bathrobe sleeve. From the confused expression on his face, he clearly hadn't expected such a question. "Umm, well, Beatrice didn't want me to get involved."

"I see. Thanks for coming forward with your information, Mr. Fittipaldi. Ortega will take your formal statement. We'll let you know if we have any further questions."

"Oh. Okay. But listen," Fittipaldi said in a confidential tone as he looked around at everyone nearby, "if you boys ever need a good deal on a tile floor, come to one of my *Tile Palace* stores. I'll make sure you get a discount if you tell them I sent you."

Beckett had to laugh. "Does that include me?"

Fittipaldi's eyes glazed over as he pulled himself upright and looked down his nose at Beckett. "Everyone except you, scumbag."

Daniels cleared his throat. "As I said, we'll let you know if we need anything else, sir."

Fittipaldi looked disappointed as he started away. Then he spun around again with an inspired gleam in his red eyes. "Hey! There was another scream a couple minutes after he threw the body in the pool!"

"Another scream?" Daniels asked.

Fittipaldi had frozen in position with his arms spread wide, as if he were preaching a sermon or telling a big fish story. "Yes, sir. It was kind of a gargly noise, like someone being strangled."

"You heard this after you heard the splash?"

"That's right."

Beckett groaned. "That was me."

Fittipaldi dropped his arms.

Daniels gave Beckett an odd look. "You waited a few minutes before you screamed?"

"Well, I found something that – "

Beckett stopped as the police diver approached. He still wore his rubber suit, his scuba tank, and his flippers, which made a strange flopping noise when he walked up beside Daniels. His mask perched securely on top of his head like a barnacle.

"We found most of the body, Lieutenant."

"Most of it?"

"A few small parts are missing. I don't think we got all of his fingers. They might be stuck in the pool drain where I couldn't see them. It's kind of murky down there with the blood and all."

Beckett shouldered past Daniels toward the sliding glass door that led to the living room. Glancing around, he spotted the one partially chewed finger segment that Jose hadn't eaten. A small patch of blood stained the concrete beneath it. He pointed. "Over here."

The diver flopped over beside Beckett and picked up the finger in his rubber glove, then nodded at Daniels. "Yeah. This is part of it."

Fittipaldi's face lost some of its color as he got a good look at the finger in the diver's hand. "Uh, if you'll excuse me – "

Ortega led Fittipaldi away around the side of the house. They heard retching noises while the diver flopped back toward the pool and Daniels turned his attention to Beckett.

"You're unusually helpful for a murderer."

Beckett ignored the insinuation. "That's the finger I found by the pool after I stepped on it. I yelled when part of it stuck to my hand." Beckett displayed his injured hand.

"Ah, yes," said Daniels. "You mentioned it earlier. However, I'm thinking you cut up the body in your bathroom, then brought it out here and tossed it in the pool. Is that right?"

"Yeah, sure. Then I called the police to turn myself in. I was just too shy to come right out and say it like that."

"Any more body parts scattered around your house that we should know about, Doctor?"

"Go ahead and look for yourself, if you haven't already. I think I stashed some in the refrigerator for midnight snacks. Finger sandwiches, you know."

Daniels didn't seem amused. "Speaking of your phone call, why didn't you call the emergency number?"

"As I told the woman who answered, I didn't want to tie up the emergency line when the emergency was over. Nobody was breaking into the house or anything. And the dead guy was already...well...*dead*."

"That was considerate of you," Daniels snorted. "We get people calling the emergency number when their pets run away. It's always nice to meet a polite murderer."

"Okay, Detective. If you really think I killed that guy, cut up his body, and dumped it in the pool, then arrest me. Otherwise, you should stop squeezing my shoes, or else I'll have to lawyer up." Beckett knew he was on thin ice, but fatigue made him cranky. He thought speaking to the man on his own terms would help.

Daniels snapped his fingers. "Ah, yes. I forgot that you're an expert on police procedure."

"No, but I do know a fishing expedition when I see it."

"Fishing expedition, is it? I see you've also been watching a lot of television. Next thing I know, you'll be telling me how the 'perp' did this and some 'skel' did that." Daniels shrugged and shifted his gaze toward the pool. "Okay, I'm not going to arrest you right now. But you aren't off the hook yet, Doctor. You're still the only suspect I've got."

"More fishing terms? 'Off the hook'? Next thing I know, you'll be asking if I'll 'take the bait.'"

"Don't push your luck," Daniels said while he strolled over to the pool with Beckett trailing along behind him.

The steaming body parts were laid out in their approximate normal positions in relation to each other. As the diver had said, a few small parts were missing from the collection; cops with flashlights were searching the rest of the yard for errant fragments. Guided by the tense angles of the stiff arms and legs, the body was assembled into a fetal position. The body lay on its right side with the arms folded across the lower part of the chest and the legs drawn up toward the torso. The clipboard man kept trying to balance the segments of the left foot on top of the right foot, but they kept falling off. It was clear to Beckett that the clipboard man wasn't a detective – his brown suit was too cheap and rumpled for Newport Beach – so he might be an evidence technician from the coroner's office.

Beckett had seen corpses before, but he couldn't help flinching when he got close enough to get a good look. The photographer's flash unit kept illuminating the gory details. His stomach fluttered as Daniels glanced at him.

"Feeling queasy, Doctor?"

"I'll be all right," Beckett muttered.

Daniels nodded and raised an eyebrow.

Beckett couldn't bring himself to look at the dead man's face right away, so he started by glancing at the other details, not wanting to let his eyes rest for too long on any one piece. The first thing he noticed was how sharp the edges were wherever the body had been sliced, reminding him of shattered glass. The cuts were oozing blood, but not in the quantity he would have expected. Maybe most of the blood had already been lost in the pool?

For a momentary respite from viewing the remains, Beckett looked into the pool. He wondered how long it would take for the pink color to leave the water. Daylight would only make the pinkish coloration more apparent. When the Carvers returned in a couple of days, they'd probably remember that the pool water was clear when they left, and then they'd ask Beckett some uncomfortable questions. He had a feeling they wouldn't like his answers. He'd already been worried that afternoon when he discovered that the trash compactor was on the fritz after Jose had dropped a phone book in there without Beckett seeing him do it. How could he explain away blood in the pool? It would take some serious eloquence to tell them what had happened without simultaneously jeopardizing his beach house privileges.

Beckett returned his attention to the corpse. The man was dressed in blue jeans, steel-toed work boots, a blue plaid flannel shirt, and a shiny green flight jacket with patches on the chest and the left sleeve. The torso was broken into six pieces. Beckett saw that the flight jacket, and the rest of the clothing, had jagged cuts through the material that matched the jagged cuts on the body. There were no signs of frayed or torn material. He thought of the way the edges of an ice cube looked when it was shattered.

Beckett calmly watched Jose race up to the body, snatch the corpse's left foot, and drag it away across the yard. "Hey," Ortega said, glaring at Beckett.

"I think he's developed a taste for it," Beckett grumbled, jogging after the dog.

The Chihuahua darted under the bushes with his prize. Beckett poked around until he spotted the dog, then made a quick grab through a gap in the hedge. With the icy foot in his mouth, Jose calmly stepped back out of reach.

Beckett pointed at the dog. "Bad dog. Drop the foot and I'll play with you later."

Jose panted and cocked his head in response.

"You're just mad because I haven't fed you yet, aren't you?"

Keeping one eye on Beckett, Jose dropped the foot and drooled on it.

"Good boy."

He slowly reached for the foot, but Jose didn't make any threatening moves until Beckett touched the corpse's foot, then he poked Beckett's hand with his nose just to spook him. Beckett jumped back and waved the foot at Jose. "Ha!"

When Beckett handed the foot to Ortega, Daniels was still examining the body. At least the foot had warmed up enough that it didn't stick to Beckett's hand when he released it.

"What was that all about?" Ortega asked, frowning at Beckett.

"Jose likes to play with his food."

Daniels got down on one knee to peer at the colorful patches hand-stitched onto the flight jacket. Portions of the patches were missing, presumably where the stitches had broken, and the remaining fragments had clean edges that looked as if they'd been cut apart with a razor blade. On the left sleeve, at the shoulder, was the top left quarter of a circular blue and white patch. Just inside a shiny, royal blue border, against a white background, were the words: "GERARD P. KUIP," with the last letters cut off. The end of a light blue design dominated the center fragment of the patch.

Seagulls screamed at each other nearby, possibly discussing the relative merits of the discarded fish heads from the local restaurants. Beckett noted the smell of chlorine coming from the jacket, relieved that he couldn't detect any stronger odors from the cold corpse.

Returning his attention to the left side of the jacket, he saw a round patch with a shiny yellow border. The left half of the patch was missing, but the right half showed the nose of a large white aircraft against a royal blue background. Below the aircraft was the word: "ARC."

A search of the jacket pockets by Daniels revealed a lump of notepaper in the zippered pocket on the left sleeve. On the exterior of the pocket were four long, narrow pouches designed to hold pens and pencils, one of which was occupied by a black ballpoint with the words: "PROPERTY OF U.S. GOVERNMENT" on its side in scratched gold ink.

"Looks military," Daniels said. "Except he's not wearing a uniform under the jacket."

"Maybe he's a civilian who works for the military. Or he was off-duty," said Beckett.

"Possible."

"Too bad there's no name patch," Ortega said, pointing at the spot high on the jacket's chest where a name patch would normally have been stitched on.

Daniels continued his search and carefully removed a slim leather wallet from one of the rear pockets of the man's pants, then waved it at Ortega.

"Great detective work. This is why I make the big bucks." Daniels opened the wallet with the end of his pen.

Stuffed in among the credit cards was a soggy driver's license in the name of Maxwell Dumas. His home address was in Mountain View, a northern California town between San Jose and San Francisco in the high-tech Silicon Valley. Beckett recognized the address because he had lived in Mountain View himself for a few years while attending Stanford.

"Poor old Maxwell came a long way to die," Ortega said. "Maybe he should have stayed home."

While Daniels and Ortega looked through the wallet, Beckett braced himself and looked at the dead man's face, or what was left of it.

The pale features defied a detailed examination. The mouth was clenched shut. Both eye sockets were partially vacant, and Beckett didn't allow his gaze to linger there. The skull had cracked into three pieces and the short hair visible between the rusty stains was brown with gray streaks. Brain matter was visible. The formerly strong jaw line, so evident in the driver's license photo, was no longer one that women would find attractive – two molars protruded through a missing section of the cheek. Beckett absorbed the details for a few seconds, long enough to be sure he wouldn't be able to forget them even if he tried, then turned away to look up at the clear sky. The surf boomed on the sand nearby, sweeping the beach clean of unpleasant memories.

Finished with his preliminary examination of the deceased, Daniels allowed the coroner's people to move in and remove the body. After placing all his parts in a black body bag is if he were so much garbage, the technicians wheeled the corpse away on a gurney. Maxwell Dumas's big moment in the spotlight was over, leaving only a bloody puddle on the concrete to show that he'd been there. Whatever Dumas had been before, no matter what he'd accomplished in his life, the Great Equalizer had reduced him to a broken husk and a big red stain. The bureaucratic maggots had done their work and removed the human shell, consigning Dumas and his past to a file folder.

Daniels stopped beside Beckett on his way out, startling him out of his meditation on life's ironies. "Don't go on any long vacations, Doctor. I'll want to talk to you tomorrow."

"I'll send you a postcard when I get to Brazil."

Daniels squinted at his face. Beckett wondered if another frozen finger was stuck to his nose or something. "And get some sleep – you look terrible."

Beckett watched Daniels walk away yawning. Just another day at the office for him. Just another death. "Yeah. Pleasant dreams, Detective."

He shook his head. Daniels would probably go home and sleep like a baby. Dumas was well into the Big Sleep with no worries. The only person who wouldn't get any sleep that night would be Beckett, and he'd feel lucky if he didn't have nightmares for the rest of his life.

THREE

The new day dawned clear and bright, as it usually did in Newport Beach. Beckett knew the exact moment when the sun rose, at 6:28, because he'd spent a restless night on the bed, staring out the east-facing window, waiting for more bodies to drop out of the sky. He'd watched the sky change color from black to pre-dawn gray to orange. From this angle, the pool was a brilliant orange mirror reflecting the heavenly light show. In a few minutes, the thin veneer of smog and haze would roll in to obscure the distant peaks of Saddleback Mountain. Exhausted and irritable, he thought the sunrise was much too pretty while he oozed out of bed into the old pair of black bowling shoes he used for slippers. He couldn't remember where the bowling shoes had come from, since he'd never taken up bowling, but they'd been with him for years and they were comfortable old friends. He never went barefoot around the house because he was prone to clumsiness and bashing his feet into hard objects.

Out on the redwood balcony overlooking the beach from the second floor of the Carver house, Beckett left the French doors open and inhaled deeply of the cool salty breeze. He leaned on the railing and devoted his full attention to a careful survey of the beach in case more undiscovered corpses lay waiting on the sand. To his right was the outlet of the Santa Ana River, a popular surfing area known as the Wedge, currently occupied by a pair of common loons – the birds, not the surfers – a great blue heron, and some least sandpipers rooting around in the surf. A brown pelican buzzed the beach while shrieking California gulls glided overhead in casual spirals. The sand looked clean and corpse-free. Beckett let his gaze drift down the coast along with the tide. Except for a lone female jogger in a yellow bikini approaching from the south, the beach was deserted.

The sandy Newport Beach coastline, lined with multi-million-dollar homes, had always fascinated Beckett. As recently as 1956, the real estate business was so bad here that two brokers had committed suicide. Now, gleaming private yachts nestled in the snug waters of the four Newport marinas. Yacht clubs, tennis clubs, health clubs, and golf clubs dotted the landscape. Private planes and business jets jockey for space between commercial flights at the nearby John Wayne Airport. Ferraris, Jaguars, Lamborghinis, and other exotic cars were crammed into parking spaces alongside the more pedestrian Mercedes's and BMWs. The local Rolls-Royce dealer sold more cars than any other dealer in the country. All this in a town with six miles of ocean frontage and seventy thousand people, swelling to over one hundred thousand during the summer; pretty good for an area of former salt marshes and tidal mud flats. Still, Beckett felt sure that corpses dropping out of the sky would not be one of the features on the cover of this year's Chamber of Commerce brochure. Murder didn't fit in well with the glitzy, crime-free image the city liked to project.

Beckett returned his attention to the yellow bikini jogging up the beach. Her tan was dark and her curly blond hair floated around her head like a cloud as she bounced along. Only a few yards away now, she looked up and smiled at Beckett with blinding white teeth. Beckett smiled back. She giggled and continued staring at him while she passed by. Beckett found this unusual until he remembered he was still naked except for his bowling shoes. It was time to go inside and get a cup of coffee.

While the coffee burbled in the coffeemaker, its welcoming aroma filling the kitchen, Beckett shuffled around, his bleary eyes peering into the refrigerator and checking the cupboards. His search turned up a can of hash and some warm orange juice. After irradiating the hash in the microwave, he thought it looked lonely on the plate, so he snapped off a sprig of the Boston fern hanging in the window to use as a garnish. He dropped an ice cube into the orange juice, which popped and cracked in half, floating in the liquid like a frozen corpse.

While he ate at the dining room table, staring out the window at the pool, the phone rang. As usual, since it wasn't his house, and since he didn't want to speak to the Carvers, he let the ancient answering machine take the call. A deep, clear voice boomed out of the tiny speaker.

"So. Left town already, eh, Doctor? I probably should have arrested you last night when I had the chance."

Beckett picked up the phone and shut off the answering machine. "Beckett here."

"Ah, you're there after all. I thought you were kidding about sending me a postcard, but one can never be too sure in this business."

He swallowed some of the hash, noting that he'd overcooked it. "I suppose not. What can I do for you, Daniels?"

"Since you haven't called me, I assume your guilty conscience hasn't driven you to confess?"

"Your assumption is correct." He looked at the cracked ice cube in his juice.

"I see. Then I have some information that may be of interest to you."

"I'm listening." He started shaping the hash on his plate into a tall mound with his fork.

"There were no mid-air collisions or aircraft explosions over this area last night. A Sea Stallion helicopter from El Toro flew over Newport Beach shortly before midnight, followed by a pair of jet fighters twenty minutes later. However, all crews are accounted for and no one is missing. The only other air traffic around midnight was a police helicopter, and I think we can safely assume that the two occupants of the helicopter are above suspicion."

"What about private aircraft?" Beckett asked. Finished making a tower out of the hash, he poked the sprig of fern into the top of it as if it were a flag.

"There were a few planes in the air, but none of them were over your house at the right time. Either Dumas was able to fly on his own without an airplane, or he fell out of a cloud."

"Or I'm lying," Beckett pointed out.

"The thought had crossed my mind. However, we discovered no signs of a struggle in your house, the murder method is unclear, and we don't have a motive for you until we know more about Dumas. And the only blood we could find was in the pool or directly beside it. Now, it's possible that you killed him somewhere else, then dumped his body in your pool, but you seem a bit smarter than that. The fact that you called the police either means that you're innocent or you're very clever."

"Thank you. I think."

"By the way, do you spell your last name with one "t" or two?"

"Two." He sipped at the steaming coffee and made a face, remembering that he hadn't emptied out the old coffee grounds.

"Ah. That's good. There's an Ed Becket in our records, one "t," who murdered three of his neighbors with a pickaxe. They never caught him, but he fits your same general description: dark brown hair, mustache, six-- foot-three, 180 pounds, athletic build, tattoo of a snake wrapped around a sword on his right arm, walks with a limp."

"Wasn't me. I don't have the tattoo or the limp."

"Glad to hear it. Of course, you could have had the tattoo removed. And you might have recovered from the limp."

"When did this axe murder occur?"

"Thirty years ago."

"So I was only four years old at the time."

"Which is why there aren't any policemen kicking in your door right now. It's possible that you started on your life of crime at that tender age, but the mustache and the height didn't quite fit the profile of a typical toddler."

"Is there some reason you're telling me all this, Daniels?"

"Just trying to make conversation. It's an old detective's trick. I never know if you'll slip up and inadvertently blurt out some incriminating piece of information."

Beckett sighed and tried another sip of his coffee. He wouldn't say the coffee had a good flavor, but he wasn't drinking it for the taste; he just wanted the caffeine. "Has your medical examiner come up with anything from the body?"

"Dumas had spaghetti for dinner, no meatballs. Might have been watching his cholesterol."

"Anything else?"

"Of course. Dr. Goldblum is one of the highest-paid medical examiners in the country. He works at the Forensic Science Center in Santa Ana – right next to the county jail, which I'm sure you'll see in the near future – and he's come up with a wealth of interesting data on Dumas. It's just that I don't normally discuss these details with the prime murder suspect."

"Oh, give me a break. Is that your way of saying you don't have a clue as to how he died in my pool?"

"Actually, he didn't die in your pool. That happened long before he reached your place. Goldblum says Dumas froze to death."

"Froze to death? That doesn't make any sense." As Beckett made the remark, he remembered the fetal position of the body parts by the pool and the cold finger segment that had stuck to his hand. Then he eyed the cube melting in his orange juice. It made sense, and he'd known that all along, even if he wouldn't admit it to Daniels.

Daniels sounded fascinated. "I thought at first that he'd been kept on ice in a freezer somewhere, but Goldblum says Dumas's interior was solid ice, even though some warming had occurred while he was in your pool. Of course, that makes determining the time of death kind of difficult, since we estimate it based on the amount of cooling of the body. And he was frozen quickly, so there weren't any bugs or eggs for our forensic entomologist to look at for determining time or location of death. For all we know, he could have been killed months ago. On the moon."

Beckett wanted to crawl back into bed and go to sleep.

Daniels continued. "Because of the clean breaks of the body segments, Goldblum thinks Dumas was shattered by hard impacts after he was frozen."

"How about one hard impact, like hitting the water in my pool?"

"As I already explained, we've ruled that out."

"Why? If he were thrown out of an airplane at a sufficient altitude, that pool water would have hit him like a brick wall. At terminal velocity, Dumas would have been moving at 120 miles per hour. I sprained an ankle once just by falling off a curb."

"Despite your sprained ankle, Dumas wasn't thrown out of an airplane."

"Then how did he get into my pool?"

"I don't know. Maybe somebody pitched him over your fence."

Beckett felt like hanging up the phone, but he managed to restrain himself. Then he remembered something. "I think I saw him through the telescope."

"Who?"

"Dumas. I was looking at Betelgeuse when I saw a dark shape blot out the starlight for half a second."

"Who's Betel...whatever you said?"

"It's a star. A red supergiant."

"Now you're telling me that Dumas came from the stars? You're going to plead insanity, I suppose."

Beckett ignored the remark. "I thought the dark shape was an airplane at first, but I couldn't see any lights on it. I think it was Dumas that I saw. And it must have been at a high altitude. You're sure the military didn't have anything flying over that they didn't tell you about, like something from Vandenberg up the coast? Maybe something that the controllers at John Wayne Airport wouldn't remember?"

Daniels hesitated. "It's unlikely."

"But possible?"

"I suppose so, but the services are usually pretty cooperative with the local authorities."

"Maybe the aircraft wasn't local. His home address was in Mountain View, and there are military bases all over the Bay area. Dumas was dressed like a civilian, but he was wearing a military-style flight jacket."

"Which he could have bought at a military surplus store," Daniels pointed out.

"Did you learn anything more about those patches on the jacket?"

"Not yet. We're trying to find out now if there's anyone else living at his home address. There may not be, since we didn't find any photos in his wallet."

"That doesn't mean much. I don't carry photos in my wallet, either. They just get bent up and torn." And he didn't have any worth carrying, but that was another matter.

"In any case, we're checking on it. But there's something else that occurs to me about your high altitude aircraft theory."

"What's that?"

"Well, we would have known about it by now if there was a plane crash or an explosion. And planes flying at high altitude are pressurized, right? So, going on the assumption that he didn't leap out of the airplane on his own after being frozen, how could the murderer have dumped the body?"

Beckett didn't have a good answer for that one. "I don't know. You're right, decompression would have been a problem. Maybe Dumas was in a bomb bay or something that wasn't pressurized."

The silence at the other end of the line told Beckett what Daniels thought of that idea.

"And why would the murderer have dumped the body over land, where it might be discovered? Why not dump it far out in the ocean where there'd be practically no chance of anyone finding it?"

"Maybe the murderer didn't have any choice regarding the location."

Daniels sighed heavily. "Doctor, I know you're just trying to help, and get yourself off the hook at the same time, but I think I'll go back to the theory that Dumas was pitched over your fence."

"But that doesn't make any – "

"Either that," Daniels interrupted, "or you murdered Dumas yourself. For all I know, Dumas is an old friend of yours. Or an old enemy."

"It's been fun chatting with you," Beckett said through clenched teeth as he hung up the phone. His anger dissipated quickly when he glanced out the window and saw Jose resting in an odd position on the concrete near the pool – he didn't appear to be sleeping. The sinking feeling in his stomach reminded him that he hadn't fed the Chihuahua last night. As he darted toward the sliding glass door, he wondered if Jose might have had a bad reaction to the corpse parts he'd eaten.

"Jose! Wake up, buddy! Are you okay?"

The dog didn't move when Beckett trotted up beside him. His eyes were closed. It didn't look like he was breathing.

"Oh, Christ."

Sure, they hadn't exactly been pals, but a certain relationship had developed between

them – no more dysfunctional than his other relationships – and he felt bad about not taking better care of the little dog.

When Beckett knelt down to place his hand on the Chihuahua's fuzzy head, he heard a gentle snoring noise. The dog opened his eyes and gave him a significant look to remind Beckett that someone trusted him and believed his story. Or maybe it was just gas.

After a hot shower, Beckett decided to visit his apartment in Fountain Valley. He wanted to check his phone messages, his e-mail, and generally get the place ready for his return.

Beckett backed his silver Mini Cooper out of the Carver garage and threaded his way through the narrow streets, thankful that his car was small and easy to maneuver. Unique two and three-story homes towered close by on both sides of the road, defended by a tight barrier of expensive cars that made life difficult for anything larger than a bicycle. Breaking free of the claustrophobic neighborhood, Beckett turned left onto Pacific Coast Highway and joined the moderate traffic heading up the coast at fifty miles per hour.

He crossed the bridge over the Santa Ana River and entered Huntington Beach. On his left was the southern end of the state beach, an uninterrupted nine-mile stretch of clean sand representing Mecca for southern California sun worshippers. It was still early in the morning, too early for the tanning slaves, so the only people on the beach were the joggers and the surfers, who looked like blond-headed seals in their black wetsuits. Except for an exhausted fat man shuffling along, the joggers seemed to be bursting with so much good health that Beckett wanted to swerve onto the beach path and mow a few of them down.

On his right, identifiable even at night by its subtle perfume, were the domed buildings and settling ponds of the massive sewage treatment plant. He'd written an article about it for the *Orange County Register*. Not wanting to waste its waste, the county contributed the dried end products of the treatment processes for use as fertilizer, keeping things green while helping the little flowers grow at Disneyland and other tourist attractions. It gave Beckett a warm feeling to know that his personal waste products were put to such a good use, delighting tourists from all over the world.

His arm hurt and he could feel a headache starting to throb at the base of his skull. The end of his little vacation on the beach was getting too weird, and it almost felt good to be going home. However, the hollow feeling in his stomach reminded him that Nikki wouldn't be there. The fact that she was married had put a severe crimp in their relationship, even though she'd been separated from her husband shortly before she met Beckett, and she had finally come to her senses two weeks ago to call it quits. He really didn't blame her for that decision: He couldn't support her in the style to which she was accustomed, their friends shared nothing in common, and Beckett snored like a buffalo with a sinus infection. Another year shot with the wrong woman. But he appreciated the time she had spent with him, anyway.

He turned right at Brookhurst, heading inland for the four-mile trip to the city of Fountain Valley – known as Gospel Swamp in a previous life. Beckett had grown up in Fountain Valley, but he preferred the older name, which had more character. Around the time of the Civil War, the area was a flat swamp dotted with islands. Revival meetings were held in tents on those islands, resulting in the name that stuck until the 1890s, when the respectable Talbert family came along and established the first post office; a stroke of creative genius, moderated by the deep humility shared by many of Orange County's affluent residents, prompted them to name the area Talbert. The Talberts also opened the first general store and drained the swamp, exposing rich farmland. Grateful for the efforts of the Talbert family, the city fathers promptly changed the name to Fountain Valley when the city was incorporated in 1957. Now, it was a different sort of swamp, full of people, cars, houses, and strip malls.

Across the street from the new shopping center, Beckett turned right on Whippoorwill and began searching for a parking space. In typical Southern California fashion, each person living in the apartment complexes that lined the street owned at least two cars, resulting in a shortage of parking spaces. Late at night, Beckett often watched drivers stoically roaming the streets, like ghostly automotive Flying Dutchmen, in their futile search for parking. Beckett's solution was to do all his traveling early in the day before everyone returned home from work. Of course, this wasn't a unique problem – in the Darwinian freeway culture of southern California, with almost twice as many cars as people, complex navigational strategies were necessary to weed out the weaker drivers from the gene pool.

On the way to his apartment, Beckett strolled past a gardener with a gasoline-powered leaf blower strapped to his back. The gardeners worked on the grass around the complex three days a week, using their insane blowing instruments to "clean up" after they mowed the grass. Beckett was convinced that this clean-up process involved blowing all the loose grass and dust through the crack under his apartment door, along with a healthy dose of gasoline fumes. He covered his face with his handkerchief to avoid breathing the blowing dust, hoping that his sinuses wouldn't seek revenge on him for bringing them there.

The noise was deafening as the gardener's swaying path put him on a course to intercept Beckett. In fact, the droning whine of the blower was loud enough to obscure all other nearby sounds. Beckett contributed to the racket by sneezing.

Out of the corner of his eye, Beckett saw the gardener lurch sideways and bounce off the wall of the building to land in the bushes. Beckett thought this was odd behavior for a gardener, but simply assumed that the man was drunk. The blower droned on, gradually getting quieter, while he turned the corner toward his apartment door. Then, over the blower noise, he heard a boom like a car backfiring. White stucco chips flew off the wall that shielded him from the street. Curious, he took a step back and saw the rear end of a red Subaru station wagon racing away. He shook his head. Someone was in a hurry.

When he opened the door to his apartment, Beckett's pulse quickened. He could smell Nikki's perfume in the still air. The pleasant fragrance washed through his nose, replacing the smell of gasoline he'd carried in from outside. He felt dizzy as the perfume sparked memories he'd been trying to forget.

Beckett shut the door and leaned back against it, studying his apartment to divert his mind while he tried to control his breathing. Built on two levels, the ground floor contained a kitchen, closets, and a small living room with a cathedral ceiling. The dark wood staircase against the north wall rose to a landing four feet above the ground floor, then reversed its direction for the final climb to the second floor loft, containing a small bedroom with a built-in waterbed and a bathroom. From where he was standing, Beckett could see the end of the waterbed through the upstairs railing, but he couldn't tell if anyone was up there. Mounds of books were

everywhere – on the tables, in the closets, on the blue carpet, and under the staircase. A few novels had defied the last earthquake to remain on the bookshelves, but not many. Practicality had forced Beckett to bulldoze narrow paths through the mounds until he had time to re-shelve all the books. He was standing on several business cards from newspaper and TV reporters that had been shoved under the door, along with two cards from industrious realtors who thought he might like to move somewhere else. One wall was decorated with personal photos: his smiling parents, his frowning older brother, his screaming sister, and an enraged prairie dog.

A photo of Nikki occupied a prominent place in the collection, her blue eyes sparkling along with her smile as she posed beside a waterfall in a red swimsuit. Her shoulder-length black hair was straight and dripping wet. One of these days he knew he'd have to take the photo down, but he didn't know what to put up there in its place – at least that was the excuse he kept telling himself.

It was clear that Nikki wasn't downstairs, so he started toward the staircase, hesitating at the first step. What did she want? Had she realized her mistake and come back to him? Had she left her husband again? He took a deep breath and trudged up the stairs.

The bathroom was empty. So was the bed. But the smell of her perfume was stronger than before.

The bed was rumpled where she'd been sitting. How long had she waited? She hadn't known he was in Newport Beach, so she must have expected to find him at home. The hollow feeling of loss returned to his stomach. If he'd been there sooner –

She'd left a note on the pillow, held in place by the spare apartment key that Nikki had kept in her purse for almost a year. It was always a wonderful surprise to return home and find her waiting for him. The fact that she wasn't there now, and that he'd missed her by only a few minutes, made him want to rush outside and look for her, but he knew the attempt would be futile.

He read the delicate handwriting on the note twice, making sure he hadn't missed anything or misinterpreted its meaning. After two weeks, she had felt strong enough to risk facing him to return his apartment key. Once she arrived at his apartment, and he wasn't there at four in the morning, she waited in the hope they could talk for a while. She waited for five hours. Here, the note was stained by tears, but the handwriting continued. Her husband noticed how depressed she'd been since they got back together, and he was getting suspicious, so they had an argument and she told him about her relationship with Beckett. She viewed her husband as a simple man with a lot of frustrations and hidden anger, but he was still mostly stable and reliable after nine years of marriage. And rich. She couldn't bring herself to leave him permanently. She'd made her choice six years ago, and was resolved to live with that decision, despite her love for Beckett. She ended the note by saying that she wished he'd been there that morning, just one final time.

Beckett gritted his teeth and tried to distract himself by counting the books piled in the narrow space between the wall and the other side of the waterbed, but he kept losing count. He dropped the note on the bed and went downstairs for a glass of white wine, which was the only alcohol he kept in the apartment. He'd never developed a taste for beer, and his bottle of tequila, or what was left of it, was still at the beach house. Looking out the kitchen window, he admired his view of the gray cinder block wall just two feet away while the analytical part of his mind wondered why the color of the wall looked even duller than usual.

The gnarled stump of a former fern he'd forgotten to water sat dejectedly by his answering machine. Portions of the plant had fallen on the bar that divided his kitchen from his living

room — the fern's subtle last-ditch attempt to attract attention before it died of neglect. The staccato rhythm of the blinking light on his ancient answering machine annoyed him, so he played his messages.

Beep.

A deep growl, then a monotone voice said, "Ed? It's Meatball. The university wants to change everything on the website. They say the javascript blows up whenever they test it with a 2.0 browser on an old Mac someone probably bought at a garage sale. This is crap. I won't do it. If they want their site to look like they bought it at Sears, they can kiss my fat ass."

Meatball was Ralph Bronkowski, the software engineer who did the programming for Beckett's business in San Francisco. Translating Meatball's message, he assumed the client wanted a minor change to the website they'd just finished. Meatball considered himself a coding artiste, so he didn't appreciate changes, especially after he considered a project finished.

Beep.

The next caller stayed on the line for a few seconds, letting the air whistle through his nose while he breathed, then cleared his throat and hung up. Probably a salesman.

Beep.

A lilting female voice: "Ed, it's Hyacinth. Meatball hasn't come out of his office since yesterday. I've been passing flat food to him under his door, but he sounds really pissed off this time. Any suggestions? Call me."

Hyacinth was his graphic designer. She shared the small office in San Francisco's trendy South of Market district with Meatball. Renaissance Gargoyle leased one corner of the former Gallo sausage factory that had been converted to office space; when local leasing rates skyrocketed during the Internet boom, landlords converted closets, supply rooms, large bathroom stalls, and any other spare space into income-producing office properties. Gargoyle's offices smelled like spicy sausage, but client visits were rare so it didn't matter. Beckett helped Hyacinth and Meatball by finding new business and handling the administrative end of things when he was in town.

Beep.

"This is Steve. It's about three o'clock on Wednesday. I'm meeting some people in Newport Beach this afternoon, so I thought we could grab some dinner tonight before I vanish into the darkness again. Call my cell phone when you get in if you're not up north."

Steve was a Hollywood investment banker friend who dabbled in film production – porn films, to be exact. They'd gone to high school together in Fountain Valley, but they'd rarely seen each other for the last five years since Steve rarely ventured out into the daylight. Beckett was sorry that he'd missed the call.

Beep.

A woman's loud and gravelly voice, "This is Dotty Hepplewhite at *TechWired*. We're going to break up your nanotechnology article over two issues, so we need another thousand words or so. The sooner the better. If you have any questions, give me a call. Thanks."

Dotty wanted more words. That was fine; it meant more money. It was the first time she'd ever asked him to expand one of his articles. Since he'd been paid by the word for so many years, it was unusual for an editor to ask him for more words than she got in his first draft.

Beep.

The whistling nose breather again. It sounded like he had some kind of sinus problem. After a few seconds, he hung up.

Beep.

The fast-talking, almost hysterical, caffeine-charged voice of Cyril Portnoy, the editor of his column for *Science Monthly*: "Ed, I sent you an e-mail about a week ago, but you haven't responded. I need the topics for your next three columns. Quickly. By yesterday, if possible. You still working on that quantum processor article? Write. Call. Help me out. Bye."

As soon as he figured out what his next topics were, he'd be happy to let Cyril know. He had a brief, mischievous urge to call Cyril and tell him he was going to do a three-part series on genetically engineered ham sandwiches. But Cyril wouldn't see the humor in it anyway, then he'd tell Beckett to go ahead and write it because he trusted him. Then Beckett would feel bad. So Cyril would have to wait until he came up with his real topics.

Beep.

Beckett's fingers tightened around his wineglass when he heard Nikki's hesitant voice: "I have to see you. I'll understand if you don't want to see me. But I think it's important. There was an argument. And I told him about us. He'll be on a business trip for the next three days. So I thought now, maybe, would be a good time. Okay? I'll call again later. Or I'll come over."

Beckett wondered how old the message was. She hadn't left the date or the time on her message, and he hadn't been back to the apartment for a week. But she sounded upset, so it was understandable. He had to assume the message was from yesterday, since she'd shown up early that morning before he got home. Her husband's business trip helped to explain the odd hour of her visit. He didn't understand why she'd told her husband about their relationship, but the reason probably fell into that large category of things he didn't understand about women. She'd said nothing about divorce in her message or in her note, and she had returned his apartment key, so their relationship still seemed to be a dead issue – just one more dead thing in his life.

Beep.

Reporters from three local newspapers, two TV stations, and the *National Inquisitor* had called to leave their phone numbers and request interviews regarding the murder in Newport Beach. The *Inquisitor* reporter also wanted to know if Beckett would admit that an alien abduction was involved.

Beep.

There were two more calls from the whistling nose breather. He snorted once, cleared his throat twice, then made a grumbling hiss that sounded like an angry bear. If it was a salesman, Beckett had to admire his persistence.

Beckett made a note to call Dotty, then reset the old answering machine to record. Finished with his wine, he attacked the pile of mail and newspapers that Nikki had brought in. The mail consisted of a postcard from the

Carvers depicting an obscure monument in Scotland, followed by credit card bills and utility bills, which he avoided opening by concentrating on the morning edition of his local newspaper.

His name was on the front page.

FOUR

al Blackthorne sorted the stack of mail into two neat piles on his black marble desk. In his hand, a gold letter opener glittered in a shaft of sunlight cut by the horizontal slats of the Venetian blinds. His desk was positioned in the office so he would always get the best light from the window to highlight the sharp features of his face. He flicked some imaginary lint from the sleeve of his black Armani suit as a polite caller on the speakerphone waited for a response.

"Mr. Blackthorne?"

"I know she's old. I know she's a widow. I don't care. Do I have to explain everything to you people?" Listening to himself, he was amused that he sounded like a banker in an old movie who was about to throw Jimmy Stewart and his orphans out into the snow.

"No, sir," said the deep voice.

Tal hung up the phone without saying goodbye. His face twisted into a smile. He knew Mrs. Bowman's house didn't need to be bulldozed so the shopping mall could be built. The Blackthorne Corporation owned all of the former farmland around the woman's home, so they could easily build at the other end of the parcel and run the parking lot around her two acres. But it wouldn't look good. The newspapers loved stories about defiant old people who stood up to real estate developers threatening to take their homes. Tal had waited almost two years for her to die or sell the house, but she wouldn't oblige him. Killing her would be too obvious. Now she'd finally made a mistake by missing too many mortgage payments. Mrs. Bowman's bank owed Tal a favor, which he reinforced by donating an armored Cadillac Fleetwood limousine with bulletproof glass, formerly used by two US presidents, to the bank manager's car collection. The Pelican's Roost shopping mall would soon be a reality.

It wasn't as if the old woman had earned the land. In 1915, the Encyclopaedia Britannica company purchased land near the coast that was generally considered worthless, mainly consisting of inaccessible ravines and hillsides. The land was subdivided into 420 parcels, which were then given away free to anyone who purchased a set of their encyclopedias. The company no doubt thought that the inducement of free land on the west coast, which the purchasers had never seen, would help their salesmen change the minds of hundreds of stubborn families who would otherwise never have bought their encyclopedias. The ironic part of the deal was that the mineral rights were included with the land. Tal could imagine Britannica's dismay, in 1920, when huge reservoirs of oil were discovered under the lots they had given away. A few years after that, the landowners each received their first $10,000 royalty checks – certainly a fair deal in exchange for purchasing a set of encyclopedias. Mrs. Bowman's father was one of those encyclopedia

buyers – his daughter had inherited the land, the house, and the oil royalties that continued until 1989 when the reservoir ran dry. Now, the land itself was more valuable, and Tal wanted to develop it.

The next letter in the stack was from the Native American Educational Fund. He flipped the letter into the charity pile so that his secretary would remember to send them some money. Blackthorne treasured his corporation's flawless reputation, and didn't begrudge throwing the odd tax deductible buck at high profile charities to enhance his image.

The speakerphone beeped. Tal pressed a button. "Yes?"

"Mr. Blackthorne? Mr. Busby is here to see you." The voice belonged to Babette, his new secretary. While she had a good set of secretarial skills, as far as he could tell, Tal's primary reason for hiring her had been that she was French. She added some class to the operation. And her attractive appearance helped decorate the office. The back rub she gave him during the interview had not influenced him at all.

Tal checked his watch; almost noon. He'd be having lunch with the mayor of Huntington Beach at one o'clock. "Okay. Send him in."

Tal looked up as the dark mahogany door to his office swung open. Framed by the doorway, a small man in a blue Brooks Brothers suit aggressively scanned the room with his birdlike eyes. Tal had never seen the man blink those bulging brown eyes, and that was a trait he found unsettling. He wasn't sure of the man's exact height, but he had to be less than five feet tall. He had a thin, wiry build and his brown hair was cut short. He had the straight posture that Tal associated with military training, although Tal had never been in the military himself and found it hard to imagine such a short person in uniform. The man's tanned face seemed to thrust forward from the rest of his head, ending in a long hooked nose. A huge gold watch glittered on his left wrist.

"Come on in, Kermit." Although the small man seemed dangerous, Tal liked to remind him who the boss was by tweaking him about his name.

"Please, sir. If you don't call me Kermit, I won't call you Talleyrand, or Tallywhacker, or whatever your name is. Call me *Condor*."

Tal sighed and forced himself not to laugh. Kermit Busby preferred his old military code name, Condor, although he had no idea why the man would want to name himself after a larger-than-average vulture that was nearly extinct. "I keep forgetting. That's some kind of a big bird, right?"

Kermit's eyes narrowed. "It's the largest land bird in North America. It has a nine-foot wingspan." To illustrate, he stretched out his arms and flapped.

"And they eat dead things."

"Well, yes, but mainly *big* dead things. Cattle, sheep, deer – stuff like that. They might take a dead squirrel or a rabbit, but only for a quick snack. They're nature's maintenance engineers."

"Charming."

"They start by eating the soft parts, like eyes or internal organs," Kermit said, his eyes sparkling. "They pop the eyes out with their beaks, then – "

As the little man droned on about his favorite carrion eaters, Tal tried to ignore him. He was revolted by Kermit's nature story, but he once again detected the psychotic qualities he needed in a chief of security for the Blackthorne Corporation. During their original interview, Condor discussed his Special Forces background, and he claimed to be a martial arts expert as well as a master of disguise. Tal had no idea how Kermit would disguise his diminutive stature, but that wasn't an important skill for a chief of security anyway.

"Their talons are strong, but they aren't built for grabbing or killing their prey," Kermit continued, probably thinking that Tal's glassy stare meant rapt interest. "If you look real close – "

Tal wondered if Kermit had an off switch. Prior to his employment by Tal, the little gnome ran his own pest control business, supposedly killing bugs or people, depending on the needs of his clients. Tal was starting to think that Kermit killed with his boring bird stories. In the long run, however, it didn't matter to Tal how Kermit got his job done. Since Tal had hired him, he'd already demonstrated his value. He might be a little dim, but he was useful.

" – also spend much of their time grooming, keeping their plumage neat and clean. Since rotten flesh is so dirty, they're particularly careful to clean their heads after feeding. There is much we can learn from these noble birds."

Tal held up a hand to stop the flow of words, then gestured at one of the overstuffed chairs in front of his desk. "Pull up a perch, Condor."

Condor squinted and looked around, then sniffed the air, tipping his head sideways in a birdlike manner. Satisfied that the room held no obvious danger, Condor stepped into the room and shut the door. As he walked over to the chair, his knees were bent and he held his elbows away from his body as if he were ready to pounce on something he was stalking. Condor would have been disappointed to learn that Tal simply thought he walked like an old lady.

"What did you want to see me about?" Tal asked. Condor sat down and stared at Tal without speaking. That unblinking malevolent gaze made Tal uncomfortable, so he had to break the silence. "Did you hear me?"

"I've got ears like a bat," Condor hissed.

Ears like a bat? Tal snorted. "No doubt. Is there something you want to tell me, or did you just drop by to lecture me about birds?"

"You're going to be so pleased," he said, smiling. "I've been out protecting your interests. And mine, of course."

Tal hated it when his subordinates tried to think for themselves. "What did you do?"

"Well, there was a little mishap in disposing of a certain payload, if you get my drift. And the aforementioned delivery landed in this guy's back yard instead of the Pacific Ocean, and he called the police, and bingo, there was a story in this morning's newspaper about the aforesaid stiff."

Tal gritted his teeth. "Would you stop trying to sound like a lawyer? It's hard enough to understand what you're getting at, and I've already got plenty of attorneys working for me. So some unknown schmuck found the body. Big deal. There's nothing to connect it with us."

"Yeah, well, it's my neck on the line, so I wanted to make sure. And the schmuck wasn't exactly an unknown. He's been on television, and the police take him seriously."

"So you took it upon yourself to do what, exactly?"

"Eliminate the witness."

Tal's mouth fell open while he stared at the little man.

Condor wriggled in his chair as if he were puffing up his feathers. "Impressed, eh? I was just doing my job. That's what you pay me for."

Tal couldn't believe what he was hearing. "You 'offed' the guy?"

"Offed?" Condor chuckled. "You can't come right out and say it, can you?"

Tal frowned. "Say what?"

"You ask me to terminate people, but you can't say the actual words."

"Well, what about you, tough guy? You say 'terminate' when we're talking

about – that subject."

"That's my training, Mr. Blackthorne. The commander in chief couldn't tell us to go out and assassinate people; he might be recorded. And who'd want to vote for a guy like that?"

Tal rubbed his forehead. "But I didn't ask you to knock this guy off! That was your brilliant idea."

Condor smiled, thinking it was a compliment. "Well, sir, to be precise, I haven't quite completed the job yet."

Tal slumped back in his chair. "You decided to whack him, then you screwed it up, is that it?"

Condor raised an eyebrow. "Negative, sir. I just had a small setback."

"What went wrong?"

"The target moved."

"You mean you missed?"

"A Mag-10 Roadblocker doesn't miss. It's a ten-gauge semi-auto shotgun with maximum penetration. I left the gardener pushing up daisies."

Tal smacked his palm into his forehead. "You killed the man's gardener?"

Condor still hadn't blinked. "You have to break eggs to make an omelet."

"This is terrible." Tal stood up and started pacing behind his desk. "I'm a respectable member of this community."

Condor spread his hands. "Hey, it happens. The light was good, but the target moved too fast."

Tal suddenly stopped and stared at his chief of security. "You did it in broad daylight? Tell me no one saw you. Please."

"No one saw me."

Tal sighed with relief.

"At least I don't think so. I don't know. The target might have spotted me. I was driving my car when I fired the shotgun, and the recoil bounced my head off the window, so I was kind of punchy for a few minutes after that. Nearly passed out a couple of times. Fortunately, I drove onto the freeway so nobody would notice how I was swerving around."

"You drove your own car?"

"Hey, it's reliable. And you never said anything about giving me a company car, so what else am I supposed to use?"

"Have you ever thought of *renting* a car? Or stealing one?"

Condor considered for a moment, tipping his head in that birdlike way. "Wow. Good idea, boss. You're a crafty one."

Tal began pacing again, wringing his hands. His reputation was on the line. If anyone saw Condor or his car and traced him back to Blackthorne, his business was doomed. White-collar gangsters couldn't just kill people in broad daylight – not in Orange County, anyway. Sure, no one was going to miss a dead gardener, but Tal's business rivals would exaggerate everything out of proportion if they found out he was involved in a blatant murder.

There was even a remote chance that Tal might go to jail, although he could probably bribe his way out of trouble. He had to make sure that Condor's target wouldn't live long enough to identify the dwarf and connect the dots back to Tal Blackthorne. "Look, Condor, maybe I should get someone else for this job."

Condor honked out a derisive laugh. "Oh, yeah? Who are you going to get? Do you think you can just walk down to the beach and find a trained killer like me?"

Tal hoped he could find someone better – that was the whole idea. "I have friends. I'll find somebody."

"Negative on that idea, boss man. Your friends in the Chamber of Commerce can't help you with this one. I'll finish what I started. The Condor waits and watches for the right moment, soaring to new heights on the wind, then he pounces on his prey." Condor swooped his hand around and grabbed the air to demonstrate his meaning. "Like that. I'll terminate the mark for you, don't you worry. The Condor guarantees delivery, even if he has to follow his prey to hell to do it."

Tal thought it would be great if the dwarf in the expensive suit did go to hell, but he refrained from saying so. He knew Condor carried a gun, so it wouldn't do to piss him off. He sighed heavily. "Okay, Condor, give it another shot."

Condor honked out a laugh. The odd noise startled Tal. "'Give it another shot?' That's a good one, boss."

The right corner of Tal's mouth went up as he attempted to smile. "Thanks."

Condor lurched to his feet, glanced around the office to make sure he wasn't going to be attacked, and darted toward the office door in the weird crouch that Tal had come to expect. When asked, Condor had explained that he walked in a crouch because he wanted to be "ready." The odd little man had never explained what he wanted to be "ready" for, but Tal was quite ready to see Condor leave.

The newspaper article was simple and direct, starting at the top of the front page alongside an article about a tornado destroying a trailer park in Oklahoma. Beckett felt honored to be given equal billing with a tornado:

BIZARRE MURDER IN SWIMMING POOL

A Mountain View man was killed Thursday night in the swimming pool of a Newport Beach home.

According to Newport Beach Police Lieutenant Moses Daniels, the body of a middle-aged man was brought up from the bottom of the pool by a police diver. The victim's name is being withheld pending notification of his relatives.

"Craziest thing I ever saw," said Emmett Fittipaldi, a next-door neighbor who claims to have witnessed the murder from his bedroom window. "I saw Beckett rip this guy up with a chainsaw and toss the body parts in the pool right in front of me." He also said that the police pulled the body out of the pool of blood in big, meaty chunks.

Dr. Edward Beckett, 34, a part-time Fountain Valley resident and science writer who has appeared on local television talk shows, was house-sitting for friends at the time the body was found in the pool. The owners of the beach house, at 138 Ocean Front Drive, could not be reached for comment.

Beckett reported the corpse to the police shortly after midnight on the Police Business line, rather than using the 911 emergency number. "It's possible that he didn't want the call to be recorded or traced," said Carla Estevez, the police switchboard operator on duty when the call came in. "He refused to call back on the 911 line. It was very suspicious. Personally, I didn't like his attitude."

Beckett was unavailable for comment, but Fittipaldi overheard him telling the police that "the body just fell out of the sky."

Details were sketchy, but Fittipaldi said there were over twenty police officers conducting the investigation in the backyard of the Newport Beach home when he was summoned to describe the harrowing events he'd seen to Lt. Daniels, who was in the process of interrogating Beckett.

Beckett was not arrested at the crime scene. When asked if Beckett was a suspect in the murder, Daniels would only say, "an arrest is imminent."

Most of the neighbors had ever spoken to Beckett, but one woman who agreed to give an anonymous statement said, "He seemed nice. Kind of quiet. He was always going in and out at odd hours, and he kept to himself."

Beckett has been an outspoken critic of the Newport Beach police. Last month, he exposed an administrative cover-up related to the contamination of DNA evidence at crime scenes by uniformed officers. Tainted evidence suspicions have forced the reopening of over six hundred police investigations. Police Chief Antonio Bedlam referred to the incident as "an administrative nightmare." Seven police department officials and a county coroner resigned from their jobs as a result of the ensuing internal investigation.

Beckett sighed. At least they'd spelled his name right. But he wasn't sure if that was a good thing or not. The article made it look like he'd killed Dumas, especially since they'd used Fittipaldi as one of the sources for their quotes. Daniels hadn't helped any by dodging the question about Beckett being a suspect. In any case, Beckett's phone number was unlisted, so he shouldn't have to worry about crank phone calls, except for the cranks in the newsrooms around town. He wouldn't be going back to the Carver house, so he wouldn't be there if curious visitors tried to see the crime scene, although he should have warned his friends.

He dropped the newspaper when a blood-curdling scream ripped through the air.

A quick glance out the window revealed nothing, so Beckett rushed outside. Mrs. Quigley, an ancient woman who lived alone just two doors down from Beckett's apartment, was standing on the sidewalk near his door, gaping in horror at something on the other side of the wall. As usual, she wore a heavy black overcoat to keep the chill off in the eighty-degree heat.

By the absence of the droning whine he'd heard earlier, Beckett assumed the gardeners had left. He was correct.

All but one.

As Beckett came around the wall, he saw the "drunk" gardener, with the blower on his back, still stretched out face-down among the bushes. Beckett rolled his eyes, then noticed that Mrs. Quigley had almost acquired enough air for another scream. She had good lungs for her age, but it took time for her to fill them up. Wanting to avoid having his eardrums ruptured by a scream at close range, he waved his arms and walked toward her, hoping her hearing aid was working.

"It's okay, Mrs. Quigley. He's just drunk."

She turned her wild eyes on his face, holding her breath as she hesitated. Beckett put his hand on her shoulder and smiled.

"I saw him pass out in the bushes a little while ago."

Mrs. Quigley looked uncertain, shifting her gaze back and forth from Beckett's face to the gardener in the bushes. Then she came to a decision and let go with a scream that was loud enough to give Beckett an instant headache.

"Stop! It's all right! Nothing to worry about!"

Then she fainted. Beckett caught her before she hit the ground and gently lowered her to the sidewalk.

"Hey! What're ya doin'?"

Crouched over the unconscious Mrs. Quigley, Beckett turned his head toward the source of the deep, angry voice. A short, thick man with a crewcut, a stained white t-shirt, and Bermuda shorts, was coming toward him at a fast waddle. Beckett had seen the man before and knew that he was a garbage man for the city of Costa Mesa, but they had never spoken to each other.

"Get away from her!"

Beckett shook his head, realizing the garbage man was confused by the way things looked. "I'm not – "

The garbage man interrupted him, grabbing his arm to haul him upright. "Damn right yer not!"

"Let go of me!"

"Tell me what's goin' on! You hurt dat old lady?"

"No!"

The screams and yells had drawn some of the other residents out of their apartments. A thin man in a three-piece suit discovered the gardener in the bushes about the same time that Beckett pointed him out to the garbage man.

"This guy's dead," said the three-piece suit, his eyes wide as he crouched beside the gardener.

Beckett shook his head. "No, he isn't. He's just drunk. I saw him fall into the bushes a little while ago."

The three-piece suit frowned as he looked up at Beckett. "I know a dead person when I see one. There's blood all over these bushes."

"What? You're kidding."

Beckett managed to twist his arm out of the garbage man's huge hand. He walked across the grass and peered at the gardener, then pressed his fingers against the man's neck to check for a pulse. He didn't have one. The gardener's face was turned away toward the wall, but Beckett didn't have any strong desire to see it anyway. The blower on the gardener's back made him smell like gasoline. There were spots of blood on the bushes and what little Beckett could see of the front of the gardener's shirt was dripping red. A pool of blood was forming on the hard dirt beneath the bushes.

"Told you he was dead," said the three-piece suit.

A middle-aged woman with red hair gasped among the small knot of residents huddled together on the sidewalk. When Beckett glanced at her, she took a step backward and pointed at him. "Murderer! I'm calling the police," she said, rushing away with self-righteous indignation.

Their short attention spans distracted by the new object of interest, the rest of the onlookers moved away from the forgotten Mrs. Quigley, still lying unconscious on the sidewalk, and shuffled closer to the dead gardener while the garbage man clamped his hands around Beckett's shoulders.

"You're getting to be a regular Typhoid Mary, aren't you, Doctor? Wherever you go, somebody dies."

Having determined by eyewitness accounts that Beckett had shot the gardener and mugged old Mrs. Quigley, the uniformed Fountain Valley cops, resplendent in their solid black uniforms, had handcuffed Beckett and made him sit on the curb between two patrol cars. The air smelled of freshly mown grass and gasoline. Three cops stood beside him, ready to subdue him if he tried to get away, when Detective Daniels approached.

Beckett looked up. "Daniels? What are you doing here? You moonlighting for the Fountain Valley police?"

"No, but there's a shortage of trained homicide detectives around here. And Lieutenant Ghandi is a friend of mine," Daniels said, indicating the cop in the gray suit examining the gardener's body.

"I suppose you told him I was a dangerous criminal."

"You mean to tell me you aren't? To me, a man who cuts up bodies and dumps them in his swimming pool is dangerous. Call me old-fashioned, but when that same man mugs an old woman and kills a gardener the next day, that tends to confirm my suspicions."

Beckett sighed. "You can't prove any of that."

"You want me to believe this was all just a coincidence?"

"I'll admit it doesn't look good – "

Daniels burst out laughing. This provoked frowns of disapproval from the "eyewitnesses," who were still standing in a protective knot on the sidewalk, apparently afraid that fourteen cops wouldn't be able to subdue the homicidal maniac who had quietly been living next to them for the past six years.

While the flash from a camera created little popping lights in Beckett's eyes, newspaper reporters from the *Daily Pilot* and the *Fountain Valley Independent*, the first press on the scene, were happily covering the biggest local story they'd had in months. Two cops kept them from getting too close to the dangerous criminal. Mrs. Quigley sat propped against the side of a red paramedic truck with a dazed expression on her face. Beckett hoped she'd start talking soon so that she could verify his innocence.

Daniels managed to bring himself under control. "Tell me, Doctor, what was it that sent you over the edge onto this killing rampage?"

Beckett rolled his eyes, noting in the back of his mind that he'd been rolling his eyes with great frequency lately. He was losing his patience. "Noise."

"Noise?"

"I hate the sound of that gardener's blower machine."

Daniels wasn't sure how to respond. "You're kidding."

"Does it matter?"

"You want to make a formal confession, Doctor?"

The three cops who were standing around guarding Beckett pricked up their ears at the word, "confession."

Beckett squinted up at the detective's face, which was hard to see with the noon sun behind his head. "I know you're used to looking down on people, but would you mind if I stand up? I'm getting a kink in my neck trying to see you."

"It's okay with me," Daniels replied. He looked at the three uniforms, who telepathically communed with each other and decided it was okay with simultaneous nods.

Beckett stood up. "Now, I don't want to ruin your day, but if you talk to Mrs. Quigley, she'll tell you I didn't hurt her."

"But you threatened her verbally? That still qualifies as assault, Doctor."

"I didn't assault her, either. I came out of my apartment after she started screaming. Then she fainted."

"That's not what the eyewitnesses said."

"You actually believe that raving bunch of windbags?"

"It's their word against yours. And you're already under suspicion for one murder."

Beckett shook his head and looked away to keep himself under control. "I don't believe this."

"*You* don't believe it? You should see it from my point of view."

Lieutenant Ghandi, who looked like a fortyish Marine drill instructor stuffed into a gray suit, motioned for Daniels to come over. Beckett walked with him, followed by his three guards.

Ghandi pointed at a damaged section of the stucco wall that screened Beckett's front door from the street. A police photographer snapped a few photos of it from different angles.

"Shotgun blast," said Ghandi, a man of few words. "Big one."

"Hmm," Daniels replied.

A disturbing thought popped into Beckett's head. He remembered the booming noise he'd heard when he entered his apartment about two hours earlier – and the car speeding away. "Subaru."

Daniels frowned at Beckett. "Excuse me? There's no need for foul language, Doctor."

"A red Subaru station wagon. I think someone tried to kill me."

"Ah. Trying for the insanity plea again, eh? You shot the gardener in self-defense after he threatened to dust you with his blower?"

"I saw a Subaru racing away after I heard a booming sound. It must have been the shotgun blast that I heard."

"Sounds to me like you're grasping at straws, Doctor. I don't suppose you got the license number of this alleged Subaru."

"Well, no."

Daniels raised his voice so the crowd of neighbors could hear him. "I suppose no one else saw a red Subaru drive past here?"

The neighbors looked at each other and shook their heads. Daniels raised an eyebrow and turned his gaze back on Beckett's face, reminding Beckett of a bug collector pinning a butterfly to a piece of wood for display.

"Did you see the driver of this phantom Subaru, Doctor?"

"Well, no. I wasn't really paying attention. It didn't seem important at the time."

"How convenient for you. So this mystery driver in the phantom Subaru just picked you out at random and took a couple of pot shots at you?"

"I guess that sums it up. The first shot hit the gardener when I walked past him. As you can see, the driver took a second shot at me when I got near my door. That seems to indicate that I was his target."

"And the helpful gardener blocked the first shot?"

"I don't think he saw it coming. In fact, I just thought he was drunk when he fell into the shrubbery."

"The blood pouring out of the man's body didn't tip you off?"

"I didn't see any blood at the time."

"Uh-huh. How do I know you didn't shoot him yourself? Maybe you missed the first time and hit the wall."

Beckett started to point at the wall, then remembered his wrists were handcuffed together behind his back, so he nodded at it instead. "You can see as well as I can. The gardener wasn't shot at close range, and neither was this wall. And I'm sure nobody has found the murder weapon around here. They already searched my apartment."

Daniels looked over his shoulder. "That true, Ghandi? No shotgun?"

"Nope," Ghandi said, working out the spread of the shotgun pellets with a tape measure.

Daniels gestured at the onlookers. "But what about these good people? They all say they saw you kill the gardener."

Beckett glared at his neighbors, who all looked away to avoid his gaze, nervously shuffling their feet. Two of them were speaking to the newspaper reporters.

Ghandi handed a notebook to Daniels and walked off in the direction of Mrs. Quigley. Daniels flipped through the notebook pages while Beckett tried to read the upside-down handwriting.

"Hmm," said Daniels.

"Is that a good *hmm* or a bad *hmm*?" Beckett asked.

Daniels rubbed his forehead with his long fingers. "According to this, each of the eyewitnesses has a different story. Some say you used a knife to kill the gardener, but none of them described the same knife. One man says you used a .357 Magnum to shoot him. Another man says you bludgeoned your victim with a garden rake, then knocked out Mrs. Quigley when she threatened to call the police."

"Like I said, someone's trying to kill me."

"With neighbors like these, it might be one of them."

"No kidding. Are you going to start looking for that red Subaru?"

"What, stop every red Subaru we see on the road and ask them if they shot anybody this morning?"

"Well, something like that. It was a station wagon, remember. Late-model."

"You have any idea how many cars fit that description in Orange County?"

"Quite a few, I expect."

"Probably a few hundred."

"Well, you're the detective. Detect. Find the guy."

"Guy? The driver was a man?"

Beckett thought about it for a moment, but he couldn't get the image of the Subaru clear in his head. "Maybe. I'm not sure."

"You're a big help. I'd think a murder suspect would be more helpful in laying the blame on someone else. It's true that shotguns are more likely to be used by male murderers, but that's not much to go on. How many people do you know who'd like to kill you, Doctor? Besides everyone on the Newport Beach Police force?"

"Nobody springs to mind."

"I see. I don't suppose you're a gang member or anything like that?"

"Sorry."

"And you don't have any criminal associates? You aren't in debt to a loan shark? You're not a drug dealer?"

"Nope."

"Well, then, since we can't come up with a motive, maybe the Subaru driver wanted to kill the gardener. Then he tried for you because he thought you were a witness."

Beckett nodded. "Possible, I suppose."

"But unlikely when we consider the events of last night. I suppose you think someone intended to kill you, but they cut up Dumas and dumped him in your pool by mistake."

"Beats me."

Daniels grimaced and rubbed his neck. "All right, Doc. Against my better judgment, I'm not going to arrest you. You leave a trail of bodies wherever you go, so I doubt we'll have any trouble keeping track of your location."

"I'll try and hide them better next time," Beckett said.

"You do that. If you're responsible for what's been happening, I figure I'll give you enough rope so that you can hang yourself. You're a clever guy, but you can only kill so many people before you start leaving billboard-sized clues with your name written all over them."

"Meaning I'm still a suspect."

"Meaning you're my only suspect. If my chief had his way, you'd be sitting on an electric chair, in the gas chamber, with needle in your arm and a noose around your neck. Fortunately, the D.A. managed to point out that we don't have any evidence linking you to Dumas. And with your recent act of civic duty, exposing a couple of faulty evidence handling procedures, it'll make us look even worse if we arrest you without good evidence."

Beckett shrugged. "Sorry I can't be of more help."

"I take it you still don't want to confess."

"I'll pass."

"I knew it. You're a hard case. You've probably left a trail of blood across fifty states. Under a different name, of course."

"Of course. I'm not stupid."

"We'll see about that."

Beckett rubbed his sore wrists while one of the uniforms unlocked his handcuffs. He noted that his neighbors were scurrying away to their apartments to avoid his incriminating gaze. "You find out any-thing more about the patches on Dumas's flight jacket? Or his relatives in Mountain View?"

"You think I've got nothing else to do but work on the Dumas case? Newport Beach doesn't exactly qualify as a small town, you know. I have other things to do."

"Well, excuse me. I assumed you'd want to get right to work on it."

"You'd be surprised how many murders go unsolved when there aren't enough clues to close the case within a couple of days."

"The murder was less than thirteen hours ago!"

"That's right. And if we had an unlimited budget, I could fly right up to Mountain View and check things out. But we don't, and I can't."

"So that's it?"

"Goldblum is still studying Dumas's body, so he might come up with more evidence that ties you to the murder. I'll just have to wait and see what develops."

"Great."

"As I said, my chief is putting the pressure on me for a quick arrest – of you – but he won't give me the money for overtime or plane fare to make a connection between you and Dumas. I already know you used to live up north, but I need a lot more than that."

"Since you won't find any connection, where does that leave me? You won't arrest me based on the flimsy conclusions you've made so far, will you?"

Daniels smiled. "That might depend on your keeping a low profile. If the press doesn't keep harping on us about the investigation, I might not have to arrest you until we have more evidence. But the way things are going, I don't think you can keep your name out of the newspaper for one full day, so it doesn't look good."

Beckett watched while the gardener's body was rolled over into a black body bag, which was then zipped shut and lifted onto a stretcher.

"Then you won't mind if I look into Dumas's background myself."

"Yourself?" Daniels frowned. "Of course I mind. This is an official police investigation, Doctor."

"And I'm a private citizen. You can't arbitrarily decide to restrict my movements unless you arrest me."

"Don't tempt me." Daniels fingered the handcuffs attached to his belt.

"Think of it this way. If I leave town, you won't see me on television talking about police harassment. And the newspapers will lose interest once they find out I'm gone. I can let you know where to reach me if anything else comes up."

Daniels considered it for a moment. "You have a point. And if your farfetched notion that someone is trying to kill you is true, it might be a good idea for you to leave town for a few days. At worst, they'll knock you off in someone else's jurisdiction. But if I let you look into this, and we end up arresting you anyway, then we never had this conversation, understand?"

"What conversation?"

Daniels nodded and walked away. "Keep in touch, Doctor."

FIVE

The United jet lurched off the John Wayne Airport runway in a steep climb. The infamous "low-noise" takeoff, which looked so unpleasant to observers on the ground, was mandatory for all the airlines. Beckett was pressed back into his seat as he watched the airport and Newport Bay fall away beneath the wing, then his stomach fluttered when they reached an altitude of one thousand feet and the pilot cut back sharply on the power, dropping the nose into a more gradual climb. From that altitude, with its marinas, the harbor, Upper Newport Bay, and the ocean, Newport Beach glittered in the sunlight like the jewel in Orange County's crown.

That morning, he'd left a note for the Carvers, who would be returning from their trip later in the day. He told them to ignore anything they might read about him in the papers and that he was going up north for a few days. They were used to him spending about half his time in Orange County and half in the Bay Area, so his note wouldn't seem unusual. With regard to the dark stains on the concrete decking beside the pool, Beckett's note explained that he'd spilled a bottle of tomato juice during a wild party.

He'd made an attempt to remove the "tomato juice" stain, after checking with Daniels to see if it was okay, but the rough surface resisted a thorough cleaning. The pool's normal filtration system had removed the pink tint from the water, but Beckett had added some chlorine to kill off any bacteria or God-knows-what-else that might have remained in the pool once the corpse was removed. The smell of chlorine was so strong that it was probably killing the Fittipaldis. He just hoped that the police had thoroughly scoured the yard for missing body parts; he had a feeling that the Carvers wouldn't be too pleased to find a toe or a pancreas among the geraniums.

The smiling flight attendant casually defied gravity by walking down the aisle, still canted at a steep angle. Beckett wondered if the airlines only hired former acrobats into their training programs. The flight to San Jose Airport would only take about forty-five minutes, so the attendants assigned to the first class section of the cabin, which Beckett could see through the gap in the curtains, were already pouring alcohol down the throats of the four passengers who could afford to pay an extra five hundred dollars for their drinks and two more inches of leg room. While wedging his knees into a more comfortable position, Beckett glanced around the main cabin and noted the usual weekday passengers, most of whom were busily tick-ticking away on their laptop computer keyboards. Due to the high number of computer nerds aboard this regular flight, Beckett was sure he'd spot at least one employment headhunter schmoozing the passengers and handing out business cards. With the shortage of skilled nerds in Silicon Valley, employment agencies had taken to extreme measures to hunt their prey, posting scouts on the regular flights between the tech centers of Silicon Valley, Austin, Texas, and southern California. The high percentage of computer and Internet professionals on certain daily Shuttle flights to and from San Jose had earned them the moniker, "the Nerd Birds."

The in-flight magazine had the usual collection of articles designed to appeal to business travelers: "Our Friend the Tarantula," "Olympic Diets to

Energize Weekend Athletes," "Empire Builders of Orange County," "Manipulating Employees into Submission," and "The Blithe Spirits of Blythe." Beckett would normally read almost anything, since he never knew when a stray bit of information he picked up might be of use to him later on, but none of the articles held his interest. He hated spiders of any kind, and felt that all tarantulas should be hunted down and destroyed with flamethrowers, so the tarantula article didn't appeal to him. The Empire Builders article appealed to his fondness for historical subjects, but his attempt to read it failed after a few paragraphs; he just couldn't focus his attention on the printed words.

After passing over Catalina Island on their gradual climb into the western sky, the jet banked to the north, allowing plenty of room to fly around the crowded airspace controlled by the tower at Los Angeles International. The pilot was a failed comedian with a captive audience; after introducing himself to the passengers over the crackling speakers, he informed them that they were going to San Jose and asked if anybody knew the way there. This created a mild panic among the more nervous fliers. Perhaps sensing the poor response from the passengers, the pilot said nothing more until they were on final approach to San Jose, when he asked the flight attendants to prepare for landing. They breezed past with their glued-on smiles, collecting plastic cups, napkins, and full bags of peanuts that nobody had managed to open.

The plane banked to the east, giving Beckett a brief glimpse of residential areas, light industrial buildings, the Naval Air Station at Moffett Field, and the southern end of the San Francisco Bay. After a final approach skimming low over the water, they dropped the last few feet and the wheels boomed when they made contact with the runway. Beckett's weight shifted forward against the seat belt while the thrust reversers, the flaps, and the brakes worked together to slow the screaming bird's flight. The commotion scared the hell out of two jackrabbits, which bounded away through the grass dividing the runway from the taxiway. When Beckett stopped looking out the window, a business card from a high-tech employment agency was on his lap; he picked it up, pulled the seat pouch open in front of him, and stuffed the card in with the dozens of other employment agency cards discarded from earlier flights.

San Jose Airport had a cozy feeling, which was probably a reflection of the area's rural past. Located in the heart of Silicon Valley, it wasn't as crowded as John Wayne Airport, probably because the local residents had a nearby international airport they could easily get to in the southern reaches of San Francisco. A second airport for Orange County had been debated for years, but no one could agree on where to put it. The last time Beckett had read about it in the newspaper, they were considering the construction of an offshore airport, but no one could decide on which city's shore the airport would be off of, or how far out in the ocean it should be built. Beckett speculated that Orange County's wealthy coastal residents wouldn't be happy unless the new airport was built in Hawaii.

With his overnight bag in hand, Beckett bypassed the luggage destruction area of the airport and picked up the rental car he'd reserved from Rent-A-Clunker. The pert young woman at the rental counter handed him a greasy key and sent him off in search of Space 89-B, which he finally discovered in the farthest and dustiest corner of the rental car lot. The car itself proved to be the dented hulk of a dirty gold Chevy Camaro with a cracked windshield on the passenger side. Judging by the car's condition, Beckett estimated that it had been built sometime in the seventies by disgruntled assembly-line workers. When he climbed into the driver's seat, he was careful not to slip on the ominous pool of oil that had formed under the car.

The interior of the Camaro held a distinctive odor of gasoline mixed with decaying former hamburgers. A wide array of colorful insect corpses lined the dashboard and the floor, which proved to be the source of the crunching noise Beckett had heard when he stepped into the car. To his surprise, the engine started right up when he switched on the ignition. It ran smoothly for about ten seconds, then coughed and died. He started it again and kept his foot on the accelerator until the engine warmed up, then shifted into first gear with great care and eased out the clutch. The car moved forward, then changed direction when he turned the steering wheel, which was better than the last car he'd rented from this place. A final test of the brakes proved that the car could stop without going through the tedious process of scraping it against the side of a building, as someone else had apparently done in the past. But, as long as the car worked, he couldn't complain for eight dollars a day. He was paying for this trip himself, so he intended to stretch every penny he could. With any luck, he'd come up with an idea for a magazine article that would help recoup his expenses.

His first stop was the Dumas residence, not far from a large shopping mall at the corner of San Antonio Road and El Camino Real. Stanford University was less than ten minutes away, so Beckett knew the area pretty well. He stopped his Camaro behind a yellow Corvette in the driveway of a two-story ranch house, with spruce and oak trees in the front yard, located at the end of Monroe Drive, a gravel road on the boundary between Mountain View and Palo Alto. The gravel road was unusual for the area, but Beckett remembered that the houses on that street fell into a sort of neutral zone that neither of the two cities would definitely claim as their responsibility. However, the gravel road lent the neighborhood a peaceful sort of rural atmosphere that was a pleasant change from the surrounding urban environment.

The presence of the Corvette increased the possibility that someone was home. Beckett hoped that someone had contacted Dumas's relatives by now, because he didn't want to be the one to bring them the bad news. This house was his only starting point if he was to find out what happened to Dumas, and get the police off his back, so he fervently hoped there was someone home who would answer his questions. With any luck, it would be the person who threw Dumas into the Carvers's pool and they would confess immediately, but Beckett guessed that would be unlikely.

Beckett switched off the ignition of his Camaro, but the engine refused to die. It sputtered and clanked, backfiring several times, finally settling down to an uneasy silence after a full thirty seconds of theatrics, like a ham actor stretching out a big death scene on stage. So much for the element of surprise; the entire neighborhood now knew he was there.

When he knocked at the screen door, a woman in her forties with a strong, handsome face opened the inner door. She wore a plain white dress with a high collar, which nicely displayed the dark tan on her skin. The whites of her dark brown eyes were red and puffy, so Beckett guessed she was the wife and she'd been informed of Maxwell's death. As if to match the current condition of her eyes, her hair was also red, but it was straight instead of puffy.

"Mrs. Dumas?" he guessed. She seemed about the right age.

"Yes?"

"I'm Ed Beckett." Not that it would mean anything to her.

"Are you another policeman?"

Beckett hesitated. He might find himself in big trouble if he said he was a cop and she later found out he wasn't. Besides, what if she asked to see his badge? On the other hand, he needed information that she might only give to the police, as opposed to some stranger who just wandered up to her door. Better to act confident and dodge the question entirely.

"Another policeman? Has someone already spoken to you about your husband?"

"Yes. Earlier this morning."

Beckett frowned and consulted the blank pages of a notepad that he pulled from the inside pocket of his blue sport coat. He'd thought the disguise of a sport coat and tie might come in handy, although he usually didn't wear such a formal outfit. The notepad had been a last minute addition to make him look official. It's amazing what people will tell you when you look like you know what you're doing, especially when you're holding a notepad.

"I see. I'll have to check with the Lieutenant on that. Would you mind answering just a few more questions for me? I know this is a bad time, but I'd like to make sure I've got all the details straight."

"I suppose it's okay," she said, opening the screen door to beckon him in.

The living room was almost white enough to make Beckett go snow blind. White, overstuffed, modern furniture was set against the white walls, which were decorated with white macramé objects. The rug and the marble coffee table in front of the modular couch were also white. A white-framed poster on one wall depicted a white Alaskan harp seal pup posing on a white ice floe. The effect was disconcerting and it made Beckett's eyes dart around the room in search of a spot of color, finally locating it when they landed on Mrs. Dumas's red hair when she sat on the couch in her white dress.

"How can I help you, Mr. Beckett? Or is it 'Lieutenant' Beckett?"

"'Mister' is fine. Or you can call me Ed. I'm not a formal kind of guy."

"All right." She reached for a white tissue from a white box on the coffee table and dabbed at the corner of her left eye. Beckett sat at the other end of the couch. "Where did your husband work, Mrs. Dumas?"

"You can call me Astrid. Max worked at Moffett Field, about four miles from here."

"He worked for the Navy?"

"No. For NASA. The Ames Research Center. He's – he was – a project manager in the Space Sciences Division."

Beckett gave her a moment to regain her composure – the reminder that Max was dead made her start sniffling again. He stood up as she dabbed at her eyes with a tissue.

"I'll get you a glass of water. Is the kitchen through here?"

She shook her head with a sniff. "That's not necessary."

"It's no trouble," he said, flashing a smile while he walked out of the room.

The kitchen was spotless and functional, with a lot of those little time-saving devices that busy people like to buy for their homes. He checked three cupboards near the sink before finding the water glasses. While filling the glass with cold water from the refrigerator, he noted that Astrid had been preparing a salad when he arrived. Lettuce, raw carrots, onions, tomatoes, and celery, most of it neatly sliced, lay beside a knife on a wood cutting board beside the sink. The vegetables smelled fresh. Through the window, he could see a manicured lawn and fruit trees in the yard.

When he returned to the living room, Astrid rose from the couch. She looked worried. When Beckett handed her the glass of water, her face relaxed and she sat down.

"Thank you, Mr. Beckett. You're very kind."

"No problem. Shall we continue?"

"Please do."

Beckett glanced at his blank notepad and sat down on the couch. "Do you know what your husband was working on?"

"Oh, he was always working on several projects. But I think he's been spending most of his time on the IRIS experiment for the last couple of months. I know he's had to work a lot of overtime lately; and they've made him work all kinds of odd hours."

"What is the IRIS experiment? Do you know?"

"It stands for 'Infrared Imagery of the Shuttle,' or something like that. He always just referred to it as IRIS, like it was a person or something."

"It was some kind of Space Shuttle experiment?"

"Well, it didn't actually go on the Shuttle or anything. IRIS was sup-posed to measure how hot the Shuttle got on reentry. It had something to do with a telescope. My son could tell you more about it, but he's at school right now."

"How old is your son?"

"Mike is fifteen. He just started high school."

"Is he your only child?"

"I have an eighteen-year-old daughter named Patricia. I haven't told either one of them about their father yet." She looked away, clearly distressed by the idea.

Beckett cleared his throat. "Well, I have to ask you a few difficult questions now. Please don't be offended, but this was an unusual death, so we have to check all the possibilities. Are you aware of anyone who might have a reason to kill your husband?"

Astrid closed her eyes and shook her head. "No. Everyone loved Max. He was a wonderful man."

"Okay. Was your husband involved in anything outside his work that could be considered dangerous?"

"Like what?"

"I don't know. Maybe a hobby or something?"

Astrid looked off into the distance. "Max collected stamps, but I've never considered that a dangerous activity."

"Nothing else?"

"No. Max was dedicated to his work and he loved being a part of the space program. He didn't really take the time for any outside activities; I had to tear him away from work for his three weeks worth of vacation each year. And he had hundreds of hours of accumulated sick leave time that he never used."

"His spending so much time at work never bothered you?"

"It used to, especially when the kids were younger, but he was always so apologetic about not being here that it was hard to stay mad at him for very long. He was always home for the important holidays and birthdays, and he was a responsible provider for his family, so I can't really complain too much."

Beckett sat back on the thick cushions of the couch, giving himself a moment to think. Tension showed in Astrid's face while she kept her eyes on him. Beckett thought there was something besides grief in those eyes, maybe curiosity, but it had always been hard for him to guess women's motivations. As far as body language went, he could only read the most obvious gestures – her crossed arms either meant she was defensive or she was cold. He decided it would make sense if she felt defensive, with a stranger asking a lot of questions right after she'd learned of her husband's death.

"There were some partial patches found on your husband's flight jacket, so we're not sure what they were. One of them started with a red 'N', so I assume it spelled 'NASA'. Does that sound familiar?"

"Yes. That's right."

"Okay. There were two others. One was the right half of a round patch, royal blue with a yellow border, and the letters 'ARC'. It had the nose of an aircraft on it, too."

Astrid nodded. "That sounds like his project patch for IRIS. There was a Space Shuttle in the middle of it."

"Was the 'ARC' part of a word?"

"It's the acronym for 'Ames Research Center'. It's normally printed with the word 'NASA' in front of it."

"All right. The third patch had what looked like a person's name on it, but it wasn't your husband's name. It said 'GERARD P. KUIP' and the end was cut off."

Astrid shook her head. "Doesn't sound familiar."

"It was on his shoulder. Left sleeve."

"Sorry. But let me check something."

She stood up and walked out of the room. At first, Beckett thought it odd that she couldn't remember the third patch, but it was a small one, and she had probably seen it so often that she had forgotten about it. He was sure someone at Ames Research Center would identify the patch if Astrid could not.

Astrid walked back into the room carrying a black and white, 8 x 10 photo. She was sniffling again, and she dabbed at her eyes with another tissue.

"I thought maybe this photo would help, but you can't see enough detail on their jackets."

Astrid handed him the photo. In the foreground, a group of people in flight jackets and blue jeans were smiling at the camera; two women and eighteen men. Some of them knelt in front, but most were standing in two rows. On closer inspection, Beckett saw that two of the men in the back row were wearing caps and white coveralls stained with grease. In the background was a side view of the rear half of a large white aircraft that looked like a Lockheed C-141. It was a type of plane that had been used extensively to transport troops and equipment in Vietnam. The plane had two jet engines on the visible wing; its fuselage sat lower to the ground than commercial passenger jets, and one open door with a short stairway was visible behind the wing. A bold blue stripe ran the length of the white fuselage, widening as it neared the tail. The number on the jet's huge vertical stabilizer identified it as "NASA 714." Astrid was correct about the photo not being close enough to make out the detail on the flight jackets; the shoulder patches were almost invisible.

"Which one is your husband?"

Astrid tapped a polished red fingernail on a tall man at the left end of the group in the photo. Max Dumas had a distinguished appearance, a strong jaw line, and a pleased expression. He was dressed the same way that Beckett remembered seeing him.

"This airplane has something to do with the IRIS project?"

"I guess so, but he didn't talk about it much. He knew I wasn't interested in the technical details of his work. I just know he had to do a lot of flying."

"Whom did your husband work for? Someone in this photo?"

"No. Karl Oberhaus rarely leaves his office in daylight, unless he has a speaking engagement. Max always said the man was a vampire who only came out at night. He's the director at Ames, so all the division heads report to him."

"Your husband was the division head in Space Sciences?"

"No, Max was a special case. He was a branch chief, which meant he'd normally report to the division head, but Oberhaus preferred to communicate with Max directly."

"Why?"

Astrid shrugged, then sat down on the couch. "I'm not sure, but I think Oberhaus used to have Max's job a long time ago. There was a lot of peer pressure on Max because Oberhaus gave him so much attention and let him work independently."

Beckett studied the plane in the photo. Could it have been the instrument of his death? And if someone in the photo was the murderer, how would he weed out the right person among eighteen crewmembers? He didn't even have any training in this sort of thing. He'd just have to hope he could gather enough evidence to provoke an official investigation into the entire crew; at least that would strengthen the case for his own innocence.

"This IRIS experiment he was working on – it wasn't a classified project, was it?"

"Sometimes it was secret and sometimes it wasn't."

"What do you mean?"

"Well, when the IRIS project started, the whole thing was unclassified, and it stayed that way for two years. Then, when they finally managed to get IRIS working right, Max got a call from NASA headquarters, in

Washington, telling him to lock up the data in his safe. He said the order came from the Air Force. The only people who could work on it after that were those with the proper security clearances. It really drove Max nuts because half his team suddenly couldn't do their jobs."

"So what did he do?"

"He made a lot of noise and pointed out how the whole project would be jeopardized by classifying it 'Secret.' It would have taken months to get the rest of his team cleared so they could get back to work again. Then Oberhaus pulled some strings and the project was declassified after a couple of weeks."

Beckett noticed that Astrid's sniffling had stopped, so he wanted to get on with the last of his difficult questions. "When was the last time you saw your husband?"

Astrid hesitated. "Two days ago, when he left for work in the morning. Max told me he'd be late coming back that night, but he didn't say why. I think they were running another test on the IRIS system."

"The detective that was here earlier, did he mention anything about your having to identify Max's body?"

Astrid looked away, blinking hard. "Well, he showed me a photograph. He got it from that Newport Beach detective. A head shot. In fact, it was just the head. I told him it was my Max."

"That must have been rough. I'm sorry."

"Is there anything else you need to ask me right now? I'd like to be alone."

"Just one more question." Beckett swallowed, knowing it was something he had to ask, even though it didn't feel right to do so. "Did you and your husband have a stable marriage? Have you ever suspected that he was seeing someone else?"

Astrid's eyes went cold and hard, which was not the reaction he'd expected. "Get out of my house."

"I just – "

"I won't let you sit there and insult me like that. Get out!"

Beckett stood up, avoiding her cold stare. "I had to ask."

"Max was the most faithful man I've ever known. Now, go away. Leave me in peace with my grief."

"I'm sorry. Thanks for your help," he said, leaving the photo of the aircraft and its crew on the coffee table.

Astrid made no move to leave the couch, so Beckett let himself out the front door. On his way to the Camaro, he wondered if he'd used the wrong approach to asking his questions. For someone who was depressed and grief-stricken, Astrid's emotions had varied considerably during their discussion. She'd shown a lot of control while talking about Max's job and his problems, but other questions had made her more depressed, which was understandable, and angry, which he didn't understand. Maybe it was his lack of experience in dealing with bereaved widows, or his usual blind spot in trying to figure out women's motivations, but something still didn't feel right. At least he now had an idea for an article he could write about NASA. Cyril would be thrilled.

Gravel popped under the Camaro's tires while Beckett drove away from the house. A white Rolls-Royce backed out of a driveway in front of Beckett, forcing him to jerk the Camaro to the right to avoid a collision. He couldn't see the driver through the tinted windows. Driving around the Rolls, his thoughts returned to the red Subaru and the dead gardener. Who would want to take a shot at him? There was a good chance that it was a random drive-by shooting, an unfortunate trend in Orange County in recent years. Gang activity had increased in areas near Fountain Valley, but a Subaru didn't fit his mental image of a standard gang vehicle. The Newport Beach police were still upset about his involvement in exposing the DNA evidence contamination problem, even though he'd started out wanting to do a simple story on Orange County's new Forensic Science Services facility. So the police didn't like him, but that didn't seem like a sufficient motivation for someone to take a shot at him weeks after the incident. That left only Nikki and her husband. She'd told her husband about her relationship with Beckett, but from what little she'd said about him, and from what he'd seen on television, Christian Enright seemed like a respectable businessman who wouldn't be prone to violence, especially since the relationship was over. The note she'd left also said something about her husband being out of town on one of his many church business trips. So, as far as he could figure, a random drive-by shooting was the only possibility.

Beckett turned right on El Camino and spotted a pay phone at a corner gas station. He had owned four cell phones in the past year, but fate had destroyed all four and he'd finally stopped using them. The first phone fell into a toilet, he sat on the second one, he ran over the third with his car, and the fourth was eaten by Nikki's pet boa constrictor. The snake, named El Bufador by his original owners, jealously protected Nikki's house from the hazards of small consumer electronics. According to Nikki, digital clocks, radios, and a Sony Playstation had all disappeared down the snake's throat, although she neglected to warn Beckett about the snake's unusual diet until it was too late. Beckett had only gone into her house for a few minutes, forgetting his phone on her couch while he used the bathroom. By the time he returned, he saw a suspicious lump in the snake's throat. When someone called Beckett and the cell phone began playing the *1812 Overture*, the snake gave him an evil look as if it didn't appreciate his musical tastes, and Beckett swore off cell phones for the rest of his life.

The aroma of gasoline filled the air as Beckett punched his editor's number into the pay phone. The phone was covered with chewing gum, paint, lipstick smears, and other unidentifiable substances, so he tried to touch it as little as possible. Even so, his index finger stuck to the last digit, the zero – when he yanked his finger free, the button remained on his fingertip.

"Cyril. Talk. I don't have much time."

"It's Beckett. I have some ideas for you. Can you get me into Ames Research Center?"

"What's it about?"

"The Kuiper Airborne Observatory," he said, scraping the zero button against the side of the phone booth.

"Did that. What else you got?"

"What do you mean? I don't remember any articles about the Kuiper."

"May, 1985, page 32, titled 'Eye in the Sky.' What else you got?"

"That was a long time ago. And this article would be more about the people who fly on the KAO."

"This isn't *People Magazine*. My readers want the science, the hardware, the thrill of discovery. What else you got?"

Beckett sighed. The zero button popped free of his fingertip when he pried on it with his thumb. "Look, I'll figure out the angle when I get there. If you let me do it, I'll give you the next article free."

"NASA-Ames. I'm calling them right now."

"Thanks, Cyril."

The gray steel of the massive wind tunnels and dirigible hangars of Moffett Field loomed into view while he drove east on the freeway. The former farmlands along U.S. 101 from Palo Alto south to San Jose generally defined Silicon Valley, which absorbed more R&D funding than any other location on the planet. The technology engine raced in high gear in this Mediterranean climate, and it received additional fuel from the military, banks, insurance conglomerates, and real estate speculators. Competition was fierce, profits were immense, and the less said about the gridlocked freeways, the poisoned landscape, and the ridiculous real estate prices, the better.

The densely packed residential areas that Beckett drove through in the shadows of the Naval Air Station didn't look like much, but the local real estate market had become overheated while Silicon Valley continued to grow. Many of those who were lucky enough to have bought their middle-class homes even ten years earlier had been able to sell their properties to become millionaires and move somewhere else. During the peak of the buying madness, a house might be listed for sale, then be sold two weeks later for twice the original asking price after receiving dozens of bids from desperate buyers. Tiny apartments that had rented for three hundred dollars a month a few years ago now went for over three thousand a month. The average cost of a lease for office space had doubled in the last year alone. It was crazy, and everyone knew it, but the local economy was loaded with cash and paper millionaires from the high-tech companies. When one tech boom slowed, another started. Sequential booms in semiconductors, computer hardware, and the Internet had recently been usurped by the growing biotechnology sector. The freeways were jammed with high-tech immigrants who lived far from their workplaces, commuting two or three hours each way so that they could afford to buy homes. Telecommuting was starting to catch on, but that wasn't evident on the crowded freeways. San Jose was the epicenter of a money quake whose effects rippled north through San Francisco and on into Marin – when each quake was over, local real estate wisdom said that prices dipped in San Jose first, then rippled north and east over the following two years. Beckett had thought many times about buying a place around San Francisco, or in Marin where he could commute on the ferry across the bay, but it seemed safer to rent a cheap motel room for his brief trips to the area.

The main gate at Moffett Naval Air Station was a simple affair with a small guardhouse and two uniformed Marines in white hats and gloves saluting cars in and out. On the rare occasion when the president visited San Francisco, Air Force One would land at Moffett and security would lock everything down, making it difficult to get around until the president had left. But this was not one of those days. When Beckett drove up to the gate behind a short line of cars, he saw a small sign that pointed him left along the frontage road to reach the NASA gate. He continued another half-mile along the chain link fence, past World War II-era barracks housing.

Gate Eighteen, the official NASA entrance, wasn't anywhere near as imposing as the main gate. Nearby, the massive steel shell of the world's largest wind tunnel overshadowed the rest of the buildings in the vicinity. One bored Marine guard looked up at his approach, scanning the dented Camaro for a Department of Defense sticker on the bumper. When he didn't see a sticker, he held up his right hand and stepped out to block Beckett's path.

"Do you have a pass, sir?" The guard's voice sounded like it belonged to a fourteen-year-old, and his face didn't look much older than that. He tried to appear menacing as he glanced around the inside of the car and managed not to cough when some of the thick blue smoke from the exhaust pipe blew past his face.

"I'm supposed to go to the Public Affairs Office."

The guard made a note on his clipboard, then handed Beckett a temporary pass to tape on the inside of his window. With a red felt pen, he traced out a route on a black and white map of Ames Research Center and handed it to Beckett. "Welcome to Moffett Field, sir. The Visitor's Center is closed. Proceed to Building 204 at the intersection of King Road and Arnold Avenue. There's parking outside the PAO. Don't park anywhere else. Don't go anywhere else without an escort. The PAO officer will provide you with a visitor's badge. This is a hazardous facility, so obey all the warning signs and stay with your escort. Low-flying aircraft have the right-of-way on the taxiways. Your escort will instruct you on specific safety hazards in the immediate perimeter of the PAO. Do you have any questions?"

"Does my escort have to stay with me when I go to the restroom?"

"Yes, sir."

"What if my escort is female?"

The guard saluted and motioned him through. "Have a good visit, sir."

As the Camaro lurched forward through the gate, Beckett glanced at the map and decided to go for a little drive around the facility before he went to the PAO. He checked the rearview mirror and saw the Marine talking to another visitor, so he randomly selected one of the side streets and drove off, leaving a trail of blue smoke in his wake. As soon as he made his turn, it occurred to him that the Marine had been speaking to someone driving a white Rolls.

F ew cars moved on the streets of Moffett Field. At eleven o'clock on a Tuesday morning, everyone was at work, their vehicles parked in the small lots beside most of the buildings. It looked like the sort of small, futuristic city that a science fiction artist would have painted in the thirties or forties with a limited palette of white, gray, silver, and black. Small office structures of dull masonry and glass were interspersed with white trailer offices and monolithic structures composed of metal spheres, tubes, and supporting steel frameworks – wind tunnel facilities used for testing aircraft and space vehicle designs. The Navy's three huge dirigible hangars loomed in the background. The largest hangar was Hangar One: Over two hundred feet tall, it had been built for the Navy's rigid airship program in the 1930s; Shuttle astronauts had seen the distinctive structure from orbit. The humid breeze from the shallows of the San Francisco Bay carried whiffs of jet fuel and oil from the runways and aircraft hangars and distributed them across the rest of the NASA facility. None of the wind tunnels were operating, but he could hear buzzing generators, the thundering prop engines of the Navy's P-3 Orions taking off to hunt phantom Cold War submarines, and an occasional boom or clang of metal.

On South Warehouse Road, across from the experimental aircraft hangar, sat a two-story structure of gray masonry wrapped in two narrow horizontal ribbons of tinted glass. A large black number high above the south entrance, faded with age, identified it as building 244, the Space Projects Facility, which originally served as the Space Environment Research Facility. Beyond it, the black surface of an aircraft taxiway ran parallel to the main runway, the only divider being a strip of tall grass that should have been cut months before. Beckett had worked on consulting jobs here several times over the last few years, and he still had a friend working in the Cryogenics Lab, but nothing ever changed. Space Projects, overshadowed by the larger Space Sciences Lab a few hundred yards to the north, sat like a gray iceberg in a sea of green grass. While it appeared to be a short structure, most of the building was underground; built during the Cold War, it had nine levels of sub-basements, with catwalks between the inner walls, providing the necessary illusion of safe refuge during Bay Area earthquakes and potential nuclear strikes. The space in the sub-basements wasn't wasted, filled with a wide variety of small labs and technical facilities so that employees could continue working even if the world outside collapsed around them. In accordance with ancient regulations that supported a post-apocalyptic work ethic, new NASA employees were still issued postcards to be mailed to Washington, DC as a change of address notification in the event of a nuclear strike destroying their homes.

Beckett parked in a small lot surrounded on three sides by tall grass, shielding his car with its temporary pass from the casual viewer. While he was in the neighborhood, he wanted to see if his friend, Tim Kyger, still worked there. As was normal practice since the funding cutbacks started in the late seventies, no receptionist guarded the lobby unless one of the staff scientists was taking a turn at answering the calls on the main switchboard.

The décor hadn't changed since his previous visit – they had the same government-issue tile floor that had been installed everywhere in the fifties and sixties; flickering light cast a bluish glow from the overhead fluorescents, balanced by the daylight that managed to pass through the double glass doors in the front entryway. A large model of the Galileo probe that traveled to Jupiter, presumably without the three-inch coating of dust he could see on this one, dominated a corner of the lobby beside two spindly plastic chairs and a corner table loaded with outdated magazines. Nobody in this building actually wore security badges, so Beckett knew he'd fit right in if he acted confident. After a quick glance around the lobby, he sauntered up the stairs behind the reception desk.

The offices in Space Projects were interspersed with former clean rooms shrouded in shadows and hanging plastic sheets. Near the dark Pioneer Mission Control center, punctuated by small offices, the walls of the second floor were decorated with astronomical mission plaques and rows of black and white photographs of famous scientists like Carl Sagan, James Van Allen, and Gerard P. Kuiper who had worked on Pioneer, Galileo, the Kuiper Airborne Observatory, or other Ames projects. As Beckett walked along, he could feel their eyes watching him, wondering if he had the brainpower to solve the puzzle of the violent act that was so out of character in this bastion of science and reason. But he didn't have an answer for them.

Tim Kyger's former office door held a different nameplate: "Franz Todlich." It didn't necessarily mean Kyger was gone, just that he had moved to another office. Long ago, the staff at Ames had learned not to get too comfortable in a particular office, and some had learned to use the periodic office migrations to their advantage. Kyger had told him that an entire project team had continued their work for three years after NASA headquarters had officially cancelled their funding – a problem that was solved by moving the team to larger offices in one of the sub-basements. When a new budget freed up funds for their work in the fourth year, they returned to the surface world, not without regret, to smaller offices where they could more easily interact with the rest of the staff. For a team that hadn't existed for so long, their project showed remarkable progress. Karl Oberhaus, the director of Ames, accepted the credit for their progress with NASA headquarters, claiming that they were simply motivated and dedicated employees who felt privileged to be working together again.

As Beckett stood there wondering where to look next, the office door opened. A mountain with black hair and a bushy beard almost stomped him flat before it realized someone was there. He held a jelly donut in his right hand, minus one bite, and a loaded coffee cup in his left.

"You're in my doorway," said the mountain, his voice booming in the hallway. Beckett detected a mild German accent.

"Sorry," said Beckett. He smiled and took two steps back.

"Who are you?"

"I'm looking for Tim Kyger."

"Never heard of him. Try downstairs."

"Are you sure? He used to have your office."

Todlich glowered at him. Some of the jelly oozed out of the donut he was holding when his grip tightened. "Do I look like a tourist guide?"

"No. Not exactly."

Todlich turned and took a couple of steps into his office. A pile of papers slid from his desk and crashed to the floor where they could join their compatriots who were trying to escape. When he turned back to face Beckett, the donut was jammed into his mouth and he held a slim Ames phone directory with an illustration of the Space Shuttle on its cover. "Here," he mumbled through the donut, slapping the phone book into Beckett's hands.

Beckett brushed the sticky donut pieces from the cover of the directory. "Thanks. You're a pal."

"Hmph," said Todlich, stomping down the hallway.

Naturally, Kyger wasn't in the directory, but he stuffed it into his shirt for later reference.

"Do you have an appointment?"

"My editor called this morning. I'm Ed Beckett."

The gray-haired woman peered through her bifocals at the details in an appointment book. Stacks of press releases, NASA folders, and videotapes crowded her scratched gray metal desk. As it turned out, the Public Affairs Office wasn't located in its own building, it was housed in a large trailer behind Administration. Years of grime coated the windows. The faded industrial carpet, a gray color that had formerly been green, told tales of an active publicity office and past glories in its bald spots and ancient coffee stains. Despite the warm day, the woman had a portable heater humming beside her desk that pushed the stale air around.

She shook her head. "No, you're not."

He blinked and swallowed the stream of threats that always threatened to spew forth from his mouth when he encountered an obstinate bureau-crat. "Yes, I am. I'm Ed Beckett."

When he started to spell his name she shook her head again. "I mean you're not on the list. Mr. Fitzgerald is very busy and you can't see him without an appointment."

Six feet behind her desk, the office door squeaked open. A tall man in his fifties stretched and yawned before he stepped out and noticed Beckett. "Oh, hello." He straightened his tie. He had the sort of predatory-friendly face that made Beckett think of used-car salesmen. "Mary, you didn't tell me I had a meeting."

"You don't. This man doesn't have an appointment."

Fitzgerald snorted. "Send him on in. I've got time."

Using a cane, Mary stood to block the narrow path that would give Beckett access to Fitzgerald's office. "No, you don't have time. He's not getting past me."

Beckett scratched his head. "It's just a mistake. My editor must have called."

Fitzgerald walked up behind Mary and shrugged at Beckett. "Mary, we've talked about this. It's okay."

"Okay, buster," said Mary, poking her cane at Beckett's chest. "Let's see some press credentials."

"I'm a freelancer. I don't have any."

Mary gave Fitzgerald a knowing look. "Want me to call security?"

"That's okay. I'll find out what he wants. If he gives me any trouble, I'll yell."

Mary pursed her lips and sat down. "Don't bother to yell if he sticks a knife in your ribs. It'll be your fault, not mine. I did my job."

With that, Mary ignored both of them and started typing on her computer. Fitzgerald beckoned toward his office, then removed a stack of press kits from the black plastic guest chair so that Beckett could sit down. Holding the press kits, he looked around in confusion, then dropped the folders on a stack of magazines. He stuck out his hand.

"Heya, I'm Larry Fitzgerald, Public Affairs Officer. What can I do to ya?"

Beckett shook his hand and introduced himself. Fitzgerald quickly dug through a pile of handwritten notes on scraps of paper, then smiled. "Cyril. Got it. You want to write about the KAO."

"That's right. I was hoping you could connect me up with the Kuiper team, have them show me around, that sort of thing."

"No prob. That's why I'm here. And you should have some literature to take with you."

Fitzgerald opened a file drawer that screeched when he pulled it out. He gritted his teeth and looked at Beckett. "Sorry." Moments later, the file drawer was empty and Beckett had an armload of information about the Kuiper Airborne Observatory. The press release on top was dated March 30, 1982.

"Thanks, I think."

"Don't let the size of the pile worry you. I'm sure you'll toss most of it anyway, preferably somewhere else. The important thing is, I get some of this paper out of my office." Fitzgerald punched a number into his phone.

"Glad to help," said Beckett, wondering if he could sneak out without Mary biting him on the leg.

After a quick conversation, Fitzgerald hung up the phone and smiled. "They're waiting for you, Mr. Beckett. Building 248. There's a visitor's badge in the press kit I gave you. I'll get you a map."

Beckett stood, trying not to drop the stack. Building 248 was right across from the Space Projects Facility. "That's okay. I can find it. Aren't I supposed to have an escort?"

Fitzgerald honked out a laugh. "Sure thing." He stood and held the door open for Beckett. "I'll escort you out of my office, then you're on your own. The Navy seems to think I have a huge staff waiting to escort people around, but it's only Mary and me. Just don't go inside any of the wind tunnels. And if you see an aircraft coming your way, don't walk in front of it. If you have any trouble, we never had this conversation."

Yoshinobu Shikei had a face like a bullet. His black hair, pulled straight back against his skull into a ponytail, only accentuated his streamlined appearance. He'd been spewing a stream of words for almost ten minutes, but Beckett still found Yoshi's accent jarring because he had a southern drawl that didn't match up with his appearance – it was like watching a Japanese movie that had been poorly dubbed into English. Beckett pretended to take notes while Yoshi discussed the fine points of the infrared array he was tweaking at his workbench. Fine gold wires and delicate chrome tools littered the surface of the table. Yoshi worked through a large magnifying glass with its own light suspended from an adjustable arm. There were no windows in the room, so the buzzing overhead fluorescents gave everything a bluish tinge. The air smelled of ozone.

"And when the tracker acquires the bright source of the Shuttle on reentry, it swings the telescope into line. If the KAO is positioned at the proper angle, the Shuttle image passes over the array and we record its heat signature. Once we've got that, Toady can analyze the data tape and generate a false-color heat map of the Shuttle underbody."

Detecting that he was supposed to say something now, Beckett nodded. "And what do you do with that?"

"Beats the heck out of me. I'm just a hardware guy. The map shows how hot each part of the Shuttle underbody gets on reentry, that's all I know. If y'all need more detail, Toady's the man."

"And who's Toady?"

A voice boomed in the doorway to the small lab. "Yoshi!"

Yoshi glanced at Beckett, then rolled his eyes at the bearded mountain entering the room. "Meet Franz Todlich, our fearless leader on the IRIS project."

Beckett stuck out his hand with a smile. "Pleased to meet you again."

Todlich looked at him like he was a bug, making no move to shake hands while he coasted his massive bulk to a stop beside the workbench, maneuvering like a supertanker. "I've seen you before," he rumbled.

"You gave me directions earlier today."

"Hmph. Lucky you ran into me, then. We've got crackers around here who wouldn't give you the time of day."

Todlich turned his back on Beckett to look at the array Yoshi was working on. "You fix this damned thing yet?"

Yoshi winked at Beckett. "Mr. Beckett is a journalist, Franz. He's here to do a story on the IRIS project."

"Journalist?" Todlich looked at Beckett with one eyebrow raised. "What rag you work for?"

"Science Monthly."

Todlich grabbed Beckett's hand and pumped it. "Love the magazine. Can't get enough of it. Sleep with one under my pillow. You must be here to interview me."

Beckett looked at Yoshi. "Well, I – "

"That's right, Franz," said Yoshi, smiling at Todlich. "We were just talking about you when you came in. I told him you were the chief scientist now."

"Now?" Beckett asked. "Was it someone else before?"

Yoshi exchanged a knowing glance with Todlich, then said, "We've had a change in our crew. Maxwell Dumas was running the IRIS project until yesterday, but Franz has taken over."

"Dumas," said Beckett, pretending to look through his notes. "That name sounds familiar."

"Dumas is of no importance," said Todlich. "I am chief scientist now."

"No, I'm sure I had a note about him. My editor specifically mentioned that I should interview Mr. Dumas."

Todlich's gaze hardened while he stared at Beckett. "Impossible. Dumas is unavailable."

"But I'm sure that – "

"Dumas was not capable of running this project," said Todlich, tapping a meaty index finger against the surface of Beckett's notepad. "Note that if you wish."

"Why?"

"He was incompetent. He could not follow orders. His massive ego kept the rest of us from doing our jobs."

Yoshi cleared his throat. "Franz still has some trouble with English. He means Max was having some trouble with our superiors. He didn't like to compromise."

"Compromise? On what?"

"Off the record?"

"Sure," nodded Beckett. Until he was in a courtroom.

"Our last test run with IRIS didn't go very well. The KAO is normally used for infrared astronomy, and each experiment team pays for its own flights. Each trip costs about eighty thousand dollars, and most of that is for fuel. They come from all over – labs, universities, wherever – but IRIS is a NASA mission. We missed the Shuttle on the last reentry and the system is still buggy. Test flights are expensive, so we don't do them very often. But the Ames director wants us to look good so that he'll look good and the project stays funded, so – "

"That's enough," said Todlich, grabbing Yoshi's shoulder.

"I don't understand," said Beckett.

Yoshi twisted out of Todlich's grasp, then turned and left the lab, slamming the door on his way out.

"Dumas was an idiot. That's all you need to know."

Beckett wanted to hear someone say it. "Maybe I should talk to Dumas myself. Where can I reach him?"

"In Hell," Todlich rumbled. "He's dead."

SEVEN

The northbound traffic on Highway 101 wasn't moving. Beckett glanced through the oily blue cloud that his Camaro generated and saw that it wasn't any better on the southbound side. The late afternoon sun beat down on the cracked concrete, baking the cars evenly on their tops and bottoms. The air smelled of gasoline fumes and hot metal. With gray concrete sound barriers on both sides of the freeway, he felt like he was parked at the bottom of a concrete trench. The glare from the sun partially obscured his view through the hazy front windshield, but there certainly wasn't any safety hazard at this speed. The Camaro's air conditioning system didn't work, so Beckett's driver's side window was down. He felt drowsy in the heat, but he kept his eyes glued on the back bumper of the car in front of him, knowing that if he didn't stay within a foot of the lead car, the driver behind him would immediately pound on his horn as a reminder. In the sea of shiny black BMWs that surrounded him, he knew he was considered an outsider because he drove an old Camaro. However, he also knew the BMWs feared him for the implied threat of a vehicle that could dent or scratch their perfect car bodies without any significant damage to itself.

Beckett sighed. He only had two miles to go to reach the cheap hotel room he'd reserved in East Palo Alto, but it would take an hour to get there at his current speed. He tried turning the radio on, but it was stuck on a heavy metal station that aired employment ads for Silicon Valley corporations such as Intel and ROLM, where the "future is now" for workers who designed cruise missile guidance systems and "surveillance-friendly" office communications.

Feeling the gridlocked hatred of all the drivers behind him in that lane, he glanced in the rearview mirror. He couldn't see what kind of car was immediately behind the Camaro, but he did see the laser death beam glare of a man in his sixties with a puffy red face. Behind him, a Rolls-Royce with tinted windows idled in stately peace, its clean whiteness a glaring contrast among the sea of black metal. The thought that he was being followed popped into his head, and that paranoia made him smile. Why would anyone follow him? The police didn't use Rolls-Royce cruisers, even in Silicon Valley. If someone was following him, they could have chosen something subtler – a black BMW perhaps, or a Jaguar. As he ran various unlikely possibilities through his mind while staring at the Rolls, he didn't notice that the cars to his left, in the "fast" lane, had actually moved up a few feet. He also didn't notice the shiny black pickup truck, a huge Dodge Ram, lining up alongside him.

In the lane to Beckett's right, hip-hop music thumped through the walls and the closed windows of a dark blue BMW that sat low to the ground – a local showing his individualism and rebellion by owning a car that wasn't black. The car in front of him, with a day-glo bumper sticker that read, "BITEME.COM," moved forward a few inches. Beckett released his brake and edged ahead to maintain the proper distance, then glanced to his left.

Something unusual caught his eye, but he was slow to respond because it didn't make sense.

To his left, mounted in the bed of the pickup truck, was a rusty white harpoon gun. It was enormous, looking like the sort of weapon that was used to hunt whales. The harpoon itself looked like a cruise missile with barbs behind its blunt tip.

And the harpoon was pointed straight at him.

A rope lanyard was attached to the back of the gun. A hand reached through the rear window of the cab and jerked the lanyard hard. Beckett's eyes widened, but nothing happened. Panicking, he jerked his head around looking for a way out, but the traffic wasn't moving. The rope jerked again and Beckett heard a loud boom.

Beckett gasped and clumsily vaulted into the back seat as he heard an incredible noise of shearing metal and the Camaro lurched sideways underneath him. The top of his head and his right shoulder bounced off the left rear window when the car rocked a second time an instant later, showering him with broken cubes of safety glass.

His shoulder and his head hurt, but he had the presence of mind to look around after he hit the rear seat. The pickup truck's engine roared and the tires smoked as the truck slewed sideways onto the asphalt shoulder, darting forward just inches away from the low concrete wall of the center divider. The truck trailed a cable. Beckett had only a moment to notice that the cable was attached to the harpoon now lodged firmly in his right front passenger door; its barbed tip scraping the ground outside the car. He ducked when the harpoon cable snapped tight with the sound of a metal spring and the Camaro vaulted to the left, accelerating for a few feet until it slammed into the back of a BMW. The metal in the car door groaned, but the harpoon held, rocking the car back and forth as the pickup truck screeched to a halt. When Beckett looked up again, he saw the Camaro had stopped moving, its left side flush against the rear of another car, so he rolled the left rear window down and pulled himself out onto the trunk lid of the BMW. Whatever the lunatic in the truck was doing, Beckett wasn't going to hang around to see how it turned out. When he slid to the pavement, he saw the driver of the pickup yelling and kicking the side of the truck. Then the driver awkwardly climbed up on the hood of the pickup, glanced back along the length of the taut harpoon cable, spotted Beckett on the ground, then cursed again and hauled himself over the center divider to the other side of the freeway.

Beckett shook his head; it still hurt and he knew he'd bumped it against the car window, but now he knew he must be seeing things. Maybe it was the angle and the distance, but the pickup truck driver had appeared to be a child.

Tal Blackthorne was having a bad day. His manicurist had shown up late for the morning appointment at Tal's office, the day's mail had brought another load of lawsuits from disgruntled homeowners with two-year-old houses that were now sinking into the poorly compacted landfill at his Lakeshore Drive development, his foreign partners were anxious about zoning restrictions along the San Francisco Bay, and now Condor was calling in with a "progress" report. Tal's speakerphone broadcast the annoying little man's voice around the office so that he could keep his hands free for rubbing his aching head while he yelled.

"A *harpoon*! Are you *nuts*? What do they use for brains where you come from? Jesus *Christ*, have you ever thought of trying to maintain a low profile?"

"You seem displeased," said Condor. "I thought you'd appreciate how clever I was."

"With a *harpoon*! Where the hell did you find a harpoon?"

"An old buddy of mine runs a marine salvage yard up here in Alameda. I got it cheap. He even mounted it in the back of the truck for me."

"Can't you just use a gun like a normal person?"

"Hey, I'm a professional. Any idiot can use a gun. I have to express my personal creativity as a master of all weapons. Don't worry, I know what I'm doing."

Tal stood to get a better angle for yelling into the speakerphone. "With a *harpoon*?"

"It almost worked. Man, you should have seen the fear in his eyes when he saw that giant dart pointed at his face. He probably pissed in his pants."

"But you missed!"

"I nailed his car. I nailed it real good. Of course, I had to leave the truck behind."

"Well, I bet his *car* won't ever bother us again." Tal slapped his forehead repeatedly. "What about the police, genius? Don't you think they'll be able to track you down now?"

"Nah. I stole the truck, and my buddy won't say anything about the harpoon if they trace it to him. But that's unlikely anyway – the harpoon wasn't registered. That's what's so cool about marine salvage – you can't trace it."

"What about your fingerprints?"

There was a pause on the line before Condor answered. "Fingerprints?"

Tal rolled his eyes with a heavy sigh. "Don't make me come up there. Are you going to take care of this or not?"

"He's as good as dead, boss. I'm on the job until it's over."

For some reason, Tal didn't feel reassured. He punched the speakerphone button to hang it up, then staggered over to his wet bar to get a drink. His neck and shoulders were tense; he'd have to see if he could talk Babette into giving him another neck rub.

Beckett's head was feeling better as he drove into a parking space by the office of the Friend Lee Motel. The neon motel sign, built in a style that was popular in the fifties, buzzed and flickered; Beckett guessed that it had been in its death throes for years but still refused to die. He liked that. The car door creaked when he opened it, then little chunks of glass fell out on the asphalt parking lot. The police had kept him busy for over an hour, answering questions on the freeway shoulder while passing drivers flipped him off for delaying their snail-paced commute. The driver of the black BMW, upon whose rear-end the Camaro had been impaled, corroborated Beckett's bizarre story with the police, so the hunt was on to find the driver of the Dodge Ram. Beckett needed food, a shower, and sleep, hoping that the day's events would make more sense the next morning after he'd had some rest.

When Beckett staggered into the office, a bald man in a stained t-shirt swatted flies on the worn plywood counter with a rolled-up newspaper. A bare light bulb hung over the desk, shining on the man's sweaty head and glaring in Beckett's eyes like an interrogation lamp. The air reeked of Lysol, and the yellowed linoleum floor made cracking sounds under Beckett's feet. The man looked up at Beckett, then looked past him and frowned at the Camaro.

"Hey, pal. What the hell happened to your car?"

"Nothing."

Slap! A fly bit the dust on the countertop. "What's that thing sticking out of the passenger door?"

"Harpoon."

"What?"

"Harpoon. You know, they hunt whales with them."

"Why's it sticking out of your car?"

"Long story. Can I check in? It's Beckett; I called this afternoon."

Slap! Another fly died on the register. The bald man turned the book around so that Beckett could sign. Brushing the fly corpse aside with a ballpoint pen attached to a chain, Beckett scribbled his name while the man put a key on the counter.

"You want it all night or by the hour?"

Beckett frowned. "All night, of course. I'll probably stay a few days."

"Whatever you say, Mr. Smith."

"Beckett."

The man frowned at the signature on the register. "You're using your real name?"

"Sure. Why not?"

He shrugged and pushed the key toward Beckett. "It's unusual, that's all. Forty bucks in advance."

Beckett counted out the money. The man picked it up and stuffed it in his pants pocket. "Room 58. Need anything else?"

"Food."

"McDonald's is down the street. Anything else?" He winked again.

"Is there something in your eye?"

Slap! Beckett had to scrape the fly off his room key as he picked it up. "An extra hundred buys you a friend. Three hundred for all night."

"That's an expensive friend."

"This here's a class joint, pal. I've got a whole photo album here so you can pick out what you want – women, men, small animals, whatever."

"I'll pass."

Slap! "Maybe tomorrow?"

"Maybe."

"I'll be here if you change your mind. Name's Lee."

"That must be your name on the sign, then. The Friend Lee Motel," said Beckett, starting toward the door.

"No, but that's why I bought this place from the Chinese guy. Already had my name on it. By the way, no spitting in the room. And if you take any towels, I'll kick your ass."

"Thanks," said Beckett, "You have a good night, too."

The room was dark when Beckett opened the door. He felt around for a light switch, but all he could find was a hole where it used to be. Using the dim light from the doorway, he walked across the room, his shoes crunching on the stiff carpet, and switched on the bathroom light. He couldn't quite place the odor in the room, but his best guess was that it smelled like a dirty wet dog that smoked cigarettes. The bathroom looked clean, as long as he didn't look too close, and there was a dusty *Sanitized For Your Protection* wrapper on the toilet. The mirror was cracked, but intact, and he barely recognized the exhausted-looking man reflected there. He washed his hands, threw water on his face, dried off, and returned to the bedroom. On the bedside table, a lamp in the shape of a Hawaiian hula dancer wearing a grass skirt cast a pool of yellow light in the corner of the room. The rotary phone had a small label on it that read, "No outgoing calls." The décor had a retro appearance – probably because it hadn't changed since the

fifties – but the bed was comfortable and didn't squeak too much. A small television rested on a platform so heavily bolted to the wall that it looked like it could survive a nuclear strike. This was the closest motel north of Moffett Field, and it was cheap, so it would do. He shut the door, locked and latched it, then propped a chair under the knob just in case.

Flat on the bed, he stared at the water stains on the ceiling and tried to decide whether to take a shower, get food, or go straight to sleep. It was a tough decision, so his thoughts drifted to his conversation with Yoshi and Todlich. Dumas had enemies, that was certain, but they didn't seem serious enough to warrant murder. Although he was new at this murder investigation game, he understood professional jealousy when he saw it, and Todlich didn't keep his feelings secret. He had to learn more about Dumas, about Todlich, and about the rest of the IRIS crew, for that matter. He closed his eyes and remembered the harpoon pointed at his face – what was that all about? Was it some random lunatic, or had he seriously ticked someone off? Maybe the police would learn something. Maybe he should just go to sleep and think about it in the morning.

He woke up only once that night, in a puddle of drool, when he heard a woman's loud moan accompanied by a rhythmic pounding on the thin wall behind his bed. He thought the woman was in trouble at first, but then she yelled, "Ride 'em, cowboy!" Beckett rolled over on his side and returned to his troubled dreams about dead gardeners.

At sunrise the next morning, Beckett discovered that the phone worked. It made a horrible ringing noise that blasted him out of a deep sleep, thinking perhaps that a fire alarm had gone off. In his frenzy to make the ringing stop, he knocked the phone on the floor and heard a tiny voice say, "Hello? Hello?"

"Yeah. Beckett."

"Heya, pal, it's Fitzgerald at Ames."

It took a moment for Beckett to register the information. He looked at his watch. "It's six-thirty."

"I like to start early. My boss is on east coast time."

"How did you know where to find me?"

"Wasn't hard. The visiting journalists always stay at the Friend Lee. And you used your real name when you checked in."

"I'm impressed."

"Well, you ought to be. I've cleared you for a slot on the next Kuiper flight with the IRIS crew.""When?"

"Two days from now. I don't know what time you'll have to be here, but I'd guess before sunrise. Usually works out better to bring the Shuttle in early, unless there's a weather delay, and the Kuiper will have to be in position to intercept their orbital track. However, there's a catch."

"I have to fly on the wing."

"Not quite. You'll have to get checked out in a chamber test, which also means we'll have to give you a physical for an up-chit. Any medical problems?"

"Not that I know of. What's an up-chit?"

"Permission to fly at high altitudes."

"What's a chamber test?"

"You don't want to know."

"Yes, I do."

"You'll learn all about it later today. If you pass, you'll get a high-altitude clearance, then you'll be safe for this Kuiper mission. Wouldn't matter if they were going to stay under forty-one thousand feet, but Meteorology says they might have to go higher this week. Also depends on the Shuttle's orbital track and the goal for each IRIS mission."

"Where do I have to go?"

"Come here for the physical at ten o'clock. If the doc says you're okay, we'll send you to an ASTC chamber with two of the women from the IRIS crew who need their high-altitude tickets."

"What's an ASTC?"

"Aviation Survival Training Center. After that, you'll all watch a flight safety video, then you'll be set."

Beckett was pleased to hear it. The test would give him some time to meet two more of the IRIS crew, and a flight on the KAO would give him a chance to see all of them in action. It was perfect. "Okay. I'll do it. Thanks."

"Don't eat breakfast. The sadists might want blood or other fluids from you."

"The what?"

"The doctors. Did I say sadists?"

"Sounded like it."

"Don't mind me. See you at ten."

"Ow!"

The ancient doctor peered at Beckett over his thick glasses. "Did that hurt?"

"Yes."

Dr. Schiff held a bizarre chrome sunburst mounted on the end of a handle that allowed it to rotate. Each point of the sunburst was needle-sharp. He rolled it on the sole of Beckett's left foot and didn't seem to care when Beckett flinched and gripped the examination table so hard that his knuckles turned white. "Did you feel that?"

"Yes," Beckett hissed through gritted teeth.

"Good."

"Good for you, maybe. That hurt."

"It's supposed to."

"What were you checking with that torture device?"

Dr. Schiff made a note on his pad. "It's medical. You wouldn't understand."

Beckett sat up on the edge of the table. He wore a light blue total embarrassment gown that the nurse had given him on the way in. He'd heard her snickering through the door after he entered the examination room. After spending two hours filling out medical histories and other forms, he wasn't in any mood for a long wait to see the doctor, but he was allowed to spend fifty minutes in the chilly examination room prior to Dr. Schiff's arrival. Making no apology for his tardiness, the doctor had proceeded with the most detailed inspection of his body that Beckett had ever received from another man, and he earnestly hoped it would never be necessary again. By the time they were through, he was sure that he'd lost at least two gallons worth of bodily fluids that had been forcibly removed during brief visits by the nurse, along with tissue samples and the remnants of his dignity. Dr. Schiff had a worse bedside manner than Dr. Hyde, which was probably why he worked for NASA as a professional medical sadist.

"Hey, doc, did you ever examine Max Dumas?"

"Dumas? I believe so. Why?"

"I'm just looking for background on the IRIS crew. Can you tell me anything about him?"

Dr. Schiff's pen leaked black ink, but he didn't seem aware of it. He rubbed his right hand on his white lab coat, leaving a black smear on the cloth. "No. Medical histories are confidential."

"Was he healthy?"

"Yes. Stand on your right foot with your hands on your waist, then hop up and down."

Beckett did as he was told. "So you cleared him for the chamber test?"

"Months ago," said Dr. Schiff. He rubbed his forehead, leaving a thick streak of black ink there like bureaucratic warpaint. "I remember because Dumas cancelled his appointment several times and made me wait. Then the brass said it was a big rush to get his exam done, as if the delay was my fault. Fat bastards sitting around in their cushy chairs in the Admin building think they can push me around, but just wait until they come whining to me with an injury, or a paper cut, or some other piddly-ass little problem – then we'll see who's boss."

"Can I stop hopping now?"

"Sure," he said, snapping out of his reverie to make a note. Then he poked different parts of Beckett's head with his fingers. "You hit your head recently?"

"Yesterday. Banged it on a car window."

"That explains the bump. We'll see if anything shows on the x-rays we took. How's the window?"

"Not so good. Ow," he winced, thinking how much the doctor seemed to enjoy poking his sore spots.

After frowning in silence for five minutes and making a variety of unpleasant worried sounds while he studied his notes, Dr. Schiff looked Beckett straight in the eyes.

"Mr. Beckett, I have to tell you something."

Beckett's stomach fluttered when he saw the concern in the doctor's eyes. "Yes?"

The doctor slid a gray medical form into his hands. "This is your Aeromedical Clearance Notice 6410 slash 2."

Beckett glanced at the form, but he didn't want to read it. "What does it mean?"

"You pass, assuming we don't find anything odd in your test results in the next hour."

Beckett breathed a sigh of relief, but he was annoyed to see the doctor stifling a laugh. "Had you going there, didn't I? And patients never think their doctors have a sense of humor."

"I haven't seen any evidence of one."

"You should have seen yourself hopping up and down for no reason," Dr. Schiff said, chuckling on his way out. "Good day, Mr. Beckett. Enjoy the chamber."

Nobody had explained to him what the chamber test involved, but the nurse had given him a concerned nod when he mentioned it on his way in. Beckett pictured a carnival Chamber of Horrors with skeletons in ragged tuxedoes popping up from behind stucco tombstones. While he removed the gown and sorted out his clothes, the nurse opened the door behind him and entered. "And this is one of our examination rooms."

Beckett heard a gasp, then scattered giggling as he turned and saw what appeared to be a Japanese tour group studying him from the hallway. Flashes from several cameras went off as Beckett hastily tried to cover himself with the discarded gown.

"Sorry," said the nurse, shrugging while she shut the door. "I thought you were gone."

Beckett rolled his eyes and sighed.

Two hours later, Beckett found himself wedged into one of the rear seats of a two-engine Cessna heading southeast to Lemoore Naval Air Station near Fresno. Lemoore had an Aviation Survival Training Center where Beckett and his two female companions would report for Physiological Flight Training, also known as the chamber test, in the wee hours of the morning. The silent pilot was a thin, gray-haired man who looked more like an accountant than a NASA pilot, which Beckett considered possible due to budget cutbacks. The two women had gone through physical exams similar to Beckett's the previous day, so the three of them spent their first hour together swapping Dr. Schiff horror stories, although Beckett got the biggest laugh when he told them about the Japanese tourists. With the ice broken, he tried to learn more about them during the flight.

Dr. Julie Ashbrook was in her late thirties with straight blond hair that ended at her shoulders, violet eyes, and a habitually skeptical expression. As the experiment manager, she was responsible for the construction and operation of the special IRIS hardware that had been mounted on the KAO to work with the big infrared telescope. She was an MIT graduate in electrical engineering, so much of what she said about IRIS was unintelligible to Beckett. Ever since she was a little girl, Julie had wanted to work for NASA and be an astronaut, and she still hoped to get into space one day, even if she had to go as a payload specialist on a Space Shuttle. She knew that one of the primary routes to a seat on a Shuttle launch was through the military, but she wasn't interested in killing strangers to reach her goal. Ames Research Center had demonstrated that senior citizens were better suited to the high G-forces of a Shuttle launch than younger people, because their hardening arteries were less prone to collapse under pressure, so Julie figured that her chances of eventually getting into orbit were excellent.

Lisa Campbell had a mild Scottish accent, curly brown hair, and green eyes. Beckett guessed she was about thirty-two. She had done her graduate work in electrical engineering at Stanford before meeting Julie at some kind of techie conference, after which they both ended up working in the Space Projects Branch of NASA-Ames. Lisa was the IRIS data systems operator, working under Julie, responsible for making sure that the IRIS hardware performed properly while they were in the air. She and Julie had spent the last year building and testing the IRIS system according to specs drawn up by Franz Todlich, then heavily modified by Max Dumas after he started on the project. Lisa loved tinkering with electronics, and a childhood interest in building radios and remote listening devices, otherwise known as "bugs," to eavesdrop on the conversations of her family and friends, had almost led her to a career in the technical branch of the Central Intelligence Agency. Her family had thought that the young Julie was telepathic, or that she could see the future, since she always seemed to know ahead of time what gifts she was going to receive for Christmas and her birthdays. Her mother, a former Las Vegas showgirl named Estelle, had wanted to build a magic act around Julie's remarkable talents and take her out on the road, but Lisa had appealed to her father, Roy, an aerospace engineer and reformed gambler, to help keep Estelle diverted long enough so that she could grow up to be a spy. Lisa never had told her mother the truth about her "talents," but she knew her parents were proud of her for pursuing a career in electrical engineering, and she had the recordings to prove it. Although she didn't build bugs any more, she had moved on to bigger and better things.

"It was a terrible thing that happened to Max," said Julie, shaking her head. She sat sideways directly in front of Beckett, who suddenly leaned forward.

"Why? What did you hear?"

Julie looked at Lisa, her voice catching in her throat. "Oberhaus told us yesterday."

"He just said that Max had been in an accident," Lisa nodded. "Someplace south of Los Angeles. And they'd let us know when a funeral was scheduled."

Julie turned and looked out the window, dabbing at her eyes with a tissue.

"When was the last time anyone saw him?"

"I saw him in the hangar the morning before our last test flight," Lisa said.

Julie nodded.

"They didn't tell you anything else?"

"No," said Lisa. "Why?"

"Well, it just seems like Dumas was a long way from home, that's all. Did he tell anyone he'd be traveling?"

"Not that I heard. He was always here working with the team. We were shocked when he didn't show up for the last flight."

"Dr. Todlich didn't seem too broken up about it."

"That bastard doesn't care about anyone but himself," sniffed Julie, continuing to look out at the puffy clouds drifting past beneath them.

Lisa nodded. "Toady's an ass."

"He designed the IRIS experiment, didn't he?"

"Sort of," Julie said with a wry grin. "Except his design didn't work. Good concept, but he was only guessing at how to build the experiment. Max redesigned the whole thing from scratch."

"Then it worked?"

"It's getting there," said Lisa. "Toady blew most of the hardware budget on the first design while we tried to make the system work with the infrared telescope on the KAO, so there wasn't much money left by the time Max got here."

"It's a limited system, but it'll work," said Julie. "Max knew what he was doing."

Beckett noticed that Julie had stopped crying. "Seems like Todlich should have appreciated Max's help."

Julie snorted and turned to look at Beckett. "Toady's an academic hack. He wants all the credit if IRIS is successful."

"Is that the only reason Todlich didn't like Max?"

Julie shrugged. "Who knows?"

"Well, there was one other thing Toady was pissed off about," said Lisa with a grin.

"Yes?"

"Two flights back, Max ate two donuts instead of one. Toady had to take a plain cruller instead of a jelly donut."

The flight had been smooth as they drifted above the clouds, but they were hitting turbulence now. The Cessna bucked and swayed, dropping a few feet every once in a while to leave Beckett's stomach behind. He was surprised when Lisa gripped his left hand and stared at the back of the pilot's head.

"You okay?"

"Yeah. Why?"

"Because your nails are drawing blood in my palm."

Lisa glanced at her hand, surprised that she was holding on to Beckett, but she didn't let go. She turned her worried gaze on Beckett's face. "I don't like small planes. I don't like turbulence. I don't know why I agreed to do this."

"Because you're a masochist," Julie said. "Just like me."

Beckett smiled at Lisa, trying to look cool while ignoring how his hand tingled. "It's probably some kind of misguided professionalism thing on your part."

Instead of the chuckle Beckett expected, Lisa gagged and vomited in his lap.

EIGHT

Tal Blackthorne's home in Newport Beach was a fantasy of sensuously curved adobe architecture and desert landscaping punctuated with waterfalls, reflecting pools, fountains, and cascading streams. Inside the screening courtyard walls, sheets of water flowed down from the ceiling on slightly angled walls of clear glass, ending in catch basins and ponds full of Koi fish that glittered under the ornamental lights. The refreshing sound of water filled almost every room, loud enough to wash out the sounds made by neighbors and traffic in the street, but quiet enough to carry on a normal conversation. The back walls of the house could be opened completely to the cool breezes from the ocean beyond his private patch of imported white sand beach. The house was a twelve-thousand-square-foot tribute to the craft of architecture, designed for an owner who would appreciate the calming beauty of water and the contrasts of desert and ocean. Unfortunately, the original owner no longer lived in the house – Tal had won it in a poker game.

Tal had his feet up on a glass table with a view of the harbor. He finished his bottle of expensive imported beer, smacked his lips, and pitched the bottle into one of the reflecting pools to join its empty brothers. This was how his evening ritual started almost every weeknight after a long day at work, except when an attractive female investor needed extra persuasion to cough up funds for one of Tal's real estate schemes. His latest effort, outside of the Pelican's Roost shopping center, was to build another overpriced housing development in Rancho Santa Fe, an "exclusive community" of expensive Mediterranean-style homes built on scrubby arid hills that were prone to wildfires and flash floods in San Diego County. Overall, his previous developments in the area had a pretty good safety record, although Rancho Santa Fe received a lot of negative coverage from snoopy news crews in 1997 when thirty-nine Heaven's Gate cult psychos killed themselves in one of Tal's homes. However, he believed that every cloud had a silver lining, so when the opportunity to purchase the Heaven's Gate house dirt cheap presented itself, Tal was there with cash in hand. Three months later, using the home's notoriety as a selling point and leaving it in the condition it was in during the mass suicide, he made a profit of almost ten times the amount he'd paid for it.

Life was good.

Without removing his feet from the table, Tal leaned over and pressed an intercom button. "Rosa, bring beer."

Rosa acknowledged his request as Tal spotted a fat man in an expensive brown suit and a crewcut tramping across his private beach with a folded beach chair. Even at that distance, the man's bushy eyebrows stood out as if two hedgehogs were sleeping on his forehead. When the man was dead center on Tal's beach, he dropped the shoes he was carrying, opened the chair, and plunked himself down in the sand to face the harbor. It was an outrage. Tal had built a fence of coiled razor wire along the perimeter of his beach to prevent exactly this sort of thing from happening – the man must have cut his way through to get in.

Tal stood and walked out on the patio. "Hey!"

The man ignored him.

"Hey!"

Tal knew that Rosa would be useless at chasing someone away, and Manuel had already gone home for the day. He didn't have any attack dogs like his neighbors because he didn't want animals around the house – the yapping rat that his wife, Peanut, carried around in her purse didn't count as a dog, and she was never around anyway. He sighed and took off his shoes, annoyed that he'd have to do the honors himself, but visualizing how good he'd feel after he chased the man away.

While he approached the man from behind, he realized how enormous the pile of flesh was that now blighted his pleasant view of the water. At fifty-one, Tal looked like a much younger man because he stayed in good shape playing tennis, swimming, horseback riding, and working out at the club – he believed that people who let their bodies go to seed should not be allowed out in public, and certainly not where Tal could see them.

"Hey, fatass!"

The man ignored him. Tal stopped one foot behind him and kicked sand on his coat.

"Get off my goddamn beach!"

Without turning around, the man quickly reached up with a hand large enough to be a catcher's mitt, grabbed Tal's belt, and slammed him face-down in the sand.

A voice with a Russian accent rumbled out of what Tal now realized to be a mountain of muscle, not fat. "Mr. Blackthorne. Good it is that you are joining me."

"Who the hell are you?" asked Tal, his face half-buried in the sand. The Russian quietly kept his hand on the back of Tal's head so he couldn't move.

"You are not able to guess? I am General Dimitri Akimov, your great friend from Moscow."

"Akimov? What are you doing here?"

"It is obvious, I would think. I have come all this way to protect my investments. We are not seeing rapid progress you promised us in San Francisco. I am hoping you will tell me of great things you have accomplished in last few days of which I am being unaware."

Tal wondered if it hurt to talk like that – it sounded like he had a mouthful of marbles. "There's no need to be concerned, General. Everything is under control."

Akimov nodded. "As I suspected. I am pleased to be hearing of this because you came highly recommended. I, myself, told our investment committee you would always act in our best interests, otherwise I would eliminate you as I have eliminated so many others who were, shall we say, not so ambitious. However, it distresses me that you are not in San Francisco. Why is this?"

"The phone is a wonderful thing, General. I can call anyone I need to do business with."

Tal had gradually lifted his face out of the sand, but the general clearly didn't like his answer, so he found himself eating the beach again.

"This must be American custom with which I am unfamiliar. In Russia, we do business correctly. We face our friends and our enemies across a table and make agreements or settle disputes. I am thinking that a developer of real estate would also want to see land he is negotiating for, is this not so?"

"I've seen it. I have photos. I've had a tour. And I've driven past there many times."

Akimov sighed. "I am hoping very much that we have not made a mistake in giving you this opportunity to make so much money."

While he didn't mind eating a little sand for such a big client – after all, he'd done far more degrading things for some of the others – the threat of losing money was like having an icy dagger plunged into his heart. "No, there's no mistake, General. You're quite correct in everything you've said. I've simply been arranging matters here before going up north."

"This pleases me."

"In fact, my advance man is up there now scouting out the situation."

"This also pleases me."

"And as soon as the government announcement is made public, I'll be there in person to gift wrap an agreement and deliver it to you personally."

"Ah. This does not please me."

Tal prepared to have his face slammed into the sand again. "Why not?"

"Money is like beautiful woman; wherever it goes, people open doors to let it through. You must make sure that proper individuals are compensated in your government to deliver this property into our hands. You must know when announcement will be made. If you are unable to do this, we will have to pursue these arrangements with someone else. We no longer have resources to force these decisions as was done in old days."

"I understand perfectly. Happens all the time. I'm already taking care of it."

Akimov grabbed a handful of Tal's hair and lifted his head. Tal blinked the sand out of his eyes and tried to smile as Akimov looked into his face. "You have only one chance with us. Do not make mistake. If you succeed, you will be wealthy man. If you fail – "

"I understand, General. No need to go into details."

"But I enjoy describing details. I am very detail-oriented."

"I'm sure you are, but I have a good imagination."

"Then let us enjoy sunset together. It is very colorful here."

Tal started to sit up, but the iron hand planted his face in the sand again.

"You will watch it from there, my friend."

At NAS Lemoore, Beckett discovered what a high altitude chamber test involved – a group of them would climb into a steel box that reminded him of an Airstream trailer, after which most of the air would be sucked out. To be precise, they'd spend some time hearing lectures about how the human body responds when exposed to hypoxia and low atmospheric pressure, *then* they'd be jammed into a barometric chamber that held ten victims and three Air Force trainers. Once they were sealed inside, they would experience the thrills of trying to get along without enough oxygen. Military aircrews and astronauts went through this sort of demented training activity all the time. As a *reward*, the Lemoore Aviation Survival Training Center sometimes offered rides on the "Vomit Comet" – a KC-135 four-engine jet used to train astronauts for weightlessness – but Beckett wasn't sure he deserved two hours in a jet that flew like a rollercoaster. Lisa agreed with him, but Julie thought it sounded like fun.

While the instructor droned on in a monotone voice about how they'd all soon be dead from a lack of oxygen, Beckett glanced around at their fellow students in the small classroom. Six young men in crewcuts and gray flight suits sat ramrod straight in their chairs with their eyes locked on their instructor target. A middle-aged bald man in a royal blue flight suit represented the astronaut corps; he grinned when he saw Beckett looking at him, then returned to tapping the keys of a laptop computer. Julie doodled on a pad while Lisa gripped the edge of the table and absorbed every word that the instructor was saying.

Beckett's eyes darted toward the instructor when he popped a balloon. His name was Mark Mills – Beckett had already forgotten his rank – and he had a constant frown on his tanned and muscular face. Mills, dressed in camouflage fatigues that didn't seem to hide him very well in the white-walled classroom, had an annoying tendency to emphasize too many words in his speech and there didn't seem to be any pattern to it, as if he did it just to amuse himself, or to keep them awake. *"Rapid* decompression at *altitudes* above thirty thousand *feet* can *reduce* the time of *useful* consciousness to *less* than fifteen *seconds*. Hypoxia *will* distort most of *your* senses, *along* with your *ability* to *think*."

Beckett believed he wouldn't be doing much in the way of thinking if they had an explosive decompression on the KAO; he'd probably panic, then black out from the lack of oxygen. He also had to wonder, if he was walking around the inside of the KAO while it was in flight, and the cabin decompressed, then the pilot dove the plane toward the ground, wouldn't that prevent him from getting to his seat?

"For you *civilians* from *NASA*," Mills said while reading Beckett's thoughts, "you *may* not have quick *access* to an oxygen *mask* during a rapid decompression *situation*. Your *pilot* will maneuver your *aircraft* into an emergency *descent* until you *reach* a lower *altitude* where there's more *oxygen* to breathe *without* a *mask*. If you *can't* reach your *mask*, you'll have to *wedge* yourself *in* somewhere and *ride* it *out* until you wake *up* again. Or *maybe* I should say, *if* you wake up again."

Mills laughed harshly at his little joke. The pilots glanced over at the civilians and grinned. Beckett wasn't amused, but Julie kept doodling on her pad. Lisa maintained her death grip on the table so that it wouldn't get away.

"In the barometric *chamber*," Mills continued, "you'll be *subjected* to the same *ambient* pressure you'd *find* at an *altitude* of thirty-five thousand *feet*. This *pressure* is about twenty-five *percent* of what you're *breathing* right *now*. To repeat, *with* oxygen, you think *normally*, but you *can* expect to be a babbling *idiot* in less than *fifteen* seconds at this lower *pressure*."

Beckett found that he was paying more attention to the odd rhythm of the man's voice than he was to the content of what he was saying. Fortunately, the lecture was almost over. Two more trainers in fatigues entered the room carrying their own oxygen masks. After the class learned how to pinch their nostrils closed and blow to clear their ears and sinuses, they were led into what looked like a storage area occupied by part of a semi-trailer, except this trailer had a heavy airlock door on the front of it. Two of the pilots playfully punched each other in the arms, but otherwise everyone was silent as they filed into the barometric chamber. The room had a low ceiling, and oxygen masks hung from the walls above the padded benches on each side for those who hadn't brought their own equipment. While the airlock door boomed shut to seal the class of victims inside with their camouflaged trainers, Beckett thought it would be a great place to test people for claustrophobia as well.

After an accommodation period of breathing pure oxygen through their masks, a humming noise started while the air was pumped out of the room. Beckett could feel the gases trapped inside his body wanting to get out, but the only pain came from Lisa's fingernails gripping his right thigh. He looked at Lisa and winked, but she didn't notice him while she stared at the tiny glass porthole across the room. The overhead fluorescents glowed through an open gridwork of structural supports to cast an unhealthy bluish pallor on everyone's skin. The bald man in the blue flight suit sprawled on his bench in a relaxed pose, his eyes casually studying the three civilians. To visually demonstrate what was happening to their bodies, a limp surgical glove tied off at the wrist had been suspended from the ceiling before they started – it now looked like a bloated cow's udder. Mills operated a small control panel by the door while the other two trainers stood at both ends of the chamber, apparently watching to see if any of the newbies exploded. So far, no problems.

Mills announced that they were ascending to twenty-five thousand feet, then half of the group unhooked their oxygen masks so that those who were still muzzled could amuse themselves by watching. It took a few minutes of writing his name repeatedly on a pad attached to his clipboard before Beckett realized he was actually doodling on his pants leg and giggling. He turned to the next page on the clipboard and saw a tough math problem where he was supposed to add ten and twelve, but he couldn't figure it out so he skipped down the page to a word problem that asked how many four cent stamps were in a dozen. He skipped that question too, thinking he should have brought a calculator. Mills said something to them, but Beckett didn't know what it was until one of the trainers walked over and re-attached Beckett's oxygen mask. Two minutes later, he felt fine except for a slight headache.

When Beckett looked at Julie's clipboard, she was busily answering the math questions, but Beckett noticed that the answers were all wrong. She kept pushing the dangling oxygen mask away from where it brushed against the skin of her face. Lisa had released his thigh at some point and was now studying the lines in the palm of her left hand.

After they'd all returned to breathing oxygen for a while, Mills told them they were at eighteen thousand feet while the trainers handed out color charts with a rainbow spectrum on each one that was bright enough to knock their eyes out. The chamber lights dimmed. Going through the same procedure as before with their masks off, the colors on the chart gradually faded. Beckett didn't feel any euphoria or confusion, but the colors continued to fade. Mills had told them in class that a person's night vision was impaired while flying at lower air pressures. When they put their masks back on, the colors on the charts returned to full strength despite the dim lighting in the chamber.

Beckett thought the test was over, but there was one more event that Mills wanted them to experience firsthand. Half of the group left the chamber, then the airlock door cycled shut. This time, they didn't put their oxygen masks on right away, they just sat on their benches and looked at them dangling over the empty benches on the opposite wall. Mills brought the chamber to an altitude of eight thousand feet, which didn't feel any different than flying on a commercial jet, and prompted the trainees to remember what they had learned in class about rapid decompression. Then Mills chuckled, which Beckett found disturbing.

With the thundering roar of a cannon, the chamber valve popped open and they were in the low pressure at twenty-two thousand feet. The humidity in the chamber turned into instant fog. Beckett felt as if his head had exploded, but he stood and groped around for the opposite wall. His heart still pounded from the adrenaline rush he'd received after the valve roared open, and he knew he was breathing too fast, but his hands brushed an oxygen hose and he traced it to the mask itself, fumbling to place it securely on his face. He still couldn't see much in the fog as he slid down onto the bench, sensing more than seeing that Lisa sat next to him. She patted his arm. Then he felt someone else's weight drop onto the bench on his other side and Julie leaned close to give him a wink.

With a loud hiss, oxygen pumped back into the chamber and the fog cleared. Everyone was seated normally on a bench except for one of the pilots who was lying on his side; a trainer sat beside his head strapping a mask to his face.

It wasn't easy being Condor. Kermit Busby's father, Augustus, had started his professional career as a Navy SEAL, then moved on to the CIA when he left the service, where he met another idealistic intelligence officer assigned to the South American desk and married her two years later. As Elvira and Gus worked together, their idealism changed over time into a practical realism while they learned to apply their operational field skills to extortion and other means of accumulating six million dollars in untracked funds to their offshore bank accounts. They eventually left the CIA to set up a greeting card business in Virginia, operating it as a money laundering front for over a year before a fluke business decision placed them squarely on the road to legitimacy. The niche market of greeting cards adorned with photos of cute animals spouting cynical messages suddenly became hot, earning them millions of dollars each year for the next seven years, and allowing them to raise their diminutive son, Kermit, in a pampered lifestyle from which he could foresee an adulthood of relative ease and comfort. Then Gus suddenly disappeared for two weeks. When he came back, his eyes were wild and his black hair had turned gray. Gus announced that he had been abducted by aliens in a UFO, probed, sent back in time to the year 1776 to meet George Washington, and finally released by the aliens so that he could donate the family fortune to the Daughters of the American Revolution. Suddenly, the business was bankrupt. When Elvira discovered what Gus had done, she killed him with a ballpoint pen, pulverized his body in a rented wood chipper, and used him to fertilize the garden of their Virginia home. Elvira was locally famous for growing high quality roses, and the flowers grew even better with the new fertilizer – a secret recipe she wouldn't reveal to anyone. This success led to her new career as a florist.

Worried that Kermit's diminutive stature was responsible for the almost daily beatings he received in school, Elvira taught him the "art" of using makeshift weapons to disable his enemies. Ballpoint pens, newspapers, and duct tape could all be used for stabbing; pocket change stuffed in a sock made an excellent sap for hitting people over the head. She also taught him to use his height by getting under his opponents where he could employ judo moves to defend himself. Kermit wasn't subtle enough to avoid getting in trouble with the authorities after a fight, so she also taught him how to establish alibis and frame others for his offenses. None of these skills helped him get dates in high school, but at least he didn't get sent to reform school.

Looking forward to becoming a Navy SEAL when he graduated from high school – and wanting to follow in his father's footsteps except for the part about the UFOs – Kermit was stunned to learn that the Navy would accept him, but not as a SEAL. Undaunted, he joined the Navy anyway when they told him he could be assigned to an Aegis guided missile cruiser attached to a carrier battle group. He wasn't sure what all that meant, but he quickly found out when he became a ship's serviceman assigned to the laundry detail on the *USS Valley Forge*. After his four years in the service, he was able to tell people that he "saw" action in the Persian Gulf during Desert Storm, even though the closest he ever got to actual combat was in providing clean clothes for the participants. But the Navy experience also triggered Kermit's entrepreneurial streak, as it had in his father, and he soon found himself stealing Navy supplies, such as toilet paper, for resale at swap meets away from the naval base in San Diego.

When Kermit's sideline was interrupted by his discharge from the service, he wanted to find a way to make money without working, and it seemed that a life of crime offered the most promise in this regard. Through contacts he'd made at swap meets, and on the Internet, he hired himself out, sight-unseen, as Condor – a hit-man for the discriminating client. Unwilling to take low-paying head shot jobs, he preferred murder assignments that would allow him to express his creativity. When necessary, old buddies from the Navy would sell him specialized weaponry that he couldn't get on the Internet, but he usually managed to turn "found" objects into weapons, except on the occasional rush job where he had to use an exotic gun. As far as the actual murders, he only had about a twenty percent success rate, but this was the kind of business where the secretive clients didn't usually talk about their dissatisfaction with his services. Even so, the demand for Condor's specialty had slowed recently, and his gambling habit burned up a lot of his savings, forcing him to consider another line of work. With a natural hatred of all living things, he became a pest exterminator, which allowed him to pay the bills by killing bugs when he couldn't kill humans. But he didn't enjoy crawling around in attics or under houses. When real estate developer Tal Blackthorne stumbled across Condor's website on the

Internet and offered him an excellent salary to do the kind of work he most enjoyed, Kermit jumped at the chance. Blackthorne had more enemies than Condor thought possible, so he could expect job security along with health insurance and a retirement plan.

Life was good.

Shiva's Place, a hole-in-the-wall Indian restaurant in Burlingame, near the San Francisco Airport, was small and dark with battered tables and a general aura of decay, but the food was excellent. Condor sat in a red vinyl booth across from a thin, athletic man in his forties with brown hair and bushy eyebrows, dressed completely in trendy black clothes and a long overcoat even though it was a warm day. The expensive gold rings on four fingers of his right hand were both gaudily decorative and efficiently destructive whenever he used them like brass knuckles to punch someone. He was Grigori Popov, a former officer of the KGB, now a trusted member of the Russian *mafiya*, whom Condor contacted whenever he needed explosives or untraceable Russian military equipment for jobs around San Francisco. Condor had located Popov on the Internet. They arranged meetings via encrypted e-mails routed through "anonymizer" servers to mask the origin locations of their messages – just in case the government was watching.

"So, my little friend, what am I selling you today?" Popov asked, pushing his empty plate aside while he sipped at his beer.

Condor straightened up in his seat and ignored the remark about his height. "Two bricks of C-4, as I said on the phone."

"Yes, yes, but what else? You are not person who makes impersonal big explosion and runs away like bunny. Can I sell you nice 7.62 mm *Dragunov* sniper rifle, or slightly used submarine?"

"Submarine?"

Popov pulled a small notepad out of his coat pocket and flipped it open. "I have two available, formerly of Northern Fleet. The *Nizhniy Novgorod*, a nuclear powered attack submarine armed with cruise missiles; and the *Bryansk*, a nuclear ballistic missile submarine of Delta IV class – your Navy would call this a *boomer*."

Condor just stared at Popov with his mouth open.

"Until recently, *Bryansk* hauled tourists around underneath Black Sea, but its nuclear warheads are still operable. Delivery is anywhere on west coast within two days. You can have one hundred thirty crew at additional cost, but they are only speaking Russian."

Condor closed his mouth. "What the hell would I do with a nuclear submarine?"

Popov shrugged. "Those are big missiles, my friend. I suspect you could do whatever you wanted."

"You're serious?"

"I've already sold two boomers to Colombian drug cartel for smuggling operations. They bought crews, as well. An excellent price I gave them."

Condor almost drooled. For a moment, his mind drifted off into a fantasy where he was able to hold up the state of California for vast sums of money to keep him from launching a nuclear strike on San Francisco or, better yet, Hollywood. Yes, threatening Hollywood would put a scare into them. He shook his head. He didn't have enough money to buy a submarine, and he doubted that Popov would accept his American Express card for the purchase. "I better just stick with the plastic explosives, but thanks for thinking of me, Grigori."

Popov flipped his notepad closed and smiled. "Maybe next time. And if you change heart, let me know. I can have *Nizhniy Novgorod* here in six days if you want something smaller. I give you good price."

Condor took a bite of the lukewarm curried chicken on his plate. Could he talk Blackthorne into springing for a submarine? Probably not. Still, he'd have to give it some thought. He liked to keep his options open. "I'll also need a sealed timer for each brick of C-4. You have any with you?"

Popov snorted. "Of course. Basic supplies in my car. Sealed timer is for boat?"

"An airplane. High-altitude."

"How about shoulder-launched surface-to-air missile? You shoot from end of runway, missile tracks heat from engine, big bang, you're gone before anyone sees you."

"No, it has to look like an accident."

"And I suppose submarine-launched SAM is out as well? I give good price."

"No." Once Grigori got an idea into his head, it was hard to stop him.

"Everyone needs protection. Submarine is best protection available."

Condor gritted his teeth. "I don't need a submarine!"

Sudden silence as a dozen restaurant patrons looked up from their meals and stared at Condor, who lowered his head to be less visible. Attracting attention was not the smartest move for a professional killer. "Sandwich!" he said in a loud voice. "Submarine sandwich."

Grigori sat back with one eyebrow raised. "C-4 is very old-fashioned. Submarine can do anything."

Condor wished he had a gun handy so that he could blow his own brains out.

Twelve hours after the chamber test, Beckett was back in the Cessna with Julie and Lisa for the late-night return to Moffett Field. They could have left an hour earlier, but Mills had warned them not to fly until a full twelve hours had passed, giving their bodies time to recover from the stresses of high altitude "flight." Beckett still had a mild headache, but the two women were fine. Now that the test was over, even Lisa seemed calm. Once again, the gray-haired "accountant" was flying the plane, his personality still as perky and bubbly as it had been on the way out.

After brief congratulations on surviving the chamber test, the three of them hadn't really discussed it very much. It had been a novel experience, and that was about it. The class had dispersed immediately after the test, with most of them going to an adjoining building before they boarded the Vomit Comet for two hours of thrills and frolic in freefall. If the NASA group had joined the rest of the class, they would not have been able to return home until the next morning, and the two women were anxious to get back despite Julie's earlier interest in the rollercoaster flight. They still had a KAO mission scheduled to intercept the Space Shuttle on reentry in the morning.

The dark sky was clear as the constellation of lights known as Fresno receded into the distance beneath them. Away from the glare of the city, a sky full of stars winked at Beckett until Julie snapped on her reading light to study one of her IRIS notebooks. Lisa leaned up against Beckett's shoulder and put one hand on his left knee while she lowered her head to look past him at the stars. He detected the scent of strawberries in her hair directly beneath his face.

"Nice view," Lisa said.

Beckett grunted in agreement while her fragrance surrounded his head.

"You know anything about stars, Ed?"

"Not much," he lied, switching to a caveman voice. "Lights twinkle in sky."

"I don't believe you."

Beckett shrugged.

"Yoshi says each star is a lost soul."

Yoshi? He didn't fit into the fantasy Beckett was developing about Lisa. "Lost soul or a ball of burning gas? Who's to say? How long have you known Yoshi?"

"You first. When did you first learn about the stars?"

"Let me think. When I was five, my dad got me out of bed on a warm August night to watch the Perseid meteor shower. After that, he started teaching me about the constellations. We had a small refractor telescope, and I could stay up later if I went out to watch stars with my dad. My mom preferred to watch stars on television."

"Nice story. I knew you were lying. To answer your question, I've known Yoshi for a few months."

"What do you think of him? I met him briefly and he seems like a nice guy."

"He's nice enough," she said, looking up at Beckett with a coy glance. "Why did you become a science writer?"

"I like variety. Did Yoshi get along okay with Max?"

Lisa blinked. "Why do you keep asking about Max?"

"Just curious. I know Max was running the project until this week, so I want to know more about the team."

Lisa leaned back in her seat, taking the scent of her hair along with her. "They got along okay, I guess. They had more contact while the hardware was being designed, but not so much lately. Julie's the one to ask about Max."

"Oh?"

Julie looked up at the mention of her name. "What?"

"Lisa says you're the expert on Max."

Julie looked at Lisa. "I worked with him."

"A lot," said Lisa. She folded her arms and looked away.

Beckett wasn't sure what had just happened. "How much do you know about him?"

"The usual things you learn when you work with somebody," Julie said. "But Remy spent more time with Max than I did."

"Remy?"

"Remy Descartes. He's KAO crew – the telescope operator. He's kind of, well, spacey, you might say, but he's okay. Max has been – *had* been – working with him a lot since we started the IRIS missions."

"Yeah," Lisa said. "Just don't turn your back on that guy."

"What do you mean?"

Lisa shrugged. "I don't trust him. He's like a split personality or something. He'll talk your ear off for half an hour, then go dead silent. You should see him creeping around the office hallways at night, muttering to himself. The only time he ever really seems normal is when he's sitting at his telescope control panel, and then you just know he's doing calculus in his head and weird stuff like that."

Beckett looked at Julie. "Is that true?"

Julie shrugged. "He's kind of creepy, but he enjoys his work, and you see a lot of strange things around here."

"Who has Todlich been working with the most?"

Julie thought for a moment. "Well, after Max, I guess Toady spends a lot of time with Celia Muerto. She's also regular KAO crew – the ADAMS operator."

"ADAMS?"

"It's the housekeeping computer on the KAO. It keeps track of everything, records data, talks to the experiments, knows the navigation information, that kind of thing."

"Celia's nice," said Lisa. "She's kind of a geek, like she lives inside her computer, but she knows how to talk to humans, too."

Julie nodded. "I think Toady likes her because she can answer his questions and then he sounds like he knows something when he repeats it to someone else."

"And Toady likes her outfits," Lisa grinned. "All the men do."

"What did Max think of her?"

"Well, he's a guy," Lisa said, then winked as she tapped Beckett on the knee.

Julie snapped her notebook shut and shook her head. "He didn't notice. Max knew better."

"That's not what Celia says."

"Celia's a tramp. Her hormones will say anything."

"Okay, forget I said anything," Lisa said, turning to look out the window again. "I still like her, though."

"I didn't say I didn't like her, Lisa. She's smart, but she doesn't dress like a professional, and I don't like the way she manipulates the men."

"They seem to like it. Toady certainly likes it." Lisa glanced at Beckett, then back to Julie. "And some of the others, too."

"What about Yoshi?"

Lisa rose up in her seat. "What about him?"

"So," Beckett interrupted, thinking he'd better throw his body on the grenade before it went off, "what time is that flight in the morning?"

Julie broke the staring contest with Lisa and looked at Beckett. "You should be in the hangar at five o'clock. Some of us will be there at four."

"That won't give us much time to sleep," Beckett grumbled, glancing at his watch.

Julie shrugged. "That's show biz."

"You could sleep in the office," Lisa said. "That's what I plan to do. There are showers downstairs and everything."

Beckett tried not to think about Lisa in the shower, but the image sneaked into his head. "That could work."

"We do it all the time," Julie said. "The Shuttle reentry gets scrubbed, or the KAO has a problem, or weather gets in the way – you get the idea. Sometimes, we're just too tired to drive home."

"You're the experts," Beckett said. "I'll follow your lead."

It was like sleeping in a tomb.

After they landed, it had taken about an hour to take the short walk over to the Space Projects building, switch on some lights, and get set up on a cot in the first sub-basement locker room. Julie and Lisa had clearly slept there before, and both of them kept extra clothes and toiletries in their lockers for these occasions. It was almost midnight, and they appeared to be the only people in the building; the hollow echoes of their footsteps on the ancient floor tiles had only added to the spooky atmosphere as they descended one level on a staircase that went much deeper underground, walked past old clean rooms shrouded in drapes of clear plastic, and opened a creaky door into the little-used locker room area. There was only one locker room, but the restrooms were separate. The regularly used cots were grouped together with two government-issue gray desk lamps someone had brought in to create a cozy little corner. It didn't really have the smell that Beckett associated with locker rooms, probably because it was so rarely used. By the time Beckett returned from the men's restroom, Lisa was asleep under a blanket on the cot right next to his, and Julie was waiting to turn off the lamp next to her cot. They said goodnight, and blackness surrounded them.

Unfortunately, Beckett couldn't sleep, even though no one had tried to kill him lately. He had the feeling that the KAO flight in a few hours would give him the opportunity to figure out how Max Dumas had died, and he wanted to be sure he didn't blow it. He was well aware that he wasn't a professional investigator, so he kept turning strategies and facts over in his mind while waiting for a pattern to emerge. He was still guessing that Max's death had been connected with the KAO, primarily because he hadn't been able to come up with any other rational explanation, but he still hadn't discovered any way that the man's body could have been hidden on the KAO and dumped over four hundred miles away in a Newport Beach swimming pool without the entire IRIS crew knowing about it. So far, except for being spotted in the experimental aircraft hangar, none of the crew had even remembered seeing Dumas on the last KAO flight the same day he disappeared.

He stared into the blackness. Past experience with insomnia had taught him it was time to take a walk. If he could feel his way out of the dark locker room without waking up the two women, he'd be able to walk in the dimly lighted hallway. He sat up, pulled on his pants, and made a mental map of how the locker room had looked before the light went out. He slid his feet forward until he bumped into a bank of lockers, then ran his hand along them while taking cautious steps in the direction of the door. Just as it occurred to him that he didn't have any shoes on, he slammed the big toe of his right foot into an open locker door, then swallowed a yelp so he wouldn't wake anyone. Limping a bit, he gingerly continued forward and slipped out through the exit into the hallway.

After ten minutes of searching, he located an office marked with the nameplate of Max Dumas. He studied the heavy silver doorknob, wondering if he could spring the lock with a credit card or jam a screwdriver into the keyhole to pop the door open – he'd never actually tried either of these techniques, but he'd seen them on television where they had worked fine. However, he didn't have a screwdriver, so that limited his options. He was curious to see whether a Mastercard or an American Express card would be better for opening doors, but when he grabbed the doorknob to give it a try, the door swung open. He reached around the corner with a slow and careful motion, then snapped the overhead lights on and jumped back, but no one was there.

The ten-foot-by-twelve-foot office could accommodate two researchers if there were a lot of people working in the building, but Dumas warranted an office of his own. Beckett remembered that there was some sort of pecking order that allowed for NASA employees to have offices by themselves when they were available, while contractors would typically be housed two to an office, or three if there was an office crunch in a particular project area. However, Dumas hadn't been deemed important enough to have an outside office, so there were no windows. Max had made full use of the available space, cramming it full of papers, books, and reports to give it more the feeling of a nest rather than a workspace. Beckett thought the books stacked on the yellowed government-issue floor tile gave the office a homey atmosphere, but he knew that was a personal bias.

The gray metal desk looked like a three hundred pound monster that would never leave the corner of the office where it had originally been installed. A matching gray bookshelf, a simple rolling guest chair with a hole in the gray vinyl seat, and a blackboard covered with colored chalk dust completed the furnishings. The air smelled of vinyl, bug spray, and dust. The corners of the desk and the walls around it held photos of the IRIS crew standing in two rows in front of the white whale body of the KAO, glossy images of the Space Shuttle underbody splashed with rainbow patches of bright color, an astronomical poster-size photo of the Crab Nebula, a couple of birthday cards, and a flattened paper cup from Matsumoto's Shaved Ice in Hawaii. An unframed family photo of Astrid Dumas and the two children was also tacked to the wall. When he turned over the photo, he saw it was stamped with a date from two years ago. A small pencil holder was jammed with mechanical pencils and black ballpoint pens emblazoned with the warning: "Property of U.S. Government." Beckett picked up one of the pens, remembering the one they'd found in Max's flight jacket, and clicked it, causing it to pop in half in his hand. He screwed it together again and put it back in the pencil holder, not wanting to anger the bureaucratic gods. They would do a thorough inventory of this office as soon as the proper papers had been filed to declare Max Dumas deceased and no longer in need of his furniture or supplies – a process that could take months, if his past experience with NASA was any guide.

Off to one side of the desk was a monument to the history of computing; a ten-year-old PC with a dusty keyboard. Considering the age of the machine, which was probably the most current desktop computer they'd been able to issue when Dumas arrived a few months ago, Beckett glanced around the office and spotted a carrying case for a laptop computer, but it turned out to be empty. There was something of a tradition in NASA that employees would buy their own computers and software for critical work, much as the Shuttle astronauts did when they went into orbit – preferring to trust their lives with recent technology rather than relying on the ancient computer hardware that drove the Shuttle's flight systems. Max had probably done the same, preferring to do most of his work on his own laptop rather than use the antique on his desk, but where was it? He flipped the switch on the desktop computer and looked through some of the papers on the desk while it booted up, but none of the diagrams or reports looked especially interesting. When the computer asked for a password, Beckett's heart sank. He tried combinations of "Max" and "Dumas," but the computer wasn't impressed. The other old standard was a birthday, but Beckett had no idea when Max had been born. As he wondered where he might find the information, he noticed the birthday cards again; one of them still sat there with its envelope postmarked three weeks earlier. On the twelfth try, the password screen successfully disappeared and he was presented with a Microsoft Outlook e-mail window. He switched to the appointment calendar, but apparently Max didn't like to use it because there were no daily entries even though he scrolled back through two months of workdays.

Back on the e-mail window, Beckett waited for a lot of recent messages to download. While the old computer cranked through the messages, he noticed that even though the blackboard had been erased, there were still ghostly remnants of the notes that had last been written there. He walked over to get a closer look, tripping on a stack of research reports. Yes, the words were hard to read, but visible, so he picked up a piece of yellow chalk and traced the outlines to make them more readable:

Mon.

5:00 F.T. breakfast mtg. here

6:00 Oberhaus ofc

7:00 calibration/star

8:00 pre-flight

9:00 t.o.

To the right of the schedule, Beckett used the chalk to trace:

J.A. cell 415-965-5091

R.O. 965

He couldn't make out the rest of the R.O. number. The Monday morning schedule seemed clear, and Beckett would have to check to see whether Dumas had met with Director Oberhaus. With any luck, that Monday would be the same day Dumas had disappeared, and Oberhaus would know why he left. If "F.T." referred to Franz Todlich, that breakfast might have been his last meal, although the meeting may not have occurred at all because Beckett remembered Detective Daniels telling him that the coroner had found only spaghetti in Dumas's stomach. And he was pretty sure that Dumas had never made it to lunch because he disappeared before the pre-flight meeting at eight o'clock.

Beckett wanted to make notes, but he didn't have anything to write on. He returned to the desk and picked up one of the official government pens, then hunted around on the desk for a pad or blank paper without any luck. He opened the top desk drawer and discovered a spiral-bound notepad. Back at the blackboard, he opened the pad and flipped through several pages of handwritten notes, then discovered a color photo taped to the middle of a page. A woman in a white string bikini stood smiling at the photographer from between two palm trees on a white sand beach. He assumed it was Astrid, but when he looked closer he saw that it was Julie.

Now Lisa's remarks about Julie being an expert on Max started to make sense. And Julie had denied knowing that much about him.

He flipped to the next blank page and wrote down everything he saw on the blackboard, tore the page out and stuffed it in his pocket, then lightly erased the blackboard again to mask his activities in case anyone came back to check. Turning back to the computer, he put the notepad back in the drawer and sat down to scan the list of e-mails that Dumas had received over the last few days. Ever since the Monday he had disappeared, the e-mails were still highlighted as unread. Scrolling down to Monday, however, was more troublesome, since Max had either not received any e-mails on Sunday and Monday, or they had been deleted. There were several e-mails listed on Saturday that Max had apparently read. But why were the Sunday and Monday messages missing? It was possible that he'd read and deleted everything those days, but that didn't appear to be his pattern judging from the hundreds of messages Max had previously read and kept for reference. There didn't appear to be any other sequential gaps in the dates as Beckett continued scrolling down through the list.

"What are you doing?"

Beckett jumped at the sound of the woman's voice. Startled, he turned and saw Julie standing in the doorway wearing only a long white t-shirt with a NASA logo on the left breast. She didn't look happy.

"Oh. Hi."

"Well?"

Beckett tried to think quickly, but he was tired. "Couldn't sleep. I was just trying this computer to see if I could get out to my e-mail."

"In Max's office?"

Beckett shrugged. "The door was unlocked. I didn't realize it was Max's office."

"Uh-huh."

"Well, it didn't work anyway," Beckett said, using the mouse to close the e-mail window, then shutting down the operating system while Julie watched. "I hope I didn't wake you when I left."

Julie continued frowning as he stood up. "No, I woke up and remembered I wanted to get something out of my office." She held up an alarm clock.

Beckett smiled. "Good idea."

"We've got three hours left to get some sleep. I suggest we go back downstairs."

Beckett padded out into the hallway. Julie glanced around to see if anything was missing, then locked the office door and pulled it shut. "You'd better come with me. I don't want you to get lost."

"Big place. It's like a maze."

Julie gave him a look while they padded down the cold tile hallway. "Are you the rat looking for the cheese?"

"Aren't we all?"

NINE

"In recognition of Mr. Talleyrand Blackthorne's compassion and his generous contributions of time, effort, and financial support, the Association for Protection of the Elderly in Society is awarding Mr. Blackthorne this year's Senior Noteworthy Ombudsman Trophy! His humanitarian life and generous nature should serve as a model for us all."

Well-meaning but tired applause filled the main ballroom of the Ritz-Carlton in Laguna Niguel as hundreds of senior citizens whom Tal had never met took the time to honor him for his dubious recent accomplishments. While he accepted a large gold trophy that looked like an angel with enormous breasts holding the Earth over her head, he still wasn't sure why, of all people, he had been selected to be honored by APES. As an Orange County real estate developer, he was always being handed a variety of awards and honors, usually as a side benefit of some long-forgotten bribe or blackmail deal, and he could always use the good publicity, but these events always seemed to bring out the worst aspects of his nature. After accepting an award, he couldn't stop himself from shoving people out of his way, cursing at people who stopped by to congratulate him, spitting at the help, or throwing drinks in people's faces – yet such behavior seemed, perversely, to enhance his reputation, and they always came back for more. He couldn't figure it out. After being awarded another Key to the City by the mayor of Anaheim, Tal had almost drowned the mayor in a punchbowl before spending a wild weekend in Palm Springs with the mayor's young blond trophy wife, but the man was such a good sport about the whole thing that Tal had almost been buried with invitations to more Anaheim award ceremonies and local celebrity tributes to Tal's "generous nature and humanitarian accomplishments." He'd started to wonder exactly how many people he'd have to shoot in the head at one of these events to make a negative impression.

The ancient troll in the funny hat who had handed him the trophy – whose name Tal had already forgotten – tried to shake Tal's hand again while posing for the cameras. Tal fondled the trophy's gargantuan hooters with one hand while using the other to knock off the troll's hat and mess with his toupee, but the man just laughed while the moment was recorded by the press corps. Continuing to smile for the cameras, Tal reached into the man's back pocket, took out his wallet, removed almost two hundred dollars, flashed the wad at the press, and slipped the cash into the side pocket of his black Armani suit. The troll laughed and shook his hand again. Tal sighed and shook his head; just for variety, he wanted someone to fight back or tell him to piss off, but that clearly wasn't going to happen here. Tal wasn't sure why he did these things, but he was fascinated by this apparent self-destructive impulse whenever it emerged to spice up one of these boring events.

When his cell phone rang, Tal grabbed a fruity umbrella drink from the tray of a passing waiter and replaced it with the gold trophy, then answered his phone.

"Yeah?"

"It's me, boss."

In response to something clever that the troll said into his microphone, the milling crowd applauded again, making it hard for Tal to hear. Tal sipped at his drink and tried to ignore them.

"What's all that noise, boss?"

"I'm getting an award."

"For what?"

"I have no idea. What do you want?"

The crowd laughed when the troll gestured at Tal and said something. Annoyed, Tal held the phone between his shoulder and his ear, then grabbed the microphone from the old man and ceremoniously dunked it in the fruity drink.

"I just wanted to report that the mission is almost accomplished as ordered."

"Almost?"

"A suitably spectacular end awaits Mr. Beckett."

"Oh, Christ. What did you do?"

"I'd rather surprise you. I'm sure it'll be on the six o'clock news."

"I doubt it. You're four hundred miles away."

"Doesn't matter. You'll still see it on the news. And there's no way anyone can connect it with us."

"You'd better be right."

"The Condor watches and waits for his opportunity. That Beckett guy disappeared for a while, but I was waiting for him when he came back. The extra time gave me a chance to plan. Now he'll get the surprise of his life – in a manner of speaking."

Tal closed his eyes and tried to think positively. After several attempts to kill Beckett, the odds had to be in Condor's favor, didn't they?

"Boss? Are you there?"

"I'm warning you, Kermit, if you screw this up again, I will be extremely peeved. And you won't like me when I'm peeved."

"The proud Condor rises like the Phoenix from the mistakes of his past. In the end, the Condor does not fail."

"I can assure you, if he does fail again, the proud Condor will be stuffed and mounted on my desk."

"No worries, boss."

In the pit of his heart, Tal knew the little turd would screw it up again, so his next call was to Babette with instructions for the plane tickets he'd require.

After a lukewarm shower and a sumptuous breakfast composed of four petrified selections from a vending machine, Beckett felt prepared to greet the new day. Lisa used the coffeemaker in her office to create a powerful brew with the ability to wake the dead, which helped to clear the considerable cobwebs from Beckett's tired brain. He'd been hoping for another opportunity to sneak into Max's office and go through the rest of the drawers, but Julie kept her eye on him so he wouldn't wander off unattended. However, at one point she had to use the women's restroom, so Beckett strolled down the hallway to an open door where he saw an office light was on.

Thwok!

Beckett peered into the office, and a playing card struck the wall near his face, quivering there with one corner embedded in the wood. It was an ace of spades. Beyond the ace, the wall bristled with maybe thirty more playing cards arrayed in uneven lines. Most of the cards were embedded in a wall poster – a huge image of a white Alaskan harp seal pup posing on an ice floe.

"Oui?"

Beckett had been so fascinated by the cards embedded in the wall that he hadn't even noticed the athletic-looking young man with the granny glasses and black beard seated with his feet up on the desk. He looked like he was ready to go camping in his jeans, hiking boots, plaid shirt, and a NASA flight jacket. He held a partial deck of cards in his left hand and the ace of hearts between the thumb and index finger of his right. Beckett leaned back to glance at the nameplate by the door – Remy Descartes.

"Sorry. Didn't mean to startle you, Mr. Descartes."

"That would be *Doctor* Descartes to you, monsieur."

"I'm guessing you're French."

"I'm guessing you're American," said Descartes, rolling his eyes. He flicked the ace of hearts from his right hand and it spun across the room in a straight line to embed itself one inch away from the ace of spades he'd thrown earlier. There was something else about the man's personality that Beckett could guess, but he didn't say it out loud.

"I don't think I've ever seen anyone throw playing cards like that."

"The cards, they are also the weapons, no?"

"You're the telescope operator, right? Shouldn't you be on the KAO?"

Descartes put his hand to his mouth in mock surprise. "*Sacre bleu*! I knew I had forgotten something!" Then he sighed heavily and threw another card at the wall, but this one bounced off and dropped to the floor.

"I'm Ed Beckett," he said, bending over to pick up the card. He handed it to Descartes.

"How nice for you."

"I'm writing an article about the IRIS project, so I'll be flying with you today."

"I can barely contain my excitement."

"Ed? What are you doing?" It was Julie standing behind him in the hallway. "You're not trying to feed the technician are you?"

"Me? No," Beckett said, nodding at Descartes. "I have to go. Nice meeting you."

Instead of answering, Descartes threw another card at the harp seal.

Julie steered Beckett toward the lobby of the Space Projects building where Lisa was waiting, her arms loaded with notebooks and a wool blanket.

"What's with that guy?" Beckett asked Julie.

"He's French."

"Ah."

Beckett accompanied Julie and Lisa across South Warehouse Road to the immense steel hangar that sheltered the Kuiper Airborne Observatory, or most of it, in any case. Almost 150 feet long with a 160-foot wingspan, the C-141 was somewhat larger than the hangar could accommodate, so a hole in the gargantuan hangar doors allowed the KAO's white "T-tail" to protrude, as if a great white whale had plunged into the building. While the ground crew prepared to push the aircraft out onto the damp concrete of the tarmac with the diesel tug, Beckett followed the two women into an adjoining ready room where Julie seated him in a dark corner with a small monitor next to a VCR. Not a DVD player; an actual VCR for a videotape.

"Do I get to watch cartoons?"

"Better," Julie said as she pushed the Play button. "Safety briefing. You've got just enough time before the director comes by for his team pep talk."

"Oberhaus?"

"Our lord and master."

The videotape started. Beckett recognized the voice of the narrator from the hundreds of nature films he'd seen in elementary school. An establishing shot showed the KAO parked on the tarmac as the sun created a golden glow on the horizon above the Experimental Aircraft hangar. Accompanied by occasional perky music, the narrator took Beckett on a virtual tour of the aircraft's cavernous interior, moving from the vehicle ramp in the open clamshell doors at the back, past the compressors that provided air to the telescope's frictionless bearings, through the meteorology equipment and seats on the lower deck, up a short ramp to the mission consoles where most of the experiment and telescope crew would be seated during the flight. Along the way, whenever the perky music swelled, the narrator would describe the gruesome possibilities that might arise in the event of a "controlled descent into terrain," otherwise known as a crash. Beckett learned that he should not wear any clothing made of synthetic fabrics while flying on the KAO, otherwise the fibers might melt into his skin during a fire. The smartly dressed crew would be wearing safety boots, jeans, and cotton shirts; plaid flannel shirts were popular among the researchers in their pathetic attempts to keep warm in the poorly heated and uninsulated interior. The only warm location during a long trip would be on the flight deck. Beckett could picture the flight crew, segregated from the rest of the mortals by a short ladder up to a closed door to their elevated private compartment, roasting marshmallows over a roaring campfire, snug in the security of their cabin while the passengers struggled to avoid frostbite and anti-freeze flowed through the toilet to keep it working.

The video went on to describe thin areas in the skin of the fuselage where battery-powered saws hung in pouches so that he could cut his way out if all the other exits were blocked after a crash. A rope ladder provided access to a door on top of the fuselage in the event of a water landing. One porthole window was kindly provided in each of the two personnel doors in the main cabin so that passengers could look outside before pulling the emergency door handles and jumping into the smoking flames from spilled jet fuel and exploded engines. There were no other windows anywhere behind the flight deck. The narrator sounded genuinely pleased, as if he had spotted a duck-billed platypus about to emerge from his dwelling, when he described the thrills of explosive decompression and the cargo net that had thoughtfully been provided at the back of the aircraft to prevent passengers from flying out into the five hundred mile-per-hour jet stream if the clamshell doors should happen to pop open in flight. The door problem was a C-141 design flaw that had surprised many airborne troops in Vietnam. With a final reminder to keep track of their oxygen masks and to remain connected to the communication system through the long cables they would drag around behind their headsets inside the noisy cabin, the videotape ended with an inspiring view of the KAO as it banked in a sweeping turn toward the sunrise after another successful nighttime astronomy flight. The music swelled, then abruptly ended when the screen went black, much like an actual crash.

Filled with inspiring thoughts of the many ways he might die while flying on the KAO, Beckett jumped when Lisa put her hand on his shoulder.

"Pre-flight."

"What?"

"We have a mission briefing before each flight. They give us a weather update, tell us where the Space Shuttle is in its orbit when we're flying a live mission like this one, and determine where we're going to intercept the Shuttle's reentry track. They've already started."

Beckett followed Lisa into a bright room with a small blackboard covered in crude drawings and what appeared to be calculus equations. Franz Todlich subtly stroked the long black hair of a striking woman standing in front of him in a tight red jumpsuit – presumably Celia Muerto, the ADAMS computer operator. Remy Descartes slouched in a chair with his eyes half-closed. Standing stiffly at attention on the far side of the room was a pilot in a gray NASA flight suit, mirrored sunglasses, and paratrooper boots who looked as if he was ready to fly a jet fighter into combat – his nametag identified him as Chuck Stone. Beside him stood his co-pilot, a glaring contrast in his sweat-stained cowboy hat, brown handlebar mustache, grimy NASA flight jacket, jeans, and cowboy boots – Robert "Rip"

Cord. Beckett didn't see anyone in the room who looked like the navigator or the flight engineer. Maybe they didn't need one, or couldn't afford one.

Julie stood at the back of the room taking notes while a gray-haired scarecrow named Gil White, the KAO mission director, read from a checklist on his clipboard, reminding them all to dress in warm layers for the long flight and to choose a pair of soundproof headphones and an oxygen mask before boarding the plane. His voice had the weary sound of a man who had read the same reminders thousands of times to new passengers. After a quick rundown of Shuttle orbital data from the tracking station in Guam and a warning that weather at the Cape was "nominal but eroding," forcing the Shuttle to land at Edwards Air Force Base, a paunchy man in an expensive charcoal gray suit sauntered into the room. He appeared to be frowning, but Beckett realized it was just the man's unnaturally thick eyebrows, brown streaked with gray, that formed a "V" of permanent displeasure on his forehead. In fact, there was more hair in his eyebrows than there was on top of his shiny head. Gil looked up from his clipboard, smiled, and introduced the director of Ames Research Center, Dr. Karl Oberhaus.

Oberhaus cleared his throat. "Good morning. This is a historic moment for the crew of the KAO, the investigators of the IRIS program, your supporters here at Ames, and NASA itself. The Shuttle program is depending on you to overcome the obstacles of this mission and 'get the data,' as the KAO crew likes to say. If your will to succeed remains strong, your team will make history today, and your efforts will provide a strong contribution to the arguments for the continued existence of this research facility as budgets continue to be trimmed at headquarters."

Someone dropped a ceramic coffee cup that exploded into fragments when it hit the floor. Beckett saw Yoshi, standing just a few feet away on the opposite side of Lisa, glance around nervously, then bend over to clean up the mess. Oberhaus looked around at the assembled IRIS team members while he nodded several times. "The guiding principle here is 'return on investment.' We must justify the expenditure of the share of national resources that we as an agency are given. We must avoid the appearance of providing a sort of corporate welfare to our civil service employees and we must sharpen the axe that will fall on research programs that are too large, too expensive, too long-term, or where the corporate return on investment may be insufficient. By completing a successful project such as IRIS, we are sending a report back to headquarters that says we are worthwhile and we want to keep our jobs. The choice is up to you. Thank you, and good luck with your mission today. Go get the data."

His speech finished, Oberhaus raised his clenched right hand in benediction, with his thumb pointed at the ceiling, then turned on his heel and walked briskly from the room to scattered applause from the team.

Beckett looked at Lisa. "Wow. What was all that about?"

Lisa shrugged. "It's the same speech he gives us every time. And it has occurred to some of us that he might be serious."

"About NASA headquarters wanting to shut off the IRIS funding?"

"About NASA wanting to shut down Ames. They can always move the KAO to another NASA facility and we could move the operation there until we're done. However, Oberhaus might find himself out of a job if they shut down Ames, and he'd probably take it out on us. Oberhaus is known for landing on his feet, but this time he's more likely to land on *our* feet."

"I get the impression he's not well-liked."

"Oh, he's okay for a petty bureaucrat. In his position, he has to keep moving through the political waters like a shark, otherwise he'll die. As long as he's our shark, he's fine, but if the shark gets too hungry, he'll turn on us."

"We'll have to distract him by putting chum in the water."

"What do you mean? Don't they use chum to *draw* the sharks?"

Beckett shook his head. "This is too confusing. Let's drop the shark analogy and go pick out some comfortable oxygen masks that will muffle our screams before we crash."

Lisa chuckled, and it was a pleasant sound that made Beckett feel warm. "Don't let the safety video get to you. We'll be fine."

"That's easy for you to say, but the local record for crashes doesn't inspire confidence."

"You worry too much. When your time comes, you'll just have to accept it."

"Maybe, but I won't go quietly."

"I will. If I can, I want to enjoy my last moments of life. I'll think about the good things."

"Then you'd better sit this one out, because that safety video made it sound as if we'll catch fire, pass out while screaming, and die pretty quickly. Just climbing into the plane might kill us. It's a deathtrap."

Lisa gave him a serious look while she selected a set of headphones and an oxygen mask with an attractive purple band. "Ed, you're creeping me out."

"Sorry. Any tips on selecting an oxygen mask?"

"Pick one that works."

They passed through the huge hangar doors onto the concrete tarmac still shrouded in pre-dawn darkness. Already backed out of the hangar, the huge C-141 StarLifter rested in a dramatic pool of light, its white fuselage gleaming, hooked up by hoses to a refrigeration truck and a fuel tanker like a patient in a hospital. The damp breeze smelled of jet fuel. As he hauled himself up the short ladder into the belly of the great white whale known as the KAO, Beckett followed Lisa's butt as it swayed back and forth in front of him in a hypnotic motion. Her tiny feet clad in hiking boots clunked against each metal rung of the ladder with a confident gait. Once inside, past the ladder that led to the flight deck, they immediately turned right in the narrow passage to walk past the tiny restroom and around the telescope chamber. The back of the infrared telescope protruded into the cabin behind a rack of electronics about the size of a washing machine that had been bolted to the floor specifically for the IRIS experiment. The telescope chamber had been sealed for hours, cooled and pressurized for the upcoming flight by a refrigeration plant parked outside.

In the comfortable-looking seats at the three telescope mission consoles were Celia Muerto, the ADAMS computer operator, Gil White, the mission director, and Remy Descartes, the telescope operator. They all looked very serious, running checks on their instruments, poking colored buttons, studying flight maps, and speaking in hushed tones into microphones pressed against their lips. While Julie poked around at the back of the "washing machine" experiment rack, Lisa slid into one of the two seats behind it where the cool blue glow of a computer monitor cast an unearthly light on her face. She tucked her wool blanket over her lap and smiled at Beckett while he looked around for a place to sit. "Back of the bus, pal."

Celia winked at Beckett and pointed down the ramp toward the back of the plane. "You can sit anywhere behind the weather instruments."

Beckett nodded his thanks, then noticed the toy koala bear tied with a ribbon to the top of the mission director's console directly under a small task light. Gil was concentrating on the flight maps spread out over his keyboard, but Celia was still watching Beckett.

"Koala bear?" Beckett asked.

Celia's bright white teeth glittered in the pool of light. "June, 1977 trip to Australia. The KAO crew discovered the rings of Uranus."

"Ah." He stifled the obvious joke that popped into his head.

"You're here to write about us, right?"

"Right."

"So you'll be staying a while?"

"That's my plan."

"I'm Celia," she said, extending her hand. Beckett smiled and shook her warm hand, but she didn't let go. "We should talk more once we're in the air. I'll come and find you if you get lost."

"I'd like that."

"Of course," she said, giving his hand a final squeeze before releasing him. She turned back to her work, leaving him with the feeling that a light had been shut off.

Beckett glanced toward Lisa in time to see her look away with a frown.

Descartes snorted. "You're making an impression, *mon ami*."

Beckett rolled his eyes and maneuvered through the cramped experiment area toward the ramp. Parts of the metal deck were marked with yellow tape striped with black, warning him not to step on anything more important than his own feet. Electrical cables were strung along the bare metal walls, secured every few feet with plastic cable ties, just like the ties police used whenever they ran out of handcuffs and had a lot of people to arrest. The plastic ties also hung from the backs of seats, sides of instrument panels, and other odd places for no discernible reason. Continuing on down the ramp, he entered a cavernous area in the back of the plane that was large enough to hold a couple of tanks or a large number of troops as these planes had been built to do in Vietnam. Two rows of seats were anchored in the middle of the floor in the back, currently occupied by Yoshi and Todlich. Beyond the seats, the huge clamshell doors were closed and a nylon net separated the doors from the cabin with the intent of keeping everyone inside if the doors should pop open in flight.

Beside the ramp was another area crowded with instrument racks and old Hewlett Packard computers where a thin man in gray hair and glasses checked items off on a clipboard while his eyes darted over the readouts. He looked up and nodded when he saw Beckett turn toward him at the base of the ramp.

"Pete Cohen," he said.

"Ed Beckett."

"I know. You're on my list."

"What do you do?"

"I'm the weather god."

Beckett raised an eyebrow.

"Officially I'm the meteorologist, but the crew thinks I can control the weather," he said with a half-smile that made Beckett wonder if Cohen was serious. "My wife thinks I can see into the future."

"Can you?"

"I can't answer that unless you have a Top Secret security clearance."

"You're kidding, right?"

"Maybe," said Cohen, giving him a significant look while he glanced at his clipboard and checked off Beckett's name. "I'm also the safety officer, so I make sure the doors are shut and nobody is stuck in the engines before we take off."

"If you can see into the future, I guess it's a good sign that you're here on the plane with us. If we were going to crash, you wouldn't be here."

"Maybe that's why I'm the security officer."

Beckett began to wonder how many of the crewmembers were nuts.

Cohen gave him a brief tour of the KAO's safety features, some of which he'd seen in the video, pointing out the battery-operated rotary saw they could use to cut a hole in the fuselage, the rope ladder that led up to the water landing hatch on the roof, the heavy emergency release at the base of the rear passenger door that looked like it could only be opened by a gorilla, the small porthole window in the door that would let them watch when the engines caught fire, the nylon "people-catcher" net, a variety of fire extinguishers to be used for different kinds of fires, and the operation of the safety belt in the empty seat next to Yoshi, who was starting to snore. If the safety tour was meant to be reassuring, it didn't work; he preferred to get on a plane, sit down, and hope for the best. Todlich just glared at Beckett while Cohen gave him the tour.

"And remember," Cohen said, pointing to one of the metal tubes on the fuselage wall, "if you see any hydraulic leaks, report it at once. It's a pink substance and it's under three thousand pounds of pressure, so don't go near it. Cuts right through your skin." He made a cutting motion across his throat. "Very unpleasant."

Beckett zipped up his jacket. "Is there any heat back here?"

Cohen pointed at a tiny vent on the ceiling at the front of the rear cabin. "Yes and no."

"I see."

"We can probably dig up a blanket if you get too cold. Most of us keep moving around during the flight, so we don't notice it as much. Now, if you'll stop pestering me with questions, I have work to do. Be strapped into your seat in five minutes for the mask and radio check."

"Thanks."

Beckett glanced out the small window in the passenger door, noting that one of the two engines of the great white bird was painted in camouflage style.

"Not very good camouflage on a white jet, is it?" Todlich boomed. He stood next to Beckett and looked out the window. Despite his size, he had somehow crept up beside Beckett without his noticing.

"Why did they do that?"

"They had a maintenance flight up to the Air Force base at Travis two days ago. The old engine blew up and Travis didn't have a white cowling handy. Takes time to paint a new one; can't just slap on a coat of house paint and call it done."

"Do these engines blow up a lot?"

Todlich shrugged. "They're getting old. The KAO should have been retired five years ago, but SOFIA isn't ready yet."

"SOFIA?"

"Stratospheric Observatory For Infrared Astronomy. Same idea as the KAO with a bigger telescope mounted in a 747-SP."

"Take your seats," Cohen announced. "Roll call."

Beckett sat down next to Yoshi, who was still asleep. The first thing he noticed was that the metal seat didn't have much padding. After tightening the safety belt around his hips, he put on his headset like everyone else was doing, smacked his nose with the lip mike, and plugged the cable into the intercom system. The oxygen mask dangled over his head at the end of a black hose.

"Beckett?" asked a voice in his head. It sounded like the pilot, Chuck Stone.

"I'm here."

"Beckett? Bite the mike."

He adjusted the mike to where it was touching his lips and spoke in a louder voice. "Yeah. Beckett here."

"Anyone seen Beckett?"

Beckett looked up and saw Cohen gesturing at the black box attached to the headset cable near his hip. He pushed the button. "Hear me now?"

"Is Beckett in the head?"

He heard Cohen over the headset. "Beckett's here. He's trying to learn how to use a headset."

Beckett heard scattered laughter and sighed. The roll call continued. Ten minutes later, the jet engines rattled the walls as the KAO thundered down the runway and lumbered into the air.

One hour into the flight, while the mission director was up on the flight deck eating breakfast and warming up with the crew, Celia summoned

Beckett over the radio. He almost hadn't noticed when she called his name, having gotten used to the constant sound of voices on the open channel discussing flight parameters, the calibration of the telescope tracker on the star Altair, weather information, and Space Shuttle position updates from the Johnson Space Center. He knew better than to remove the headset, not so much because he wouldn't hear about any emergency information, but because the thunder of the jet engines necessitated ear protection in the uninsulated cabin; he could feel the vibrations through his whole body. But the noise didn't seem to bother Yoshi, whose evident excitement about the flight was rubbing off on Beckett at close proximity, so Beckett was dozing off when Celia called his name. Beckett blinked, stood up, and carefully walked up the ramp with the coiled headset wire in his hand. When his feet hit the ramp, the pilot made another vertical course adjustment, climbing as quickly as possible and allowing Beckett to discover why those little plastic cable ties were hanging all over the place as he frantically grabbed for something to hold onto so he could maintain his balance. When his ponderous weight returned to normal as the pilot leveled off, Beckett continued his progress toward Celia.

With the mission director out of his seat, Beckett had a secure place to spend the next few minutes in the busy experiment area behind the telescope bulkhead. Careful not to kick anything or push buttons on the console while he dodged the oxygen masks hanging overhead, he plopped into the seat beside Celia. He plugged his headset into an intercom outlet and Celia switched them to a private channel so they could have a conversation.

Celia gave him a sultry smile. "Nice of you to come up and see me, Ed."

"My pleasure."

"Want to know what I do?"

"Sure."

She tapped on the monitor in front of her. "This is ADAMS, the Airborne Data Acquisition and Management System. If we were flying a normal astronomy flight, the experimenter might ask ADAMS to record and analyze data, but this group has its own IRIS computer system to do that, then they interpret the data when we're back on the ground. Today, all ADAMS has to do is fly the aircraft, keep track of the KAO's position, predict the Space Shuttle's reentry course track with updates from Houston, operate the telescope, and maintain housekeeping records for about a hundred in-flight parameters."

"Isn't there an autopilot in the cockpit?"

She smiled. "Yeah, we call him Chuck."

"That's it?"

"No, Chuck has an autopilot, but ADAMS has control when we're on a flight track determined by the mission. The telescope can only look four degrees ahead or behind a line perpendicular to the aircraft's flight. If our target is a star like Polaris that never varies more than a degree from due north, there's no problem tracking it. If we have to track something like a planet for a few hours, the plane has to turn on a steady arc to keep the telescope lined up, and that's too much work for a regular autopilot. Even then, the telescope operator has to help the computer maintain its lock on the target."

"What about the Space Shuttle? How do you track that?"

"We basically get position updates, project a point where the KAO can intercept the Shuttle's reentry track, and try to be there at the right time with the telescope pointing the right way. Then it's Remy's and Lisa's responsibility. We only get one shot at the Shuttle per mission because it's flying at about Mach 16 when we cross its path; if we're off a little bit we have to wait for the next flight."

"Have you missed it before?"

"Twice. The KAO telescope wasn't built to do anything but astronomy, and neither was the tracker, but it's the only way to get this kind of information. The Shuttle was never tested at actual reentry speeds before it was flown; it wasn't possible to hit those speeds in a wind tunnel. They start their reentry at about Mach 24 while they're still at four hundred thousand feet."

"And what will they do with the information if the mission is a success?"

"The thermal protection system was over-designed to keep the Shuttle crew safe. The underbody hits about twelve hundred degrees Fahrenheit at peak heating shortly after it hits the atmosphere. With the kind of data we can pick up with the KAO's telescope, IRIS might be able to shave off several thousand pounds of tile from the heat shield, and that's weight that could be used to lift heavier payloads into orbit. It costs about ten thousand dollars per pound to lift something into orbit on the Shuttle, so that's a big savings."

"If IRIS works."

"Right."

Beckett pondered the ADAMS system for a moment. It seemed like there ought to be something there that could help his investigation. He wanted to ask if the computer could identify Max's killer. "What kind of housekeeping information does ADAMS store?"

"Constant altitude information, course track, weather, calibration data, telescope positioning, KAO fuel and environmental data – things like that."

"Anything about the passengers or the crew?"

"No, just their total weight. The pilot needs that for fuel calculations."

"Do you save all that information after a flight?"

"Sure. Sometimes the experimenters need it for reference, so everything gets taped and added to the library in the KAO operations office, or the 'cave' as we call it."

"Hmm." He'd have to listen to the audio from Dumas's last flight, although he didn't expect to hear the killer confess over the intercom to the rest of the crew. But there might have been some speculation among them regarding Dumas's absence from the mission. The project manager wasn't actually needed to operate any of the equipment during a flight, so it would have been easy for Todlich to step in and assume Dumas's responsibilities. Back on the ground, Oberhaus had probably named Todlich the official project manager out of expediency because no one else knew as much about the mission who also had management experience.

"You have nice eyes."

Beckett was startled out of deep thought. "What?"

"I like your eyes."

He could feel Lisa staring at the back of his head. He looked over his shoulder and she frowned at him. Seated beside her, Julie continued staring at the monitor in her experiment console. This was very confusing; he knew Lisa couldn't hear what Celia was saying. It was even more confusing when Celia gently put her hand on his left knee. "Ed, will you write about me in your article?"

For a moment, he couldn't remember what article she was talking about, but then his cover story came back to him. "Oh, sure. You've been very helpful."

Gil tapped Beckett on the shoulder, gesturing that he wanted his seat back, so Beckett smiled and stood up carefully, holding onto the back of the seat and shifting his weight to accommodate the sudden banking of the huge aircraft. While the plane bumped and rolled, the end of the telescope that protruded through the bulkhead into their pressurized cabin swayed back and forth to maintain its lock on the star they were using as a calibration target. Beckett was disturbed when he realized that the gyro-stabilized reflector in the telescope was actually steady while the aircraft itself moved around it. Gil sat down, unplugged Beckett's headset, and plugged in his own. Beckett coiled up the cable and looked around at the others intent on their work. Without a link to the intercom system, all he could hear was the rush of air and the thunder of the engines through the fuselage.

To his right, Remy Descartes munched on a chocolate croissant at the telescope operator's console while reading the newspaper. Over his head, the image from the tracker on the telescope showed the star, Altair, dead--center on the monitor screen. Since Descartes didn't look busy, Beckett tapped him on the shoulder. Descartes gave him an annoyed look and continued chewing. Beckett removed his own headphones and gestured at Descartes's ears.

"What? You can see that I'm busy," Descartes said, lifting one earpiece as he swallowed. It was hard enough to understand his French accent normally, but the food in his mouth and the noise in the cabin made it even harder.

"I was hoping you could tell me a little bit about what you do here. For my article."

Descartes stared at him long enough that Beckett figured he was going to tell him to get lost, but apparently he'd just been processing the information to determine a proper response. He plugged Beckett's headset cord into the intercom box and switched to a private channel. "Okay, but only if you promise to spell my name correctly. The journalists, they are always coming on the flights and spelling my name wrong."

"I promise," Beckett said, nodding solemnly.

"You know that most of the infrared radiation from space is absorbed by the water vapor in the atmosphere, right?"

"Sure."

"Well, we're above ninety-nine percent of that water vapor as soon as we fly above thirty-nine thousand feet. We have a thirty-six-inch reflector telescope mounted in that chamber over there, and it looks out through a viewing hole in the fuselage so we can observe the full infrared spectrum in the sky. We cool down the telescope chamber before takeoff so that the mirrors don't warp from the temperature change when we open the viewing port; we also get a cleaner infrared signal that way." He gestured at the glowing star image in the monitor over his head. "Right now we've got the instrument pointed at Altair for calibration. When we're ready for the encounter, I'll aim at the part of the sky that the Shuttle is supposed to pass through. If we're close enough, the IRIS tracker will pick up the hot glow of the Shuttle and realign the telescope to get a good image on the infrared array."

"You don't get any blurring from the jet engine vibration?" Beckett asked.

Descartes shook his head. "The telescope, she rests on pneumatic shock absorbers and rides on a compressed-air bearing so it's isolated from any direct contact with the aircraft. We might feel turbulence, but the telescope will remain motionless. The telescope chamber, it is like a little world all by itself." He took a bite out of his croissant and looked up at the star on the overhead monitor.

Beckett nodded. "You worked with Max Dumas quite a bit, didn't you?"

Descartes coughed and sprayed a few chunks of his croissant on his console.

"You okay?" Beckett asked, slapping him on the back.

Descartes swallowed, brushing crumbs off the console onto the floor, then frowned at Beckett. "Why are you asking about Max?"

"Background. He was the project manager for a long time, and I heard you knew him pretty well." Beckett saw something flare in Descartes's eyes, but he wasn't sure if it was anger or fear.

"Max had many flaws, but he was a good scientist," Descartes said, glancing at the rows of numeric ADAMS data on one of his monitors.

"What kind of flaws?"

When Descartes looked at him again, his jaw muscles were tight, and there seemed to be some kind of conflict going on in his eyes that finally settled into a look of suspicion. "This is none of your business. Who do you think you are, accusing me of – "

"Remy!" Todlich shouted, his bulk looming behind Beckett. "Have you run the position update yet?"

Descartes glared at Beckett, then pulled his headset plug and switched over to the public intercom channel, leaving Beckett startled by his outburst. How had he accused Descartes of anything? The man seemed guilty of something, but what? Backing up a bit to let Todlich peer at one of the console monitors while he coiled his cable, Beckett noticed Julie watching him, but she quickly looked away.

Beckett plugged into one of the intercom boxes along the wall, pondering what Descartes had said and wondering who he should talk to next. Then he heard Gil White's voice over the headset. "All right, people, listen up. Dryden Flight says the orbiter reentry is scrubbed. Bad weather at both landing sites. We're going home."

Grumbling and shaking their heads at each other, the team members sat back in their seats and started shutting down the equipment.

The plane lurched. Cohen, the meteorologist, had said something about his studying clear air turbulence, so he probably liked the bumpy ride, but Beckett's stomach didn't – it lurched whenever the plane did. But, as it turned out, this lurch hadn't been prompted by turbulence.

With an incredible sound of thunder, a shockwave pounded through the cabin, hurling papers, notebooks, blankets, clothing, and cups of coffee toward the back of the plane in a sudden whirlwind that roared past like a freight train, lifting the bulky Todlich off his feet. Beckett threw his arms around the headrest of Descartes's seat to steady himself against the powerful gust pulling at his body while the startled Todlich flew down the ramp toward the sudden light at the rear of the plane and disappeared, accompanied by the screams of those who were still in their seats, sharing their fears with everyone else through the headsets. The regular crew members grabbed for their dangling oxygen masks as the clear air in the cabin turned to fog and the floor turned at a steep angle. Gasping, Beckett wondered how he could get to the oxygen mask dangling over his seat in the rear of the plane, assuming the rear of the plane was still there in the howling wind that buffeted everyone in the cabin, and the deck tilted further, putting his seat and his mask almost straight uphill while something wrapped around his neck trying to strangle him. His seat might as well be miles away for all the good it would do him now. The wind pulled at his arms, trying to pull them out of their sockets, and pounded at his eardrums as if he were caught in a crashing wave like a surfer at the beach. His panicked brain tried to remember what they'd said in class – was it ten seconds, eight, six before the lights went out in his head? He couldn't remember. Not that it would matter with the plane diving straight at the ground. And he realized that the headset cord was wrapped around his neck like a garrote, squeezing while he strained against it to hold on to the seat in front of him, and then his head bounced against something and the headset flew off, releasing the pressure on his neck, defying gravity as it tried to blow uphill past his legs toward the terrible abyss of light, finally pulling free from the intercom box and shooting away, just as Beckett was about to shoot away when his tired arms finally broke free of the chair, or the chair broke free of the deck. Then his arms went numb, and his body lurched in the air, slapping at the deck plates as he sailed upwards toward the raging light, buffeted by sound and wind beyond anything he'd ever experienced.

A dark silence flooded into his brain.

TEN

Expecting to wake up dead, Beckett was happily surprised for a moment when he opened his eyes to discover that he was still breathing onboard the KAO. He felt a lot of sore spots and cuts on his freezing body, along with the coppery taste of blood in his mouth where he'd bitten his tongue, but nothing appeared to be broken, even though he found it difficult to move. His happiness faded when his foggy brain conjured a vision of his body trapped in the web of a giant spider, but he was actually hooked in the nylon net that stretched tightly across the gap over the open clamshell doors at the rear of the aircraft. Wind buffeted his body and boomed in his ears, and when he twisted his head around to see what was behind him, he saw the glinting surface of the San Francisco Bay gradually rising to meet them, and he noticed that the clamshell doors were not merely open, they were *gone*. A few feet away, Franz Todlich and Pete Cohen were also stuck in the net, facing out, upside-down and apparently unconscious. Beckett's ears hurt and he had a headache that pulsed with the pounding of his heart, but it was nice to be able to feel anything after the KAO's high-speed plunge toward the ground. It was an experience he didn't want to repeat.

The blue waters vanished, replaced by the concrete runway at Moffett Field. Beckett braced himself, hoping the contact of the KAO with the ground would not be violent enough to shake him loose from his precarious perch. The landing gear boomed when it hit the tarmac, then Beckett's stomach lurched along with the aircraft as it bounced, resisting the pull of gravity, and finally boomed a second time when the tires made contact once more. His weight shifted forward in the net while the pilot slowed the ponderous weight of the C-141 screaming down the runway. Beckett knew that the extra length of the Moffett runway could accommodate the largest of aircraft, and the pilot was probably going to use most of it to slow the heavy bird. Metal parts rattled together and the thunder from the engines increased, slowing them, and Beckett wished his head would stop spinning as he smelled burning rubber from the smoking tires. His weight bounced in the nylon net, and he tensed his arms to make sure he didn't slip out. He heard an unearthly wail and looked through the net again to see a yellow fire truck pacing them on the parallel taxiway. The KAO bounced and jerked as it slowed, but Beckett was happy to see that there weren't any flames or additional pieces of the jet falling off as they rolled along. He had no idea where the enormous clamshell doors had gone when they fell off the jet – he didn't even know if they'd been over land or water at the time – but he was glad that the safety regulations required a net above the rear loading ramp, and that he'd been in the plane rather than on the ground when the tons of metal came down.

The giant aircraft shuddered to a halt a few hundred yards away from the experimental aircraft hangar, well within reach of the stationary firefighting equipment but far enough out that an explosion wouldn't harm any of the buildings or the planes. While firefighters swarmed toward the back of the KAO, a different sort of swarm occurred inside the plane.

Celia's long black hair stuck out in all directions as she ran down the ramp and threw her arms around the groggy Todlich, sobbing on his chest while he blinked in surprise. Cohen sat on the floor near Celia's feet, rubbing his neck. Yoshi and Lisa held on tight to each other, staggering down the ramp while several pairs of arms lifted Beckett out of the net and set him down on the deck. The firefighters had cut through the net now, and one paramedic checked out Todlich and Cohen while the other one went up the ramp into the forward compartment. Everyone seemed to have glazed looks on their faces, and Beckett supposed that he did, too. When Julie came down the ramp with a worried expression, Beckett was pleased to see her relief when she spotted him and knelt down beside him while the paramedic checked his vital signs. "Ed! Are you okay?"

Beckett grinned and nodded at the paramedic. "Ask him. I've got a headache, but I don't think anything's broken."

The paramedic, whose badge identified him only as "Carl," nodded as he felt around Beckett's chest with a stethoscope. She gently placed her hand on Carl's shoulder. "When you're done here, Remy is still unconscious up front."

"My partner's up there now," Carl said.

Julie nodded, then smiled at Beckett. "I'm glad you're okay."

"And how was your flight?" Beckett asked. He liked the attention he was getting from Julie and he didn't want her to leave.

"Better than yours," she said. "I just stayed in my seat with my oxygen mask and watched my life pass before my eyes."

"Oh, was that your life? I think I saw it too, and I knew it wasn't mine."

Carl stood and jogged up the ramp to help his partner with the staggering Remy, whose face was black-and-blue with bruises. When Julie saw him, she patted Beckett on the chest and walked over to the base of the ramp.

"Looks like you've been in a fight," Julie said, crossing your arms. "And you lost."

Beckett sat up, surprised by her tone of voice – familiar and condescending, as if they'd known each other a long time.

"Stupid American pilot was trying to kill me," Remy said. "I thought NASA pilots knew how to fly."

Chuck Stone cleared his throat at the top of the ramp. "Wasn't my fault."

Remy's eyes widened as he turned around and saw the pilot. "You could have killed all of us, Mr. Hotshot Pilot."

"He's the one who saved us," Julie said, poking Remy in the chest. "And it's just like you to start pointing the finger – "

"Oh, yes, I'll point the finger, but not the one you think – " Remy began.

Julie's eyes narrowed. "You're hysterical."

"Oh, am I?" The paramedics had to hold Remy back when he tried to lunge toward Julie, then a hypodermic needle appeared in one of their hands and it plunged through Remy's sleeve into his upper arm. His eyes were wide, but he stopped struggling to stare at his arm. "What did you do?"

Carl pushed him toward a seat. "Like she said, you're hysterical. I gave you a sedative."

"I'll sue. Sue you for...that medical thing they sue doctors for," Remy mumbled as he sagged into his seat with his eyes closed.

Julie shook her head and walked back over to Beckett, who was using the shredded safety net to help himself stand up. He felt shaky, and the headache was causing a little nausea, but he felt better in an upright position. Julie put her arm around his shoulders to help steady him.

"If you don't mind my asking, what was that all about?" he asked, pointing toward Remy with his chin. Beyond the unconscious telescope operator, the firefighters had opened the passenger door and lowered the stairs.

Julie raised one eyebrow and sighed. "Remy? He's rude, vindictive, and a jerk. Someone has to keep him in his place when he gets out of hand, and it might as well be me." She looked uncomfortable, and turned her head to watch Lisa and Yoshi start down the passenger stairs.

"Why you? Isn't Todlich in charge of the team?"

"Remy's more afraid of me. He's my ex-husband."

Tal Blackthorne carefully walked down the passenger steps from the white Learjet onto the white tarmac beside the small aircraft hangar. The acrid odor of jet fuel mixed with the salt smell of the San Francisco Bay, and he saw the silvery waters receding from the mud flats on the far side of the runways. The sun was setting, giving the hangar buildings a golden glow. A short distance away, Condor leaned against the front fender of a black limousine wearing a matching black suit, sunglasses, and driving gloves. Tal hoped the little man knew how to drive without wrecking the car, and he was willing to save the price of a chauffeur to find out, especially since he didn't need any extra witnesses to some of the activities he had planned for the next couple of days.

Other than basic greeting noises, Condor said little as Tal climbed into the back seat of the limo, and that seemed odd. Normally, Kermit would have already bored Tal out of his mind with inane comments about the weather, Tal's flight, the traffic, or whatever else popped into his head. While Condor jogged around the car and jumped into the driver's seat, Tal tried to study the man's face, but he carefully avoided eye contact while hiding behind his sunglasses, even though it was almost dark outside. When the smoked glass privacy divider started to rise behind the front seat, Tal used his own switch to roll it back down.

"Did you do the job?" Tal asked.

"The traffic getting here was murder," Condor replied, pretending not to have heard Tal as he swung the limo around toward the exit gate.

Tal waited without saying anything else, knowing what answer he expected. He popped open a bottle of beer from the small refrigerator by his seat and started drinking to prepare himself for this conversation. If he'd known how to contact any other hit men that weren't somehow connected with one of the various mafias that operated in Orange County or Los Angeles, the little man would have been on the unemployment line by now. The fact that the little man was crazy also played a part in Tal's decision not to fire him; after all, Kermit was armed, and Tal had a feeling he wouldn't take rejection very well.

"There were some technical difficulties," Condor finally answered, pretending to concentrate on his driving while they drove onto the airport access road.

"Such as?"

Condor glanced in the mirror and licked his lips. "Well, getting onto the airfield was no trouble; security isn't what it used to be around here. Then I placed an explosive charge on the C-141 that the target was on this morning, and it went off and all, but the damned thing came back and landed normally."

Tal choked and sprayed beer out of his mouth. "You did *what*?"

Condor kept his eyes on the road. "It's okay. I am a professional, you know. I was trained to handle explosives."

Gasping, Tal dabbed at the beer on his suit with a napkin. He knew he couldn't possibly get drunk enough to deal with this guy on a rational level, but he opened another beer anyway. "Marvelous. Attacking a government aircraft. Let's just call the FBI hotline and tell them where to find us."

"I covered my tracks, boss."

"The FBI has people who investigate bombings for a living, you meathead! If they find any evidence at all, they'll probably know everything about you, including your shoe size and what you had to eat for breakfast three weeks ago, before you've even had time to fart! They've even got bomb sniffing dogs, for Christ's sake! *Dogs*, Kermit! Vicious, slobbering, hungry *dogs*!"

Condor stared at Tal in the rearview mirror, but the sunglasses hid his expression. When he spoke again, his voice was low and calming, as if he were speaking to a rabid animal. "Hey, everything's cool. They won't find us. Maybe you ought to take a pill or something."

"Take a pill?" Tal cackled. "I don't think they stock cyanide pills as standard items in limousines these days, do they? Here, let me check." He made a show of briefly looking around the interior, then glared at Condor's head. "Nope. No cyanide." He popped an ice cube out of the bucket in the refrigerator and tossed it at the back of Condor's head, where it hit the back of his hat with a satisfying thump.

"Ow!" Condor hunched down lower in his seat, holding one hand over the back of his head.

Tal drank some more beer to calm himself. "So you set a charge and the aircraft came back. Would you mind explaining how you know what happened on the aircraft?"

Condor hesitated, then rose higher in his seat. "I monitored the air traffic control frequency and heard the NASA pilot's report. Then I watched the runway from a safe distance. When they landed, the fire trucks came out, but there wasn't any fire."

Tal felt a dark calm settling over his mind. "How is that possible? Maybe your so-called bomb never went off, did you think of that? You told me you were a demolitions expert, and a SEAL, and all kinds of other crap, and you can't even bring down an undefended plane."

"Hey, it happens. Bringing a jet down isn't a walk in the park, you know. I know the bomb went off because parts were missing after they landed."

"Why didn't you just blow up the entire aircraft?"

Condor hesitated, almost as if it hadn't occurred to him. "Style. I wanted to make it look like an accident. Those jet transports were always popping their clamshell doors in Vietnam, sucking people outside. I must have scared the hell out of them, though."

Tal took another drink. "Scared to *death* would have been acceptable, but your little brain can't seem to grasp the concept."

"Hey, there's no call for short jokes."

"I'm not joking. I didn't get where I am today by pussyfooting around when there was work to be done, or opponents to be disposed of. Now, I'll have to take matters into my own hands, and I wouldn't expect a bonus for this if I were you. In fact, I'm starting to wonder if you wouldn't be better off driving a taxi or flipping burgers somewhere. You'd make a great short-order cook." Gun or no gun, he had to put the dwarf in his place.

Condor glanced in the rearview mirror again, almost running two black BMWs off the road as he merged onto the freeway. Horns blared. "Now, boss, there's no need to get excited and make decisions you know you'll regret."

"Oh, I doubt that I'd regret it."

"Look, I'll take care of it in a few hours, okay? I know where the target is staying. Since he's so hard to kill, I'll surprise him in his bed with a lead sleeping pill. In the cheap dive he's in, they may not even notice his corpse for a couple of days. Until he starts to smell."

Tal nodded his approval. "That's more like it. Quit jerking around and get it over with."

Condor gave him a hesitant smile. "The Condor always gets his prey, boss. I can do this."

Tal snorted, then pushed the switch on his armrest to start raising the divider window. As it rose, Condor turned, lifting his face to see over the smoked glass, and quickly asked a question. "Hey, boss, you want to buy a submarine? I can get a good deal."

Ignoring the question, Tal closed the divider, fervently hoping that Beckett would be terminated before General Akimov arrived. He'd have to prepare a backup plan in case Kermit failed again. Since the Russians were coming, there could be no mistakes.

Alongside Moffett Field in Sunnyvale, a windowless turquoise-colored structure sat among the sprouting mushrooms of communications dishes beside Highway 101. Known locally as the "Blue Cube," the command center of the Air Force Satellite Control Network operated fifty-four defense satellites that provided military intelligence, communications, weather, and navigation information. The Blue Cube housed about fifteen hundred military and civilian employees, one of whom was Ralph "Meatball" Bronkowski, a software engineering contractor who also had a part-time job with Ed Beckett. Now on his fourth beer, Meatball slumped in a restaurant booth with Beckett at the Jolly Knight, a popular watering hole near the Blue Cube that attracted a wide variety of tech employees. With such a high concentration of technical skills regularly visiting a public place, the Jolly Knight also drew various kinds of headhunters that circulated among the crowd – employment recruiters and foreign spies – all wanting to make friends with the digerati. Everyone knew this, so the tech companies and the government had their own spies in the restaurant – security watchdogs and counterintelligence officers – all wanting to make friends with those who wanted to make friends with the employees, who were mainly there for the cheap beer, free appetizers, and human contact. The owners of the Jolly Knight didn't really care about the occupations of their customers, they just knew they had a good thing going that brought in a lot of revenue.

Beckett felt comfortable among the mostly male Jolly Knight crowd, even though he didn't look exhausted or pale enough to fit in with these people who regularly worked twelve- to sixteen-hour days. Meatball was a typical example: under six feet tall, weighing in at around 250 pounds, long brown hair tied back in a ponytail, a stiff bottlebrush mustache, the fishbelly complexion of someone who rarely saw the sun, thick glasses in bent wire frames, blue jeans, and a *Star Trek* t-shirt that had seen better days. When Beckett was able to make eye contact with Meatball, which was rare, he saw bloodshot gray eyes, and he'd always imagined that the color had been drained out of them by staring into computer monitors for most of his thirty years. He'd known Meatball for years, ever since he was a lowly programmer instead of a lofty software engineer, and he always looked the same. As Beckett told the story of the KAO's explosive decompression at forty-one thousand feet, Meatball hung on every word, categorizing the experience as one he would have enjoyed if he ever felt the need to leave his office.

"And then what?" Meatball asked.

"We made it back."

"Nobody was killed?"

"No, just a few injuries."

Meatball looked disappointed. "Still, what a rush, huh?"

Beckett nodded. After his second glass of wine, he was finally starting to relax. Everyone else from the KAO flight had gone home, understandably wanting to be with their loved ones, but Beckett hadn't felt like returning to the Friend Lee Motel right away, and he'd set up this meeting so that his friends could help him out.

Some of the noise in the room died down as Hyacinth Cummings strolled into the room, completely oblivious of the attention she was getting. Dressed in a long-sleeve white shirt, black vest, and black skirt combination that suggested a tuxedo, she scanned the room until she saw Beckett waving her over to the table. She had short, straight black hair, a complexion so white that it belonged on a corpse, and lips that glowed with bright red lipstick. When she got closer, Beckett saw her alert green eyes, somewhat obscured by her unusual contact lenses featuring gold spirals that seemed to pull you into her pupils. Thin and tall, she towered over the two men at the table and smiled. "Am I late?"

While Meatball grumbled and munched on a breadstick, Beckett moved toward the middle of the booth to let her sit down. "No, I was just telling Meatball about my big adventure."

Hyacinth sat down with a serious expression, and the room's noise level went back up to normal. "You look okay."

"The wine helped, I think." She had already pulled the entire story out of him when they spoke on the phone two hours ago.

Hyacinth leaned over and kissed Beckett on the cheek. "I'm glad you're all right."

Beckett grinned. "Typical day for me. Dodging murderers, surviving aircraft explosions, driving over here on the freeway – danger is my life."

"That's what it sounds like."

"Hi," Meatball grunted, waving his arms once to get her attention.

Hyacinth turned her head and looked surprised. "Oh, hi, Meatball. I thought you were still in the Gargoyle office, so I slipped some food under your door."

"Cool. I'll get it tonight," he said in his typical monotone voice. A smile flickered across his face. "Thanks."

"Everything okay with the new website?"

Meatball used one of the employment recruiter business cards stacked on the table to pick breadstick bits out of his teeth. "Yeah."

Hyacinth nodded. "I gave them some new art, and Meatball fixed the code, so they're happy now. You have some more work for us?"

Beckett looked around to make sure that no one at the neighboring tables was eavesdropping. He knew that the tables were regularly bugged and debugged by various intelligence agencies and industrial spies, but they were after bigger fish, so he wasn't going to worry about it. "I need you to help me out. I feel like people are following me, and I can't be every place at once. And if I don't solve this problem in the next day or two, the odds for my survival won't be good."

Meatball took a calculator out of his pocket to work out the odds while Hyacinth ordered a glass of white wine from the waiter.

Beckett slid two pieces of paper across the table to each of them. "I've listed some names and information there. I know background investigations are a little out of your normal lines of work, but it's basically research, and a lot of it can be done on the Internet."

"Cool," Meatball said, still punching numbers on his calculator.

"Meatball, I'd also like you to hack into the net at Ames and see if you can recover some old e-mail records from a few days ago. Can you do that?"

With a slight frown, he continued working on the calculator. "Not if it's been deleted, although they might be recoverable depending on the server OS. I don't know. I'll poke around and think of something."

"Security won't be a problem?"

Meatball snorted.

Hyacinth studied the papers. "You don't want me to do anything illegal, do you?"

Beckett shrugged. "No. Not really. Depends on your interpretation, I guess."

"I'll have something for you tomorrow," she said, blinking her spiral eyes at him.

Meatball looked up from the calculator. "Twenty-two thousand to one."

"What's that?"

"The odds against your survival for two more days."

After another hour of food and drink while he explained the Dumas situation, Beckett paid the bill, tried to phone in a report to Detective Daniels who had already gone home, then walked Hyacinth and Meatball out to the parking lot. The wind off the bay was chilly, but Beckett hadn't brought a jacket because his mind had been occupied with other matters when he packed his overnight bag. They all said goodbye, Hyacinth drove off in her red Honda and Meatball in his black BMW, then Beckett walked over to his Camaro. The rental car was easy to spot in any parking lot now, with the harpoon sticking out of the front passenger door at a sharp angle, its tip almost touching the ground. He turned the key in the driver's side door lock, but the door was stuck again, so he removed the clear plastic he had taped over the hole where the former window had been, and started to climb in.

Off-balance, half in and half out of the car window, there wasn't much he could do when someone with sinus trouble and a whistling nose dropped a pillowcase over his head and grabbed his arms from behind, then quickly tied his wrists. Beckett started to yell, but a fist slammed into his stomach while he was yanked backwards out of the car. Then they kicked him in the side and he saw tiny flashing lights in front of his eyes. He tried to draw his legs up in a fetal position for some protection, but hands grabbed him under the arms and dragged him a few feet – the stuffy nose whistling madly with the effort – then roughly dropped him into the trunk of a car and slammed the lid shut.

The Friend Lee Motel was the sort of place where roaches went to die. Flies avoided it because they didn't want to be seen there. They had a swimming pool in the middle of the parking lot, but the water had been replaced with broken lawn chairs and old beer cans. The

"U"-shaped motel faced the 101 freeway across the street, apparently to get the maximum benefit from the traffic noise that echoed between the two stories of anonymous numbered doors. Hookers worked out of some of the rooms, while drug dealers worked out of others – it was like a small business co-op building. Condor couldn't believe that anyone would choose to stay there voluntarily, but Beckett had made Condor's life easier by doing so.

Condor had parked the limousine down the street at the McDonald's so he wouldn't attract attention. He called the desk clerk at the motel around eight o'clock to get Beckett's room number, then called the room to make sure Beckett wasn't there. He now sat with his back against the wall in the shadows behind a broken Coke machine on the second floor, looking down at the parking lot and Beckett's door. Around midnight, he had popped the cheap lock on the sticky wooden door and quietly checked around inside the room to make sure Beckett wasn't there, and he was now starting to wonder if the man was going to show up at all. Decent people were already in bed by three in the morning, and that's where Condor wanted to be, too. Huddled there in a black trenchcoat over his suit, he'd started to doze off a few times, but the creaking of bedsprings, moans, yells, and various animals noises that he heard through the walls had startled him awake each time. For making him sit out there in the cold, he would make sure Beckett died in a lot of pain when he shot him with the micro-Uzi automatic pistol that rested snugly inside his coat.

Although he'd expected Beckett to arrive in a car, he was relieved when the man finally showed up, on foot, keeping to the shadows along the wall as he walked past the office and on down to his room. Condor admired his caution. Even in the poor light downstairs, he could see by the man's stealthy walk that he was ready for an attack, and that meant that Condor would have to wait a little longer before he broke into the room. No problem. He'd never met anyone who could wake up fast enough from a sound sleep to dodge a bullet. The only issue for Condor would be the noise. He had a silencer on the gun, but if he took the time to shoot Beckett in the knees and other places before he finally killed him, the man would start screaming like a little girl, and it might be loud enough to draw unwanted attention, even in a dump like this.

Condor watched Beckett while he hesitated at the two doors before his own, trying the knobs as if he were drunk. When he stopped outside his own door, he glanced around to make sure no one would jump him from behind, fumbled around a bit, probably looking for his key, then went inside. The light didn't come on in the room, but that just meant he was still being careful. If he thought of blocking the door shut with a chair shoved under the doorknob, Condor would simply go through the window, which he had already unlocked from the inside on his previous visit. Condor wasn't going to lose his job just because his target was paranoid. Of course, if it occurred to the man to check his window locks before he went to sleep, then Condor would be screwed, but failure wasn't in his vocabulary and he preferred to maintain an optimistic attitude. He knew that his experience and training would pull him through, or at least keep him from getting whacked on one of his own hits.

With his hand inside his coat, Condor slowly made his way down the stairs, then ducked into the shadows along the walls and crept toward Beckett's door. This was the moment he lived for, when the adrenaline raced and put his nerves on alert just before the hit, anticipating success, ready for anything. He almost stumbled over a folded lawn chair propped outside the door to one of the rooms, but his finely-tuned reflexes kept him upright, and he caught the chair before it clattered to the concrete. Yes, he was ready now, and he would enjoy watching Beckett die.

He reached inside his coat and removed the gun, holding it high in the air in his right hand while he slowly turned the doorknob with his left, holding his breath, thinking positive thoughts. It was unlocked! Everything was going his way this time. Beckett was as good as dead.

When he entered the room, he was startled to find his target crouched over the bed going through his overnight bag in the dark. The man looked up, and Condor reacted with his professional reflexes, firing a burst that threw his target over the bed. He hit the wall on the other side with a satisfying thump, knocking a framed painting off the wall that slammed into the back of his head. The thump wouldn't draw any attention because the walls on both sides of the room were already resonating to the beds bumping against them, accompanied by a chorus of squeaking bedsprings and grunting noises. Grinning, Condor looked outside to make sure nobody had seen him, then shut the door halfway, still allowing a dim shaft of moonlight into the room from outside. He knelt beside the body with his gun ready to fire, but the crumpled figure wasn't breathing. Condor took off one glove and reached around to feel for a pulse at the man's neck, but he didn't have one. Dark fluid seeped from the exit wounds in his back where the soft-nosed nine-millimeter bullets had tumbled through him. He stood up before he got any of the blood on his clothes, stuffed the gun back into its holster, put his glove back on, then carefully locked the door and shut it on his way out.

Another job well done. His boss would be pleased.

Christian Enright – Chosen of Eternity, Bringer of Light, and Friend to All – smiled his trademarked smile, took a step forward, whistled through his nose, and punched Ed Beckett in the stomach.

Enright wore a white three-piece suit that nicely complemented his short blond hair and tanned complexion. His capped teeth were unnaturally white and large, almost glittering in one of the few shafts of early morning sunlight that had managed to squirm through the high canopy of the thick redwood trees and fall to the floor of the quiet forest. He was a big, athletic man in his mid-forties, and his chiseled face was known throughout the country due to his daily appearances on the Friendology Network cable channel, one of the many companies he owned that supported the good work of his Friendology empire. His main studio was in Huntington Beach, California, but each of the religious retreats that he operated had also been built with broadcast facilities so that he could tape his shows when he was on the road. The Santa Cruz Redwood Retreat was one of twenty-three luxury meditation centers that allowed his followers the chance to get away from it all and study the Friendly Teachings. Regular Friendology contributors with the largest donations were allowed to take up residence at the meditation centers, giving them the chance to study at the feet of Friend Enright during his visits.

Beckett grimaced and drew himself upright – fighting the pain in his stomach, his side, and his throbbing head – using the ropes that bound him to the redwood tree for support. So far, he had not enjoyed his experience at the Santa Cruz retreat, and meditation did not calm his mind. He tried to focus his eyes on the white Rolls-Royce parked nearby, but the waves of pain rolling back and forth through his body made it hard to concentrate. He'd spent much of the night in the trunk of the car, his head resting on the spare tire while he inhaled the odors of leather and gasoline, but his sleep had been sporadic, haunted by nightmares where somebody beat him up and locked him in the trunk of a car, then waking to find that the nightmare continued. Around sunrise, Enright had hauled him out of the trunk, tied him to the redwood tree, and removed the pillowcase from his head.

This was what he got for sleeping with Enright's wife, Nikki.

At least he didn't have to wonder who was following him around in the white Rolls any more. Or who was trying to kill him.

"You know," Beckett said, "I really expected you to be more of a talker. I've seen you babble for at least an hour straight on television."

Enright punched him in the stomach again, and his nose whistled when his fist made contact. "There are many paths to enlightenment, Mr. Beckett. Pain is one path, and vengeance is another. I give you the gift of mental clarity, administered by my hand, and my own spiritual awareness grows as a result. Words are unnecessary to make my point."

"So, you're saying that you feel good about beating me up," Beckett said through gritted teeth. Enright's whistling nose reminded him of the non-verbal messages he'd received on his home answering machine in Fountain Valley. "How did you find me, anyway? I know you followed me in the Rolls, but I didn't see you *everywhere* I went."

"I have many Friends," he said. "I sent out an alert to my flock with your name and description, and you eventually came across one of my followers. Celia Muerto, to be exact." Enright punched him again, then paused for a moment to take two snorts from a nasal inhaler he carried in his pocket. "Celia cared enough about you to call me. And I cared enough to bring you here and show you the shining path; to teach you the way of righteousness and honor. To know yourself through pain is to know the Eternal. After I liberate your negative energies, we can free your soul."

Beckett coughed. "I'd like to point out that Nikki was separated when we started dating. And she never wore a ring." He gasped and bent over as Enright slugged him again. The nylon rope that held him to the tree was smooth, but he could feel it biting into his flesh, cutting off the circulation in his arms, and his back was being rubbed raw by the rough bark.

Enright patted Beckett's head, then pulled his head back by his hair. His whistling nose was only inches away from Beckett's face, and his breath smelled of eggs and sausage. "Your unenlightened spirit may not be aware of it, Mr. Beckett, but I am your friend. Despite the wrongs you have committed against me, the heartache you have caused, and the darkness in your soul, I forgive you as one friend would forgive another."

Beckett smirked. "And that's why you've been trying to kill me? With friends like you, who needs enemies?" He winced as the big fist slammed into his midsection again, wondering why he couldn't stop himself from making remarks like that. The man was obviously nuts, and the best Beckett could do was to goad him on, hoping Enright would get bored and stop punching him. On the other hand, he had to wonder why Enright had switched to the direct approach, opting to beat him to death rather than watching while one of his followers killed him. Maybe the failed murder attempts had pushed Enright over the edge, forcing him to take the risk of killing Beckett himself to make sure the job was done right. And a beating was a more personal experience with a long tradition that probably felt more rewarding to a religious zealot.

Beckett heard a ringing sound in his ears, which was no big surprise, but he felt better when Enright pulled a cell phone out of his pocket and answered it. "Friend Enright." He listened a moment, studying Beckett's face with calm confidence, not displaying any anger or outrage that would have allowed Beckett to see him as human. Beckett's beating was simply another item on Enright's To-Do list for that day. "Okay, I'll be right there," he said. He turned off the cell phone and smiled at Beckett. "If you'll excuse me, I have to tape my show right now."

Beckett coughed. "No problem. Take your time. You need a break."

Enright punched him in the face, leaving several small cuts from his diamond rings, and walked off down the path, presumably toward the studio that Beckett couldn't see. With his tormentor gone, Beckett had time to reflect on his many injuries and on what a crappy week he was having. And the odds were against him surviving another day, according to his trusted Meatball. On the bright side, if Enright managed to kill him, at least he wouldn't have to worry about being arrested for the murder of Max Dumas.

He struggled against the ropes, trying to loosen them, but all he managed to do was get circulation back into his arms, which now tingled in a maddening way as blood flow was restored. He had to wonder, was the time he'd spent with Nikki worth this sort of abuse? He shrugged. Yes. If the circumstances had been different, he might even have married her. But there was a lesson here somewhere, and he thought it involved running background checks on any women he might meet just to make sure they weren't married.

When he heard footsteps on the path in the otherwise silent forest, he figured there had been some delay in taping Enright's show, so the man was coming back early to resume Beckett's pounding. It was a pleasant surprise when he saw an elderly man coming toward him with a small backpack and a fishing pole. He wore a plaid flannel shirt and waist-high wading boots that hung from suspenders. Fishing lures jingled on his straw hat, and he held a corncob pipe between his teeth. Beckett wondered if he was hallucinating a gray-haired Huckleberry Finn. His eyes bugged out when he saw the white Rolls-Royce. "Well, I'll be a pickled biscuit," he said. He reached out and touched the silver winged lady hood ornament – the Spirit of Ecstasy – with his index finger.

"Hi," Beckett said. He didn't want to startle the man.

Old Huck looked up at the sky, frowned, then looked around and spotted Beckett tied to the tree. "Eh?"

"Good morning."

Huck rubbed his eyes and took a few steps closer, squinting at Beckett. He jerked his thumb at the Rolls. "Nice little hot rod you got there."

So he didn't know it belonged to Enright, which was probably a good sign. "Could you help me out, here?"

Huck stepped a little closer, then frowned when he noticed the ropes. "What are you doing?"

"Trying to restrain my enthusiasm," Beckett said. "Do you have a knife?"

He cupped his hand to his ear. "Eh? Wife? No, I'm not married."

"*Knife*," Beckett said clearly.

"Knife?" Huck tipped his head and puffed on his pipe. "Of course I've got a knife." He reached into his backpack and withdrew a shiny Bowie knife with a twelve-inch blade.

"Great. Cut the rope." He squirmed a little bit to demonstrate his restraint.

"Gut the Pope?" Huck's eyes widened and he took a step back. "You high on goofballs or something? That why you tied yourself to a tree?"

"Look, I've got money. I'll pay you to cut me loose. Cash."

"Cash, is it? You need money to buy more goofballs? Well, you're barking up the wrong tree, mister."

Beckett wanted to scream. "Look, I've been kidnapped by a maniac in a white suit who tied me to this tree, and he wants to beat the crap out of me as soon as he's done taping his television show. I barely survived what could have been a plane crash yesterday, and some child in a pickup truck tried to kill me with a harpoon the day before that. I'm not having a good week here, so I'd really appreciate some help if it's not too much trouble." Having said all that, he suddenly realized that he sounded crazy. Now, Huck would probably run away to save himself.

"Well, why didn't you say so," Huck said, stepping forward to cut the ropes.

Beckett staggered away from the tree, rubbed his wrists, and took a few deep breaths before grabbing Huck's hand to shake it. "Thanks, pal. Thanks very much. Here." He reached into his back pocket and pulled out his wallet, then took all the cash – about forty bucks – and held it out to the old man.

Huck puffed on his pipe and stared at him. "What am I supposed to do with forty bucks?"

"Take it. It's all the cash that I have. Just my way of thanking you."

"Thanking me?" Huck raised one eyebrow. "According to you, I just saved your life. For forty bucks, I ought to tie you up to that tree again."

"Look, I appreciate your helping me, but unless you take credit cards, I really don't have anything else of value out here in the middle of nowhere."

With a wild look in his eyes, Huck gave him a crazy smile and nodded at the white Rolls.

Hyacinth Cummings felt creepy. Engaged in her new career as a stalker, she had followed Franz Todlich's black BMW from his house to the Mediterranean-style hotel, the Westin Palo Alto, trying to learn more about him as Ed Beckett had requested. At first, she thought Todlich might be meeting Celia Muerto there, but he trundled past the front desk without registering or asking for a key, then started up the stairs. Allowing enough distance so that he wouldn't spot her, she waited until he completed his slow and arduous climb to the first landing, panting all the way, then followed him. Dressed in a black, sixties-style suede leather miniskirt with fringe on the sides, and a matching top and vest, she smiled at the front desk clerk on her way past so that he wouldn't question her. On the top floor where the two-room suites were located, Todlich stopped by the open window at the end of the hallway and knocked on a door, where he was then admitted by a child wearing a black suit. Hyacinth looked around to make sure no one was watching her, and that there were no security cameras that might alert a guard, then crept down the hall to listen at the door. She heard the muffled voices of two men, but she couldn't understand what they were saying.

A room service tray on the floor held a coffee pot, two cups, two water glasses, and a half-eaten club sandwich. She picked up a water glass and held it to the door, then pressed her ear against the base of the glass. Unfortunately, all she could hear were the two muffled voices, but now they were echoing through the glass. She shrugged and put the glass back down on the tray, feeling a warm breeze through the open window. She looked out and saw a slanted red tile roof that overlooked the uninhabited pool area, although most of the pool was below her line of sight. Holding her shoes, she climbed through the window. The clay tiles were warm against her bare feet. She looked down toward the pool, but there was no one there to see her. Staying low to the roof in a crouch, she worked her way along Todlich's hotel room wall, keeping her right hand against the stucco while holding her shoes in her left. She gasped and dropped to all fours when one of the tiles came loose and rattled all the way down the roof, finally plunging over the side. Then she heard a *ploop* noise when the tile hit the water. She waited a moment, catching her breath as her heartbeat returned to normal. When she was satisfied that no one in the pool area had noticed the flying debris, she continued on her journey, testing each tile before she stepped on it. When she reached the edge of the roof, she held onto a downspout from the rain gutter and glanced around the corner at a small balcony with a white metal table and two chairs. The closed curtains billowed out through the open sliding glass door, and she could hear indistinct voices in the room. By this point, she figured she had probably gone to all this trouble to find out that Todlich was visiting his ex-wife and his young son, or something like that, and then she would probably fall off the roof. Beckett had asked her to do some weird things in the past, but even though he was a good friend as well as her employer, she planned to hit him up for a big bonus for this little escapade. She was a graphic artist, not a trapeze artist. But, what the hell, she needed the exercise, and it was kind of fun, in a way.

Sitting on the edge of the enclosed balcony, she stepped down on one of the chairs so she could reach the floor without making any noise. The neighboring balcony was obscured by a solid, waist-high wall, and curtains were billowing through that open door as well. She quickly moved past Todlich's open door, hoping they wouldn't see her shadow on the heavy curtains, and positioned herself by the opening.

"But I'm not interested in meeting your Russian friends," Todlich said. He sounded nervous.

"You don't get a choice," said another man. "They want everyone there tonight. Think of it as a progress report."

"I still don't see why – "

"Why? Because you're being paid an awful lot of money, that's why."

"I was paid to help you with Dumas, and that's all," Todlich said firmly. "Speaking of which, you still owe me the second half. I did my part."

"Well, your part isn't over yet. You'll get paid after Akimov pays me, and you'll show up for the meeting tonight at the blimp hangar. You got a problem with that, or does my assistant have to give you the Dumas treatment?"

Todlich hesitated. Hyacinth jumped as something brushed against her back. When she turned, she saw a calico cat standing on the low railing. "*Meow*," it said.

Hyacinth put her index finger to her lips and whispered. "Quiet."

"*Meow*," the cat insisted.

Worried that she would be discovered, she was about to shove the cat off the railing when a muscular man with shoulder-length brown hair and sunglasses stepped out on the neighboring balcony to look down at the rear garden. He looked like a weightlifter with way too many muscles. Although she couldn't see all the way down, he didn't appear to be wearing any clothes.

"*Meow*," said the cat.

The weightlifter glanced at Hyacinth, looking over the tops of his sunglasses, then smiled. "Heya."

Hyacinth smiled back, glancing worriedly at the open door beside her, wondering how she could escape with this meathead watching her. She started petting the cat to keep it quiet. It arched its back, happy to be there.

"Nice day," the weightlifter said. He had some kind of a New York accent. He reached his meaty paw across the gap to shake her hand. "I'm Arnold. Nice ta meetcha."

Arnold, she thought. Of course. She quickly shook his hand and grimaced.

"You here for the biotech conference?" he asked.

She shook her head and looked away, trying to hear what Todlich was saying without looking like she was eavesdropping.

Arnold leaned forward to look her over. He smiled again with his perfect teeth. "Ah. You here for the Miss Universe competition?"

She rolled her eyes, wishing he'd go away or explode. Then she heard footsteps coming toward the door, and a new voice saying, " – yeah, I'll check it out."

Not knowing what else to do, Hyacinth shoved the cat to one side and jumped over the railing to join the weightlifter, stumbling when she bounced off the table, then awkwardly slamming her head into Arnold's stomach. He grunted, but held onto her as he staggered against the railing, then her momentum knocked him down on his back. She scraped her knees on the balcony floor when they hit, but the rest of her body was padded by Arnold's chest. When she twisted her head around to look back, she saw the top of the kid's head coming through the door and out onto the balcony, too short to see over the railing.

"Whoa," gasped Arnold. He didn't seem angry, just surprised. "I had you figured as the quiet type."

"Hey," said the kid, whose voice seemed deeper than it should be. He shoved the cat off the railing and it dropped out of sight with a screech while he lifted himself up to peer over the edge. "What the hell are you two doing? Keep it down over there."

"Piss off, shorty," Arnold barked, pushing Hyacinth off his chest so that he could stand up.

"You piss off," said the little man, glaring at Arnold. "We're trying to have a meeting here, and you're out there screwing like rabbits."

Arnold walked over to the edge of the railing, leaving enough room so that Hyacinth could start crawling into the hotel room. "I eat little guys like you for breakfast," Arnold said.

"I'm not surprised," said the man. "But I shoot guys like you for lunch." He lifted a gun above the railing and pointed it at Arnold with his finger on the trigger.

On all fours, Hyacinth scurried under the curtains into the thickly carpeted bedroom of Arnold's suite, then bolted for the door. She'd learned enough. Graphic artists could take a lot of abuse, but "human target practice" wasn't in her job description. She'd wait for Todlich in her car. With her doors locked.

There was a little green park in Sunnyvale, just off Lockheed Way near the south end of the Moffett Field runway, an afterthought built by those who had created the nearby Blue Cube, protected from any children in the park by a high fence topped with razor wire. A small boy with black hair, about ten years old, stood with his hands on his hips, calculating the best way to climb the steel bars of the jungle gym. His mother was on her back in the grass reading a novel. On a wood bench nearby, Meatball Bronkowski stared into the monitor of his laptop computer, tapping on the keys with his beefy fingers, sweating in the hot afternoon sun. He looked up only when he saw the white Rolls-Royce stop in the parking lot. The front passenger door opened and Beckett stepped out. He spoke to the driver, an elderly man wearing a straw hat loaded with shiny fishing lures, then shut the door and smiled as the Rolls drove away.

"You have a chauffeur now?" Meatball asked when Beckett sat down beside him.

"Hitched a ride," Beckett said, not wanting to worry Meatball with the details of his adventures with Christian Enright. He knew Meatball wouldn't notice his bruises because he rarely looked Beckett in the face, and the tape around his stomach and ribs, applied during a brief stop at the hospital, was invisible under his shirt. "You come here often?"

"Nah. Don't like the sun, don't like noisy kids. But they wouldn't let you in there," he said, nodding his head at the main gate to the Blue Cube. He handed Beckett a sheet of lined paper covered with handwritten notes. "This is for you. Directions to Hangar One at Ames. Hyacinth wants you to meet her there."

Beckett peered at the note to make sure the handwriting was legible, then stuffed it into his shirt pocket. "What else you got for me?"

"I tried breaking into the Ames e-mail server. Found the files for Max Dumas, but the messages on the days you wanted had been deleted."

"Oh." Beckett's shoulders sagged. Another blind alley.

"But the Mars system administrator is a friend of mine," he said, typing on the keyboard.

"Mars?" He noticed that the laptop had an external Iridium satellite internet modem.

"Each computer center at Ames has its own servers tied to the local network, and each center is named after a planet. The network node for the Space Projects branch is Mars."

"Okay. So?"

"So my friend backs up the e-mail server every night, and he loaded the files you wanted onto a password-protected directory so I could take a look at them. Want to see?" He turned the laptop so that Beckett could see the screen.

Buried in among the junk mail, memos, jokes, and advertisements that Max Dumas had received, Beckett found a love note from Julie, an offer from Todlich to meet for breakfast in his office at five o'clock on the morning of Dumas's disappearance, and a brief note from Remy Descartes: "Dear Pig: Your affair with Julie, it must stop immediately. I protect what is mine. You are warned now. Stay away."

Descartes had sent the threat the night before Dumas's death.

But Todlich was probably the last person to see Dumas alive.

And someone had considered these e-mails important enough to delete them from Dumas's desktop computer. Apparently this person didn't take the time to hunt down the individual e-mail they were trying to erase, which would have been more subtle, so he – or she – just deleted every message that Dumas had received on the Sunday and Monday before his death. And he knew from his own attempt to use the desktop machine that anyone who used Dumas's computers needed to know his password, or know enough about him to guess what it was. The password was a variation on Max's birth date, and Julie had sent him the birthday card that Beckett had seen on Dumas's desk, but other co-workers probably knew his birth date as well, so that didn't help much.

Beckett checked the "Sent Messages" folder to see if Dumas had responded to Todlich's breakfast invitation. He hadn't, but Dumas could have called Todlich or spoken to him to accept the invitation. He took the page of folded notes out of his pocket and verified that "F.T." had been listed on the blackboard on the five o'clock portion of Dumas's schedule, followed by a meeting with Oberhaus at six, assuming the schedule he'd seen there had been for Dumas's last day at work. But Detective Daniels had told Beckett that the coroner found spaghetti in Dumas's stomach, which suggested that, unless he had very strange eating habits, breakfast was not his last meal. Unfortunately, it also neither proved nor disproved breakfast with Todlich. Or maybe the spaghetti didn't have any meaning at all, and he should forget starting a career as a detective. At any rate, he could try asking Astrid Dumas to see if she remembered what Max had eaten for dinner the night before his last flight, assuming she still wasn't mad at him. And he still needed to speak with Oberhaus to see if Dumas had shown up for their six o'clock meeting.

Beckett had seen the laptop computer case in Dumas's office, but the computer itself had been missing. Where had it gone? Anyone careful enough to delete e-mails on the desktop computer might also have stolen the laptop and disposed of it, but he'd have to keep an eye out for that as well.

Beckett saved the interesting e-mails to the hard disk on Meatball's computer, then handed it back to him for safekeeping. He could get them printed later when he presented all his evidence to Detective Daniels, who was probably wondering what Beckett was up to about now. With just a little more information, Beckett felt that he could uncover who had been directly responsible for the death of Max Dumas, why they had done it, and how.

Assuming, of course, that someone didn't kill him first.

ELEVEN

Equipped with a long-term visitor's permit arranged by Karl Ober-haus, the limousine carrying Tal Blackthorne had sailed smoothly through Gate Eighteen into Ames Research Center. Condor remained with the car while Tal walked off with his briefcase through the human-size door into Hangar One, the enormous white dirigible hangar built in 1931. The hangar's ceiling lights were on, giving the structure an unearthly glow in the darkness with shafts of brilliance shining up through the skylights in the domed black roof. When Tal stepped through the door, he had to stop for a moment for his brain to adjust to the size of the interior space. The floor area of the hangar was large enough to hold seven football fields, and the roof was two hundred feet above his head, curving in a graceful dome lined by skylights and supported by metal struts that criss-crossed the inner walls all the way down to the floor. Despite the concrete floor, there were few echoes in the vast chamber, so Tal had the feeling he was still outside. There were enclosed office spaces along the walls, but the empty eight-acre space was also big enough to be used by local hot air balloon enthusiasts for practicing takeoffs and landings. With the massive doors closed at both ends of the hangar, the tethered sixty-foot tall balloons were able to fly in a wind-free environment. In a weak moment, Oberhaus had given the balloonists permission to use the hangar once a month, and Tal had already argued with him about it.

The scale of everything seemed wrong, so Tal felt a slight sense of vertigo as he continued walking toward the offices. Oberhaus had told him on a previous visit that the offices all had roofs with small skylights because clouds would occasionally form under the high ceiling and a light mist would fall. As Tal looked around, he was thinking of how the space could be converted into a futuristic condominium development that climbed the walls and centered on a central garden in an open atrium. There were two smaller blimp hangars on the other side of the runways, but they were made out of wood and too dark inside to be used for housing. The rest of the base would be converted to single-family residences, and one set of plans allowed for retention of the runways if Tal determined that the upscale development would do better with its own airfield for private aircraft. Tal had already greased the skids to minimize any restrictions imposed by the environmental impact report, since he could clearly see that the wetlands at the north end of the runway would be a nuisance. With four of the six local planning commissioners now on his payroll, he anticipated an easy road through the city's bureaucracy so that he could build whatever he damn well pleased. So many possibilities. If the sneaky Russians didn't screw him over, this could be the largest and most profitable development project of his entire career. If Tal could successfully screw the American public out of this choice property in the middle of Silicon Valley, buying it for only a fraction of what it was worth, a grateful federal government might even award him a Congressional Medal of Freedom. He could almost imagine plucking the toupee off the president's shiny head during the award cere-mony, then dropping it on the head of one of the Secret Service guys who would certainly have tackled him by then.

When Karl Oberhaus stepped out of one of the offices to meet him, Tal saw that something was wrong. The director appeared to be frowning, as always, with his bushy eyebrows forming a "V" above his nose. A fringe of brown hair, streaked with gray, adorned the rim of his skull, and the bald top of his head reflected the light from the high ceiling. He wore a tailored dark blue Armani suit that did a reasonably good job of hiding the belly that wanted to peek out above his belt. He had a habit of shooting his cuffs when he was nervous, and he shot them repeatedly as Tal approached, warning him that something was wrong. Tal moved his briefcase to his left hand, smiled, and shook the man's cold hand.

Oberhaus paused to wipe his damp forehead with a white handkerchief. "I can't say I like your friends, Tal."

"General Akimov is here already?"

Oberhaus nodded. "Dr. Todlich is here, too, but they don't seem to have hit it off very well. For the last ten minutes, the general has had Franz's head in a hammerlock under his arm, asking all kinds of questions that the man can't seem to answer."

Tal sighed. "He's a weak link. We knew that when he took over from Dumas."

"It's too bad Max didn't understand the new goals for Ames. He spent all that time improving the IRIS system so that the mission would be a success. When I told him it had to fail so that we could shut down the research program at Ames, he actually yelled at me. At *me*! And we'd been friends for years. He took it all so personally. Scientists can be so shortsighted when it comes to political realities." Oberhaus looked at the floor and shook his head. "I tried to explain it to Max, but he refused to see the big picture. What a waste."

"This is no time to get sentimental," Tal said, trying to peer through the crack in the conference room door to see if Akimov was beating the crap out of Todlich. "If we show any weakness, Akimov and his pals will eat us alive."

"Yes, I'm sure you're right, but murder is such an *extreme* solution. I was quite fond of Max, you know."

"Fortunately, you're more fond of money. Don't let an attack of ethics ruin your retirement."

Oberhaus jerked as if he'd been punched in the face. "I'm only doing what's best for NASA and the space program."

"And your wallet."

Oberhaus harrumphed. "You'd better hope no one ever figures out that your assistant knocked off one of our scientists, even if he was clever about it, or the money won't help you."

Tal shrugged. "Ames is a dangerous place. Wind tunnels, experimental aircraft testing, all kinds of scary machinery – the place is a death trap. Dumas just happened to be in the wrong place at the wrong time. With the wrong attitude."

"I'd rather not talk about Max any more, if you don't mind."

"Just remember the money. Wealth beyond your wildest dreams. Now, let's not keep the general waiting."

Beckett lay on his stomach on the filthy roof of the conference room watching Oberhaus enter with a new arrival who had an air of self-confidence about him. The pills they'd given Beckett at the hospital had reduced the pain in his stomach to a dull ache, but he was still careful about his position when he stretched out. The left side of his face itched, still slightly swollen where Enright had punched him that morning. He edged forward a bit to get a better view of the whole room. The makeshift conference space had a bare concrete floor, a coffeemaker perched on a stool, a whiteboard, two long folding tables placed end-to-end, and several gray folding chairs jammed into the narrow space between the tables and the gray walls. A Russian general named Akimov sat at the table drinking from a tiny paper cup of coffee. Franz Todlich sat beside Akimov, smoothing his rumpled hair and rubbing his sore neck. Todlich's face was red and shiny with perspiration. Beckett didn't understand everything about Todlich's relationship to Akimov but, judging from their earlier conversation and the beating Todlich had received, it didn't appear to be a happy one. The closest table held a large architectural model showing the planned real estate development that would be built at Ames after the base was closed and vacated by the government. The model builders had taken the time to create an idyllic small town fantasy of detailed structures with homes, apartments, streets, gardens, stores, theaters, banks, streetlights, trees, dogs, and happy people waving to each other on the sidewalks. Hangar One, re-painted in pastel colors and hung with decorative lights, formed the centerpiece as a town hall and condominium complex with a soaring atrium.

Hyacinth was stretched out beside Beckett, peering down through the dirty skylight to watch the action. She had already updated him by whispering in his ear, which was a pleasant experience he wanted to repeat in the future. The flimsy roof material barely supported their weight, but they could hear through it quite clearly. As long as they avoided making noise by moving around too much, the attendees at the meeting would never know they were there. The noise of Akimov's altercation with Todlich had masked the sounds of Beckett's arrival, and the two men talking outside the conference room had fortunately not looked up during their conversation to see Beckett crawling overhead like a giant spider, but leaving again would be tricky if the meeting didn't break up soon.

Beckett checked his watch, noting that he had half an hour before he was supposed to meet Julie in the KAO hangar. Hyacinth had followed Todlich all day, finally ending up in Hangar One. From there, she had called Meatball on her cell phone with the information about this meeting, managing to position herself on the roof of the office before Akimov or Oberhaus showed up. Todlich had used the office before anyone arrived so that he could type up a status report on the IRIS mission. Although Hyacinth had not been able to read the monitor screen on Todlich's laptop computer, he had given Oberhaus a copy of the report when he arrived.

The Russian raised his arms and smiled magnanimously. "Ah, my good friend, Mr. Blackthorne. Good it is to see you again. I am explaining our plans to Doctor Todlich."

Todlich flinched when Akimov glanced at him.

"I heard. And you can call me Tal, general. Do you like the model of the development?" Tal gestured at the display on the table.

Akimov dismissed the elaborate model with an airy wave. "It is amusing toy for little girls with dolls. I am not little girl."

"I had noticed that," Tal sighed. He'd hoped the general would appreciate the progress they'd made in planning the development. "But the model is a very useful tool, general. Some people aren't as imaginative as you are. They don't see the possibilities unless we show it to them."

"Model is waste of time now. Bribes first, government announcement second, land purchase third, then girls can play with models."

"Yes, well, the bribes have been made, we have the planning commission on our side, and the government will announce the closing of the base very soon."

Akimov raised one of his massive eyebrows. "How soon?"

"Within weeks," Tal said. But Akimov didn't look pleased. "Days, maybe. It partially depends on when the IRIS project gets canceled." He looked at Todlich significantly to divert attention from himself.

Todlich flinched again when Akimov frowned at him. "Yes, I was discussing this with good doctor."

"I'm doing the best I can," Todlich said, edging away from Akimov. He was sweating like a pig. "I helped the little man get to Dumas. I've sabotaged equipment. And the plane almost crashed yesterday. I could have been killed."

Oberhaus showed his approval with a nod. "That was good, Franz. A crash would have shut us down for good. But I think you're missing the general's point. We don't want your best, we want your worst."

"It must be my accent," Akimov said with a mischievous gleam in his eyes. "People misunderstand me."

Tal cleared his throat and walked over to the coffee pot. "I'd like to point out that my assistant arranged the airplane mishap, not Todlich." He poured coffee into one of the tiny paper cups, then hunted around for a low calorie sweetener.

"I didn't mean to imply – " Todlich began. "Wait a minute!" He rose from his chair, his face red and trembling, his eyes wide as he shouted: "You're saying you tried to crash the KAO? With me on it?"

Akimov reached up with one enormous hand and pushed Todlich back down in his chair. With this reminder, Todlich contained himself immediately and flinched away from Akimov.

"You are not understanding," Akimov rumbled as his eyes pinned Todlich against the chair. "Much is at stake. Do not be selfish pig. Consider your comrades and their needs. Consider how your name would have been honored by your government if plane had crashed. Consider what I will personally do to you if you are not maintaining your silence."

Oberhaus sat down on the edge of the table to loom over Todlich, and he spoke with a reasonable, friendly tone of voice. "Franz, nobody wants to kill you. The KAO wasn't supposed to crash. But I do have to question your motives after the incident. You haven't explained who was responsible for getting the KAO repair arrangements made so quickly. Gil says you'll be ready to fly tomorrow, pending FAA clearance."

Todlich looked pale as he glanced at Akimov, then back to Oberhaus. "That wasn't me. That was the KAO crew. Blame them. They're the ones who keep that old bird in the air."

Oberhaus nodded. "Okay. But you do understand that the next mission must fail, right? We need headquarters to cancel this thing. If we wanted a success, we would have stuck with Dumas."

"Yes, I understand." Todlich nodded glumly and looked at his watch. "Are you done with me? I have another meeting."

Oberhaus looked at Akimov. "I think we're done with you, Franz."

Akimov dismissed Todlich with a wave, not even bothering to hide his disgust.

Tal finished stirring his coffee, took a sip of it, then spat it out in the garbage can. The cup quickly followed. Then the coffee pot went after it. "I'm just waiting on the closing of the base. Senator Greenbach already has the announcement drawn up, and he'll call me before he sends out the press release, but he's waiting on you guys."

With a grunt, Akimov lifted his ponderous weight out of the chair before aiming his blowtorch stare at Tal. "This is not all you wait for, my friend."

Tal looked puzzled. "What do you mean?"

"My secretary showed me interesting newspaper article. Body of Maxwell Dumas was discovered by this eyesighter."

"You mean an *eyewitness*," Oberhaus said.

"Yes. I am thanking you, director. In any case, this troubles me."

Tal shook his head, unconsciously taking a step backward when Akimov's eyes narrowed. "I took care of it, general."

"And how was this?"

"My assistant disposed of the threat."

"I did not hear of this," Akimov said, looking skeptical. "You are having proof?"

"Well, it just happened early this morning. It should make the news by tomorrow after someone finds the body."

On the roof, Beckett had a puzzled expression. It sounded like they were talking about him, but he didn't recall being murdered that morning, unless Christian Enright was in on this whole thing and there was some miscommunication as to whether he had killed Beckett or not. It didn't seem to make sense that Enright would be a real estate developer's assistant, but maybe he was branching out into new areas. This was all too confusing, and the pain pills weren't helping him think more clearly. He needed to talk to Detective Daniels, dump all the information in his lap, and let the police work it out. Assuming Daniels believed him, of course. But Beckett knew he needed to give the police more to work on than assumptions and guesswork. He needed evidence, or a confession, or something like that. And he still didn't have any idea how Dumas had ended up in a pool in Newport Beach, which was a little detail he was sure Daniels would want worked out.

Beckett looked at his watch. It was time to go meet Julie in the KAO hangar, and he could use Todlich's departure from the meeting to help mask the noise of his exit from the roof. He looked at Hyacinth, who smiled and gestured that she would remain there until the meeting was over. As Todlich clattered chairs around in his attempt to work his way out of the corner where he had been trapped by Akimov, Beckett stood up and stepped on a metal beam that jutted out from the hangar wall, then slid along it toward the wall where he could climb down the support struts to the floor and make his escape. The ten minute walk over to the KAO, following Todlich, would give him some time to think.

The runway was busy that evening. During his hike over to the KAO hangar, Beckett saw an ER-2 gently touch down at the end of the runway as if it were a fast-moving butterfly. An updated version of the U-2 spy planes built by Lockheed, the NASA ER-2, looking like one long jet engine with wings, was used for high-altitude atmospheric research. The two in-line "bicycle" wheels carried the weight of the aircraft until it slowed down. Extra weight would shorten the amount of time that the light jet could stay in the air, so the spindly-looking "pogo" auxiliary wheels in the middle of each wing were dropped when the aircraft lifted off from the runway. Beckett watched two Jeeps race along beside the narrow jet as it slowed down, then two men jumped out and attached the pogo wheels to the wings before it slowed down enough to flop over to one side.

Distracted by the frantic activity of the ER-2's landing team, Tau lost sight of Franz Todlich in the darkness. The man didn't seem very aware of his surroundings, so it had been easy to follow him from the old dirigible hangar along Zook Road, which ran parallel to the runway. Gusts of wind brought a whiff of rotting vegetation from the wetlands by the bay while the tall grass along the road waved in the breeze. A full moon coated everything with a blue patina of light.

Where the taxiway crossed the road, Beckett saw a sign that said, *Yield to Aircraft*. When he started across the taxiway and heard a big propeller chopping air to his left, he turned to see one of the white experimental helicopters stealthily creeping toward him just ten feet off the ground. Unlike other helicopters he'd seen, this one had stubby wings below two jet engines so that it could fly like a jet after the rotor blades lifted it into the air during takeoff. With ejection seats that fired straight up after explosives blew off the big rotor blades, the RSRA helicopter pilots liked to say that, in the event of an emergency where the crew of three had to bail out, they'd send the navigator first just to make sure that the blades were all gone. Beckett jogged a bit to get out of the approaching helicopter's path.

A few hundred yards ahead, he saw the KAO's white T-tail, marked with the NASA 714 call letters, sticking out of the brightly lit hangar. Something about it looked odd, but it took a moment for him to realize that the rear clamshell doors that had mysteriously disappeared on the last flight had now been replaced. The new doors were painted with camouflage colors, which made them stand out against the rest of the white aircraft.

When Beckett entered the rear of the hangar, one of the maintenance guys in white overalls blotched with grease was looking up at the closed clamshell doors. Julie and Celia were standing next to him drinking coffee and eating potato chips out of a big bag as if they were watching television. Celia brushed crumbs off her white t-shirt, which was labeled with the words, "Vacuum Sucks," and the potato particles continued their descent to her tight black jeans. Julie was wearing tennis shoes, blue jeans, and her NASA flight jacket – quite similar to the one Max Dumas had been wearing when he died.

"I think it looks funny," Celia said as Beckett approached.

"It was the best that Travis could do on short notice," said the maintenance man. He pulled the brim of his white baseball cap down lower over his eyes to hide his irritation. "We got a quick turnaround so we'd have a shot at the next Shuttle reentry."

Celia frowned. "Who's Travis?"

"Travis Air Force Base," Julie told her.

"Travis does the big repair work for us," said the maintenance man. "They have a fleet of C-141s up there, but they're all military. Everything's painted with camouflage colors."

"But it looks ugly," Celia complained. "Look at it."

The maintenance guy sighed and walked away.

Celia spotted Beckett. "Don't you think it looks ugly? Couldn't they take the time to paint it white?"

Beckett shrugged. "As long as it can fly, I'm sure the color doesn't matter."

Celia snorted and climbed up the passenger ladder behind the wing, taking the potato chips with her. Watching her go, Beckett's stomach grumbled, but the dull ache from Enright's beating had reduced his appetite. "What's with her?" he asked Julie.

"I don't know. Low blood sugar. Where have you been?"

"Looking for trouble."

"Looks like you found it." She moved closer to peer at the scratches on his face, and Beckett detected the scent of jasmine. "The life of a science writer must be more exciting than I thought. What happened?"

"Cut myself shaving. How are you feeling after yesterday's thrill ride?"

Julie sipped at her coffee and shrugged. "Not bad. It was kind of exciting, in a way. But I know we've got a great pilot, so that probably makes me feel more secure. He started by flying C-141s in and out of combat zones, and he flew NASA experiments through hurricanes with a DC-8, so he's got plenty of emergency experience."

He had to admire her attitude. "So you're ready to go up again?"

She brushed her blond hair back over her shoulders with one hand. "Tomorrow, if the FAA says the cargo doors are safe. If the weather cooperates, Houston wants to bring the Shuttle in on orbit 115, which is tomorrow morning. In that case, if they're going to land in Florida, we'll intercept them over the Gulf of Mexico. Otherwise, they'll land at Edwards in the wee hours of Sunday morning."

That didn't leave him much time. He wanted to tell her to cancel the next flight because he had no idea what the conspirators might do to the aircraft to ensure the mission's failure, but he had no proof to show her or the police. If he had to explain it to her without any evidence, he would, but he wanted solid facts so she wouldn't think he was a nut job. "Have you seen Todlich?"

"No, but he's usually with Celia. Why?"

"I just had a few questions for him. For the article."

Julie's violet eyes twinkled when she smiled. "I didn't think you'd come back after all the excitement, but I was hoping you would."

"You were?"

Celia poked her head out of the rear passenger door and waved. "Julie! Are you coming, or what? We're ready to run the test."

Julie touched Beckett's arm. "I have to go, but if you need a ride later, let me know. We should be done soon."

Beckett remembered that his harpooned rental car was still parked at the Jolly Knight. Meatball had dropped him off near Hangar One after their meeting in the park. "That would be great, Julie. Thanks."

She smiled and jogged away.

Beckett walked through the cavernous hangar and out the door on the other side, thinking Todlich might have gone to his office in the Space Projects building. A single streetlight illuminated the small parking lot, and he could see through the tinted windows of the building into the offices where the lights were on. Todlich's office faced the runway, so Beckett couldn't see his window from the front of the structure, but lights were on in two of the downstairs offices: one looked empty, but Remy Descartes's office was occupied. After making sure that no one was outside watching him, Beckett strolled behind the bushes that lined the front wall and spotted Descartes having an animated argument with a woman in his doorway who was wearing a long white dress – Astrid Dumas. It was obvious from Descartes's threatening e-mail that he hadn't liked Max Dumas, but what was Astrid doing here? Unfortunately, Beckett couldn't hear anything through the thick glass, as the windows had been designed to screen out the many loud noises from the runway and the nearby wind tunnels.

Returning to the front door, he found that it was locked, so he walked around to the west side of the building and discovered another locked door to the high bay, a former satellite testing facility. Wondering if he'd be able to get inside before Astrid left, he spotted one of the engineers leaving by the north exit, and got him to hold the door until he jogged up and darted inside.

"You know what I think?" Astrid said in a loud voice. "I think you were just using me, and that's why you haven't been over since Max was killed."

"Oh, don't be stupid," Descartes said with a voice full of contempt.

Beckett could hear their voices pretty well in the tiled hallway, but he quietly walked up to the corner and leaned up against the wall where they wouldn't be able to spot him if they stepped out of the office.

"Stupid? You're the one who stole Max's laptop computer, not me!"

"He didn't need it. He was already dead by then."

"And if the police showed up and found out you had his computer, who do you think would have been the number one murder suspect, genius?"

Descartes hesitated before responding in a lower voice. "The stupid American policemen, we have heard nothing from them. There is nothing to worry about."

"Well, they spent plenty of time with me, and you're just lucky no one saw you at my house."

Beckett peered around the corner, but he saw only Astrid's back in the doorway of Descartes's office. Then he suddenly heard soft footsteps approaching from behind.

"Ed? What are you doing?" Julie asked.

"Oh, hi." He straightened up and smiled at her. "I was looking for Todlich."

Julie frowned. "His office is at the other end of the building." She looked around the corner. "Is that Astrid?" Before Beckett could respond, Julie firmly took his arm and led him toward the exit where he'd come in. "I'll give you a ride home."

Julie had to steer her old Volvo around a knot of eight hookers standing in the driveway of the Friend Lee Motel so that she could park near Beckett's room.

"Tell me this isn't really where you're staying."

"It's cheap," Beckett said, thinking he should have just had Julie drop him off at his car in the Jolly Knight parking lot.

Beckett pointed and she pulled into a parking space. "How can you sleep here? Rough place. The neighbors don't worry you?"

"They have businesses to run, so they don't bother me." He blinked and leaned forward in his seat, trying to make out what was hanging across the door to his room. Then he frowned – it was yellow tape that said, "Police Line – Do Not Cross."

Julie saw it too. "You were saying?"

"Hang on a minute. I have to see what this is about," he said, climbing out of the car. He started toward the room, then changed his mind and walked over to the office.

Slap! Lee swatted the newspaper against the plywood counter to kill two flies who were on a date. Four more flies buzzed around the bare light bulb hanging over his head. He scratched under the arm of his stained t-shirt and looked at Beckett with a bored expression. "Yeah?"

"Why were the police in my room? There's tape all over the door." The linoleum floor crackled as he walked over to the desk.

"Police?" Lee asked. Then he recognized Beckett. "Jesus! You're back from the dead!" He dropped the newspaper, and his right arm disappeared under the counter. When it came out again, Lee aimed a shotgun at him.

"Hey," Beckett said, taking a step back. "I paid in advance."

"We don't allow that kind of thing in our rooms, pal. This here's a class joint." He reached under the cash register and pressed a button, or at least that's what it looked like from Beckett's side of the counter.

"What kind of thing? What are you talking about?"

Lee snorted. "And you was dumb enough to come back. You forget something? We thought it was you when we found it."

"Found what? You're not telling me anything!"

"The body. Like you don't know. Tried to fool me by registering with your real name, huh? You whacked some guy in your room so the cops would think you were dead. Well, it didn't work, pal. The cops'll be here any minute."

Beckett now understood what the real estate developer had been talking about with Todlich and the Russian. Enright, or someone else who worked with the real estate developer, had tried to kill him again, but they got the wrong person.

"Blood all over the damn place," Lee growled. "I get a rate from a crew that cleans up crime scenes, but the carpet and the bed are ruined. And you're gonna pay for it, pal. I'm not getting stuck with this one."

Beckett didn't know what to say. Somebody had died in his room, and it could have been him.

"I might even sue your ass," Lee said, waving the gun barrel in a circle. "Heard you was killed on the radio, and they gave the name of the motel. Thing like that is bad for business."

"I didn't kill anybody."

"Yeah, that's what everybody says. Problem ain't whacking somebody, it's hiding the body afterwards. That's how you amateurs always get caught. Especially when you go back to the scene of the crime like a moron."

Beckett didn't like the way this was going. If the police came, they'd end up talking to Detective Daniels in Newport Beach, and then he'd be toast. Too many deaths around one person tended to imply at least some degree of guilt, or at least that's what he'd think if he were a cop. Maybe he could get Julie's attention to distract Lee somehow? Maybe he could duck down low and bolt for the door before Lee took a shot?

His plans for escape suddenly vanished when the hookers in the drive-way scattered and a patrol car screeched into the parking lot.

TWELVE

The holding tank in the Santa Clara County Jail held four prisoners in addition to Ed Beckett. Escher Mobius was a wealthy twenty-two-year-old hacker who had been picked up for bringing down major websites with denial-of-service attacks, dressed all in black with his pants tucked into unlaced combat boots, glaring at everyone else in the cell. Emmett Wolverton, a fortyish engineer who worked for a major computer chip manufacturer, wearing a yellow pullover sweater and gray slacks, was accused of stealing a truckload of bagels from his employer. Hans Mellon, notable because of the swastika tattooed on his bald head, was in his mid-fifties, wore what appeared to be a German SS officer's uniform from World War II, and had been arrested for the clumsy embezzling of millions of dollars from the venture capital fund where he was a partner. Bronko Ludovic was a postal worker in his thirties who claimed, in broken English, that he had been framed for using his delivery truck to mow down eighteen pedestrians on a sidewalk before dumping a load of mail into the bay.

Except for the lack of Latino gang members and stockbrokers, this was pretty much the crowd that Beckett had expected to meet in a Silicon Valley jail. They were now engaged in a sort of impromptu group therapy session that was starting to make Beckett wish he had a cyanide pill hidden in one of his teeth.

"They must have been good bagels," Hans said to Emmett, whose face was buried in his hands.

"It wasn't about the bagels," Emmett mumbled. "It was about being treated like a cult member, being told what to think, being forced to eat bagels and coffee every Friday morning like some sort of sick variation on a Catholic mass. Were we eating the body and blood of the CEO who split the stock for our sins?"

"We call that 'team building' where I come from," Hans said. He spoke without any trace of a German accent, and sounded like he might be from Vermont.

Mobius spit on the floor. "What the hell would you know about it? Emmett displayed his individuality by showing The Man what he could do with his bagels. He didn't want to be stamped or numbered or filed, he just wanted to follow his own road."

"All roads lead to prison," Bronko said in a gloomy voice as he pointed his right index finger at the ceiling. "The government controls our minds through the US mail."

"Is that why you dumped all your mail in the bay?" Hans asked.

"The signals can't reach our minds from underwater," Bronko said with a nod.

"Hey, geek," Mobius said to Beckett, who was wondering if he could knock out one of his cellmates, switch clothes with him, and escape under a fake identity. Probably not, he decided. Then he realized Mobius was speaking to him. "You haven't told us why you're in stir with us."

Beckett raised an eyebrow at Mobius. "Did you really say, 'in stir'? Did you get that from an old Jimmy Cagney movie or something?"

Mobius spit on the floor again. "Don't change the subject. Why are you in here?"

"I killed a man just to watch him die," Beckett said. "I blew his head off in a motel room in East Palo Alto." He tried to make his eyes bore a hole in Mobius's forehead, but the skull was too thick for him to make a dent. "Then I ate him."

That made an impression. Beckett smiled inwardly while the rest of the inmates moved farther away from him. If he was going to be stuck in here, he figured he might as well establish his reputation early, although it was hard to believe that a room full of criminals would accept anything he said as the truth. Of course, they weren't very good criminals, which was why they were in jail in the first place.

"What's your name?" Emmett asked. He seemed suspicious.

"Edward Beckett."

Emmett frowned. "I heard you were dead. I was listening to the radio before they arrested me. They said somebody killed *you* in a cheap motel room in East Palo Alto."

"That's what I wanted everyone to think," Beckett said ominously.

However, his effort at gaining respect turned out to be unnecessary. A guard called his name, led him down the hall to a room where they gave him a brown envelope containing his wristwatch and wallet, then out through a series of locked doors to freedom.

Julie Ashbrook was waiting for him in a pool of light from the streetlamp when he staggered down the steps to the sidewalk. "Ed, are you all right?" She stepped forward and hugged him.

She felt good and she smelled nice. Beckett took a deep breath and looked up at the dark sky. "I am now. Did you pay my bail?"

"I was going to, but you seem to have a friend who pulled some strings to get you released."

"Who?"

"I don't know. Your guardian angel, I guess."

"Maybe so." He nodded, then gazed off into the distance. "You know, I lost track of the time in there, and it passes slowly when you're behind bars with vicious criminals, always watching your back, unable to relax for fear that someone will stick you with a shiv or pry the gold fillings out of your mouth. After a while, you forget what it's like on the outside, what a woman's touch feels like, what a child's laughter sounds like. How long was I in the big house?"

Julie gave him an odd look. "About an hour. Maybe less."

"Oh." Remembering the brown envelope in his hand, Beckett put on his watch and returned the wallet to his pants pocket. "What now? A jailbird like me can't go back to the scene of the crime without stirring up bad memories."

Julie took his arm and led him toward her Volvo parked at the curb. "You're staying at my place tonight."

"You wouldn't lie to an ex-con, would you?"

"Have I ever lied to you before?"

"How would I know?" And it was a good question.

She opened the car door for him. "Get in the car, perp."

Neither of them noticed the black limousine, parked half a block away, that pulled out to follow them.

In Beckett's dream, he was hanging onto the tall tail of the KAO as the massive four-engine jet plummeted toward the Carver's back yard pool in Newport Beach. The engines were on fire, streaming black smoke, but they smelled like coffee and donuts, which seemed odd. They were about to crash when someone touched his shoulder and he woke up. Julie was kneeling on the floor beside the couch, dressed only in a short red silk robe and white panties dotted with purple flowers, which was more than he was wearing. He picked up the sheet he had kicked off onto the floor during the night and subtly used it to cover himself.

"Good morning," she said brightly. Her hair brushed his forearm as she placed a hot cup of coffee in his hand. "Drink this. You'll feel better."

How could he not feel better after waking up to a sight like this? "Thanks. You're nice."

He rubbed his eyes, then glanced around at the simple white wicker furnishings, the heavily loaded bookcases where stuffed animals from *Bloom County* and *Winnie the Pooh* peeked out from between the hardbacks, the dirty dishes overflowing in the small kitchen sink, the *Air & Space*, *Smithsonian*, and *Aviation Week* magazines stacked haphazardly on the coffee table.

Julie smiled. "Toady called to say that the Shuttle reentry was scrubbed for this morning. There's a hurricane near the Cape, and rain at Edwards, so we have the day off."

"Oh?" He could use a day off, but he'd have to keep the investigation going, even though he'd like to spend more time with Julie. He sipped at the coffee, which was strong and good.

"Donut?" she asked, gesturing at the open cardboard box on the coffee table.

"Wow. The service here is much better than it was at the Friend Lee Motel."

"I would have made eggs or pancakes or something, but you wouldn't have liked the results. I didn't want you to think I was trying to poison you." She picked up a cream-filled éclair and bit into it.

Beckett picked up an apple fritter. "This is fine. Thanks for letting me stay here last night, and for picking me up at the jail, and everything else. How did you know that I love apple fritters?"

"I didn't. I bought a dozen assorted."

"Clever."

She stared at the fritter and sighed. "Max also preferred fritters, but he'd eat most any kind of donut as long as it didn't have too much mold on it." Her smile faded, and her eyes grew distant.

"Julie, you knew him pretty well, didn't you?"

She shrugged. "How well can we really know anyone? We were having an affair, but I'm sure you already figured that out for yourself." She pointed at the framed photo on the wall over the couch, showing Max Dumas with Julie on a white sand beach, similar to the photo that Beckett had found in Max's notebook hidden in his desk.

He sat up higher on the arm of the couch. "Was he worried about anything before he disappeared? Did anyone hate him enough to kill him?"

She took another bite of her éclair and chewed slowly. "You know Remy didn't like him. Neither did Astrid, really. Max said he and Astrid had slept in separate rooms for over a year before he met me. When Max found out that Remy and Astrid were having an affair, he didn't interfere, but he started seeing me. That was after my divorce from Remy, who still thinks he owns me or something, so he got jealous when he found out about Max."

"How did you get involved with someone like Remy?"

"I don't know. He was French, and he seemed so sophisticated with that smooth accent, and I was lonely. A lot of men get scared of my brain when they learn that I have a PhD in electrical engineering from MIT, but Remy didn't care because he's just as technical, and the French aren't intimidated by anyone. You know how it goes. He has his good qualities – it's just that they're buried so far under the bad qualities that it's hard to see them. All we ever talked about was work. Then I got drunk one weekend when we were in Las Vegas, and I woke up married to him on Monday."

"Do you think Remy was jealous enough to kill Max?"

Julie sipped at her coffee and almost snorted it through her nose. "Remy? He's all talk and no action. He might bark like a Doberman with a French accent, but he's really just a poodle."

Beckett couldn't help thinking of the other little dogs in his life, and he saw the similarities between them and Descartes. But the Frenchman's conversation with Astrid still nagged at him.

"Astrid seemed pretty broken up about Max's death when I spoke to her," Beckett said.

Julie smirked, wiping away a bit of cream that stuck to the side of her mouth. "Astrid may have been upset, but it wasn't because of any real affection for Max. It probably had more to do with the delay in Max's life insurance claim while they're investigating the cause of his death. And she's a pretty good actress. She has a degree in drama, and she performs with a little theatre group near Stanford. She got raves for her Lady Macbeth."

Beckett remembered that Astrid had been preparing a salad when he dropped by the house to interview her. And she might have seemed upset because she'd been chopping onions. "You have any idea why Remy would have taken Max's laptop computer?"

She didn't even have to think about it. "Because he got there first."

"What do you mean?"

"When someone quits, the vultures move in. Funding is tight, so our equipment budgets are limited. Our office computers are so old that if anyone leaves, we all rush in to see if we can get better hardware for ourselves. Kind of like a salvage operation."

"But Max didn't quit."

"No, and that's why his personal laptop was still around. So Remy got there first, and it probably had all kinds of useful IRIS project data on the hard disk that Remy could use. And I know Remy had borrowed it in the past." She paused, looking at him over the rim of her cup as she drank her coffee. "Can I ask you something?"

"Anything."

"You're not a science writer, are you?"

"Of course I am."

"Then prove it. What prompted you to pursue a career in science?"

"Mud pies and sex."

Julie blinked. "Okay, that's not the answer I expected. Why mud pies? I won't ask about the sex part; it sounds dirty."

"When I was five, and we still lived in Oklahoma, there were two eight-year-old girls who lived next door. They were twins: Donna and Danni Hogaboom. I've always liked older women. Anyway, like many females throughout my life, they enjoyed tormenting me."

She playfully poked him in the chest. "Let me guess. By making mud pies?"

Beckett shook his head. "They didn't just make them, they made me *eat* them."

"*Yech*. Did they hold you down and feed you?"

"No. They just told me to do it, and I did. I started to catch on over the next few days, so they started tricking me by saying they were chocolate pies, or by putting whipped cream on top. And they always made them in pie tins so they'd seem more authentic. Anyway, they used to roll around in the grass laughing while I'd eat an entire pie."

"Why did you keep doing it?"

He shrugged. "Why do people slow down on freeways to look at car accidents? I had some kind of sick fascination with the whole mud pie process. As I got older, and I started to wonder how girls operated, I tried to analyze my mud pie experiences: What was the psychology behind their manipulation of me – why did they feel the urge to do it, and more importantly, at least to me, why did I allow myself to be manipulated? Was there some mineral in the mud that my body craved? I approached each question with the same dedication and scientific commitment with which

Albert Einstein approached the theory of relativity. I even tried eating my own mud pies, but it just wasn't the same."

Julie plucked a plain raised donut out of the box. "What happened to Donna and Danni?"

"They went into marketing. For McDonald's, I think."

"So you wanted to become a scientist instead of a baker, but you couldn't decide which science you preferred."

"Something like that. I kept winning science fairs in school with projects like *What Mud Pies Are Made Of*, and *Fear of Pheromones*. Digging in the mud had given me the idea that I might like archaeology or paleontology, but I didn't like the idea of digging for the rest of my life, so I moved on to other natural sciences. I got into big trouble in a high school science fair because I built a nuclear reactor, even though it didn't work because they wouldn't allow radioactive isotopes on campus. I almost got expelled after the FBI showed up to interview me, but it all worked out in the end; my science teacher got me admitted to Stanford when I was fifteen." Looking into Julie's eyes, he was shocked to see that she didn't have the glazed expression he normally associated with women who asked for his life story. When he was out on a date and they were drinking, his date would normally pass out, or pretend to, before he was even finished talking about elementary school.

"Lisa went to Stanford, too," Julie said. "Were you in the electrical engineering program?"

"Among other things. I tried taking some career aptitude tests, but they basically said I could do almost anything that didn't involve team sports. Before they died, my parents had managed to put together a hefty educational fund, so I managed to stay in college and study different subjects until I was thirty. Stanford kept trying to make me graduate, but I couldn't decide what career I wanted. Some of my counselors said I lacked focus." He wanted to stop talking about himself, but she seemed interested, and he felt a need to tell her everything, maybe as a warning, before their relationship went any farther.

"So you became a science writer."

"I became a lot of things. I've even done some work for NASA. But yes, I'm a science writer at the moment."

"Okay, I believe you, but if you're Doctor Science, then why are you asking all these questions about Max's death? That's all you seem to talk about."

"It's a long story." She couldn't want more?

"I've got time."

He was ready to trust somebody, and he knew it would help to run some of his suspicions past her to see if she agreed with his conclusions. So he told her.

Beckett stood on the balcony outside Julie's apartment, looking down at a calm blue swimming pool that had caught a reflection of the orange dawn sky. The air was cool, but he wore one of Max Dumas's old sweaters that he'd borrowed from Julie. He had told Julie the truth about himself, and she hadn't thrown him out for deceiving her, if in fact he had ever managed to fool her. They were planning to spend the day together. Julie had a sailplane at a small airport in Fremont, so she was going to take Beckett for a ride over the bay before they went hiking in the hills. He knew there were other things he should probably be doing to further the investigation before tomorrow's KAO flight, and he needed to get an update on what else Hyacinth had learned by eavesdropping on the conversation in the hangar, but he was tired and needed a break. And Julie seemed pretty nice, so he wanted to take the opportunity to know her better before events forced him to leave again. He knew it was selfish, and short-sighted, but he felt he owed it to himself because he planned on having a life after the investigation was over and his life returned to normal – whatever that meant. As soon as Julie got out of the shower, they would leave.

When Beckett heard footsteps behind him, he thought Julie was approaching in her hiking boots, but then he heard the whistling nose of doom and turned around.

"Hello, sinner," said Christian Enright.

Before Beckett could reply, a large fist slammed into the left side of his face, accompanied by a particularly merry nose whistle, and someone turned the lights off.

When he woke up again, Beckett found himself in a pleasant setting that was disorienting. Instead of looking down at the blue swimming pool by the apartment building, he was gazing at a much larger pool, and this one had waves exploding against a rocky beach over one hundred feet below him. The high cliffs topped with scrubby grasses and a few cypress trees had been molded into streamlined shapes by the constant winds. They were all alone, just north of Santa Cruz, where the grassy hills rolled down to an abrupt ending above the ocean. Beckett knew that the Pacific Coast Highway was somewhere nearby, but it was obscured by tall grass and he couldn't hear any traffic noise because of the howling wind. The air smelled of salt. Seagulls buzzed the cliffs. A white Rolls-Royce sat nearby.

Beckett was tied to a tree. And his face hurt.

He looked at Christian Enright, who was smoking a pipe while he gazed out to sea. Still dressed in an immaculate white suit, he looked like an admiral remembering his days on the ocean, whistling an old sea shanty through his nose, even though the farthest he'd ever been away from shore was the middle of Newport Harbor on his fifty-foot yacht. A heavy rock sat on the edge of the cliff by his white shoes, and a rope connected Beckett's ankles to the rock's destiny.

"I see you got your car back," Beckett said.

"No, this is another one," Enright said, glancing at the Rolls. "I keep two at every airport where I travel."

"Of course."

"It's an image thing, you know. My followers expect it. They want me to live well."

"Certainly."

"The cars are all owned by the Friendly Corporation, so they don't cost me a thing. I love the tax code. What a great country."

"Yeah." Beckett nodded, tugging at the ropes around his body that dug into his sore stomach. "I'll have to try that sometime."

Enright threw his head back and laughed, pumping fragrant smoke out of his lungs and whistling like an excited football coach. The smoke dissipated quickly in the strong breeze. "That won't be necessary. You won't need a car where you're going."

"So you're finally going to kill me?" Beckett asked. "You're not going to beat me up first?"

"I think you've learned your lesson, Mr. Beckett. And your remorse over the entire affair is going to drive you to jump off this cliff into the sea."

"Well, I don't actually feel all that bad about it."

Enright placed one of his feet on the precariously balanced rock. "Yes, you do. I have a retreat full of my followers here in the redwoods, and they all heard you say how depressed you are, and how you felt suicidal at breakfast this morning."

"It's funny that I don't remember any of that."

"Yes, well, the important thing is that my followers remember, isn't it?" He took a switchblade out of his suit pocket and snapped it open.

"The man who was shtupping your wife commits suicide near your retreat after confessing everything. You don't think the police will find that suspicious?"

"Perhaps. But the local police chief and several of the officers on his staff are followers of mine, so I think they'll believe me when I say you showed up here begging forgiveness, then I forgave you in front of a room full of people. Unfortunately, no one stopped you from leaving the retreat despite your evident depression. And we feel real bad about that, too, Ed." Enright sawed at the ropes holding Beckett to the tree while keeping one foot ready on the rock. His nose whistled rhythmically with each cut.

"Nobody's going to wonder why I tied myself to a rock before jumping?"

"You don't know much about suicides, do you, Mr. Beckett? It's quite common for the serious suicide to do this sort of thing so he doesn't change his mind at the last moment. And you're a serious fellow."

As soon as the ropes were cut, Beckett planned on grabbing Enright. Either he'd get the knife and cut himself loose, or Enright would go over the edge along with him. He felt bad about the whole idea, but the leader of the Friendology cult wasn't giving him any choice in the matter. Besides, he wanted to get back and spend the day with Julie.

Beckett tensed as the ropes fell free.

Enright yelped and sailed over the cliff like he'd been shot out of a cannon. The mournful whistle from his nose receded into the distance. A cloud of dust followed him.

Beckett was startled, since he hadn't touched the man. And the wind was so noisy that he couldn't hear the body hit the rocks or the water, even though he listened for it. He didn't have time to watch him fall, because the switchblade had landed right next to his feet, and the rock was wobbling on the edge of the long drop. He started slicing at the rope like a lunatic, hoping the wind wouldn't shift and send him or the rock over too quickly.

Then he saw the front end of a limousine out of the corner of his eye; a small fact he had overlooked in his shock at seeing Enright sail through the air. And he saw the kid in the black suit get out of the driver's seat and wobble toward him. The kid who had fired the harpoon at him from the pickup truck. But it wasn't a kid, it was a very small man who was laughing so hard that he could barely walk. And he had a gun in his hand.

"Did you see that? Great hang time!" he cackled. "I love this job!"

Beckett frantically hacked at the last fibers of the rope while he pulled the end tight and lifted it a few inches, hoping it wouldn't overbalance before he was ready.

"Beckett, you're one of those guys who makes friends wherever you go, aren't you?" Tears ran down the man's face as he tried to control himself, raising the gun, but then he doubled over and laughed some more. "Everyone wants to kill you!"

The little man was so full of himself that he didn't see the rope. He tripped.

Beckett's switchblade sliced through the last strand and hit the dirt.

The rock went over the cliff, dragging the rope behind it. Beckett didn't wait to see the result; he turned and lunged toward the limo. He dropped into the driver's seat, but the engine was off; no key in the ignition. He spotted the white Rolls and sprinted for it, glancing around to make sure the little man with the gun wasn't racing to intercept him.

The Rolls started immediately. Enright had left the key in the ignition just as he had last time, unconcerned that someone might steal it. Then a bullet shattered the passenger side window, showering him with glass. The right rear door thumped when a slug tore into the metal.

As he drove off, Beckett got a brief glimpse of the little man's head and arms perched on the edge of the cliff with the gun gripped in one hand, waving wildly as if he wanted Beckett to come back and get shot.

But he wasn't laughing any more.

Erik Oberhaus's spacious office in the administration building was a simple affair: a standard gray metal desk faced two guest chairs and a round table that seated eight. On the other side of the room, three couches circled a glass table covered with aviation and space magazines. Except for the window behind the director's desk chair, which had a lovely view of a short strip of grass bounded by sidewalks and asphalt roads baking in the afternoon sun, the walls were covered with bookcases, on which a few aircraft and Space Shuttle models were displayed among the hardback books and project binders. To one side of the desk was the only high-tech piece of equipment in the room: A monstrous treadmill borrowed from the life sciences unit – they no longer needed it because astronauts and pilots were rarely tested at Ames any more. Even the enormous whirling centrifuges – which simulated the G-forces of rocket launches or high speed aircraft maneuvers – were now used only for special types of human physiological research, and as rides for visiting senators traveling with their girlfriends.

When Tal Blackthorne entered the director's office, he found Oberhaus dressed in a sweaty t-shirt and shorts while jogging on the treadmill. He was wired up to the heart monitor, which beeped happily at a steady rate and displayed the number of heartbeats per minute on an old analog dial. Since Oberhaus couldn't hear Tal when he sat down, Tal had to stand within smelling distance of the director to carry on a conversation. But this was a man who could make him a lot of money, so he was willing to put up with a few inconveniences until Ames was shut down and the man no longer held any power over Tal.

"What was that howling noise I heard outside?" Tal asked.

"They're running some tests this week in the big wind tunnel – the eighty by one-twenty." Oberhaus spoke in a relatively steady voice while his feet pounded the treadmill with the steady gait of a hamster on crack running in a wheel. "So, what's this I hear about your eyewitness coming back from the dead?"

Tal sighed and looked around the room for some form of alcohol he could drink, but there was nothing in view except a pitcher of yellowish water, which didn't look very appetizing. "I'm taking care of it right now. Kermit is swooping in for the kill, or so he tells me."

"How much does this eyewitness know?"

Tal wasn't about to tell Oberhaus that he had no idea how much the man actually knew, except that he'd spent enough time snooping around the KAO crew that he could probably put all the pieces together at any moment and blow their whole plan out of the water. "Enough to be dangerous, but not enough to put us away," he said reassuringly.

"The news on the radio said he was arrested for killing himself. They made a big joke out of it. Turns out someone killed a burglar in this guy's room, but they don't have any suspects at the moment. You wouldn't happen to know anything about that, would you, Tal?"

Tal shrugged. "Anybody who lives in East Palo Alto deserves what he gets, as far as I'm concerned. And that includes motel dwellers."

Oberhaus switched off the treadmill and slowed his pace until the belt stopped. The beeper went silent when he unclipped the heart monitor. Then he poured some of the iced yellow water into a glass and gulped it down while Tal watched. "Want some Gatorade?"

Tal smirked. "Not unless it has vodka in it."

Oberhaus gestured at the treadmill. "Your turn. You need some exercise."

"What?"

"Get up on the treadmill."

Tal flapped his suit coat at Oberhaus. "I will not. I'm not dressed for it."

"You want me to call Akimov? He hasn't called me, so I guess he hasn't heard the news yet."

Tal jumped up on the treadmill and switched it on to a slow speed so he could walk. Oberhaus stepped over to the speed control and cranked it higher so that Tal had to jog.

Oberhaus took a drink and watched until Tal started puffing. "Tal, old buddy, I'm curious as to why it's taking your assistant so long to take care of this problem. He's had days, and the man is still alive."

"The problem is that my assistant is an idiot," Tal said. There wasn't any point in lying about it, otherwise they'd attach more of the blame to Tal directly.

"You know, there were some marvelous rumors from headquarters after they heard that the KAO almost crashed yesterday."

"Really?" Tal loosened his tie.

"A KAO crash would be considered a spectacular failure. With everything else that's been happening here, and the general lack of research activity, I think a real crash would shut us down faster than you could say 'FAA investigation'. Not that I'd ever suggest such a thing, of course."

Tal awkwardly removed his suit coat. "I know. I already told my man to set some charges on the KAO when he gets back."

Oberhaus increased the speed control on the treadmill so that Tal had to sprint. Tal was breathing faster, although clearly not fast enough for Oberhaus, and the hair on his forehead was soaked with sweat in the stuffy office. "He's following the eyewitness?"

Tal sure hoped he was. Not all that surprised to learn that Beckett was still alive, he'd sent the apologetic Kermit to the jail facility as soon as he'd heard that Beckett had been arrested. Kermit followed the man back to the apartment of one of the women on the IRIS crew, so Tal had told him to wait for a better opportunity the next morning. "Kermit reported in from Santa Cruz, ready to punch the guy's ticket. If Kermit fails, I'll dispose of both of them myself."

"Good," Oberhaus said, cranking the speed control to maximum to make a point.

Tal yelped and flew off the back of the treadmill.

The sun was setting when Beckett parked the white Rolls-Royce in the small parking lot outside the Space Projects building, then spotted Julie walking across the street to the KAO hangar. He quickly hopped out of the car. "Hey! Julie!"

She turned as she opened the metal door to the hangar, frowned when she saw him, then continued through the doorway and slammed it shut. This subtle maneuver gave Beckett the impression that she was ticked off about his sudden disappearance from her apartment, so he jogged after her.

A refrigeration truck pulled into place near the telescope chamber when Beckett climbed the forward ladder just behind the raised flight deck. He wound his way to the right past the tiny restroom and the wide telescope chamber that seemed almost as wide as the fuselage, careful not to hook his foot on any of the cables that snaked across the floor, and finally popped out into the main cabin where Julie sat behind the IRIS hardware in back of the telescope's pressure bulkhead. Yoshi tinkered around with the hardware at the instrument pressure dome in back of the bent-Cassegrain focus while Lisa crouched beside him, her hands buried among the circuit boards and wires plugged into the back of the washing machine-sized IRIS instrument rack. Descartes stared at a monitor over his telescope operator's station where the IRIS tracker image showed a crosshair target moving around.

Beckett walked straight over to the back of Julie's seat and spoke quietly. "Sorry about disappearing from your apartment like that."

Lisa looked up over the rim of the instrument rack with both eyebrows raised, glancing back and forth at Beckett and Julie, but Julie didn't respond, continuing to type on the computer keyboard.

"I couldn't help it," Beckett said. "I wanted to stay, but I got tied up."

Julie pursed her lips and typed harder on the keyboard, nearly breaking the keys. "You don't need to explain anything to me."

"Yes, I do," Beckett said, crouching down so his mouth was near her right ear. "You remember I told you about Christian Enright? Well, he found me again."

That got her attention. Julie turned in her seat and looked at him directly for the first time. Her eyes went wide when she saw his partially swollen left eye and the big bruise on his cheek where Enright had punched him. "Are you okay?" She put her hand on his arm. "I thought you just changed your mind and ran away."

"I'm fine," Beckett said, tingling where her fingers touched his arm. "But Enright isn't so hot. The kid who was chasing me turned out to be a small man, and he ran over Enright with a limousine. Well, I guess he didn't run over him exactly, but he hit him with it, so Enright sailed off a cliff into the ocean."

"Oh, brother," Lisa mumbled, rolling her eyes before she crouched down behind the instrument rack again. Yoshi and Descartes weren't paying any attention to the conversation, and Beckett was trying to keep his voice low enough so that they couldn't hear him.

"That would explain the car you were driving," Julie said, rubbing his arm. "And what happened to the little man?"

"I left him in Santa Cruz, hanging off the edge of a cliff. I couldn't help him because he kept shooting at me."

"Did you call the police?"

"And tell them what I just told you? They'd put me away."

Julie nodded. "It does sound kind of fantastic. Maybe you could tone it down a little."

"I don't have much credibility with the authorities at the moment. All I can do now is figure out how Max died. I have an idea who did it, but I still don't know *how*. Can you go over everything you do to get the KAO ready during the last few hours before a mission?"

Julie shrugged. "We do what we're doing right now, which isn't all that dangerous."

"What else do you do to get the aircraft ready?"

Julie tapped her fingers on the console, thinking before she answered. "We take on fuel, of course. Other than that, we just get the telescope precooled and ready to go. But Remy could tell you more about that."

Beckett glanced at Descartes. "I don't want to bother him right now."

"It's okay. He's doing some calibration; nothing critical. Just talk to him about work, tell him how impressed you are with him, and he'll tell you everything he knows." She leaned over and lightly brushed her hand over his bruised cheek, then gently kissed the bruise. "To make it heal faster," she said. Her eyes sparkled.

Beckett sighed with pleasure, forgetting where he was for a moment, then blinked, smiled at Julie, cleared his throat, and turned his attention to getting information from Remy Descartes. Once again, Descartes seemed quite normal and enthusiastic when he discussed his job or the equipment on the KAO, and he ended up giving Beckett a detailed tour.

Outside in the hangar, Beckett followed Descartes up a metal stairway to the platform used for telescope maintenance. The rolling platform pressed snugly against the KAO's fuselage, its floor just a few feet below the open telescope cavity on the port side, just ahead of the top-mounted wing. From this vantage point, Beckett could look straight down into the telescope's thirty-six-inch primary mirror, and Descartes pointed out the small IRIS tracker used only for the Shuttle intercepts. The sliding cover door on the fuselage was open now, but the compartment would be precooled and sealed before takeoff, not to be opened again until they were at telescope operating altitudes, above most of the atmospheric water vapor, at thirty-nine-thousand feet or higher. A spoiler was raised before the chamber door opened in flight, damping the turbulence caused by the gaping square hole in the side of the aircraft.

When Descartes described how the refrigeration truck pumped super-cooled nitrogen into the telescope chamber to precool the optics before each flight, Beckett began to realize what had happened to Max Dumas. Beckett had fooled around with liquid nitrogen in the lab at Stanford, soaking flowers or pennies in the liquid before shattering them, so it didn't take a big logical leap to imagine what it could do to a human body.

"How long does it take to cool down the telescope before a flight?" Beckett asked. With a flight time of maybe an hour from Ames to Newport Beach, he was wondering how Dumas could have disappeared in the morning and ended up in the Carver swimming pool late that night.

"Hours. Many hours, depending on whether the aircraft is parked outside in the sun or inside the hangar. When we stage the IRIS missions out of Hawaii, the KAO must be parked in the sun in the hot climate, so the telescope, it takes longer to cool, you see? For our usual astronomy flights, or a night landing of the Shuttle when we're running a IRIS mission, we start the precool in the morning so it will be ready for takeoff after dark."

"Do you have many Shuttle landings at night?"

"Not many. The Shuttle, it was supposed to deorbit in the afternoon last time, but it got delayed into the evening. We were all here early in the morning, but we did not get off the ground until after sunset. That was a very long day for us, and we were short one person."

Beckett nodded. That was the flight Dumas had missed. "And you always do a precool before a flight?"

"Yes, unless we're just moving the aircraft to stage a mission from a different location. But if we're going to open the door and expose the telescope to the atmosphere, we must precool. The mirrors and the support structures, they would cool at different rates during the flight, warping the optics and degrading the image. And because the infrared emission from a star or a Space Shuttle must mix with the infrared radiation from the telescope mirrors, we get the cleaner signal by precooling the entire chamber and sealing off the cavity before the flight. The telescope, it is already at the working temperature when the chamber is exposed to the cold upper atmosphere. When the port is opened, the pressure difference allows the chamber to purge itself of any remaining nitrogen. Inside, behind the pressure bulkhead, we continue to breathe as if we were at nine thousand feet. You see?" Descartes answered his cell phone when it buzzed, then excused himself to jog down the stairs and dart back inside the aircraft.

And there it was, thought Beckett, leaning forward on the rim of the open telescope port, peering down at his reflection in the mirror several feet below. Somehow, probably unconscious, Max Dumas had been frozen inside the telescope chamber, never to wake up again. When the telescope port was opened at high altitude, the pressure difference had popped Dumas out into the sky like a beer can hurled out of a pickup truck. After a forty-thousand-foot plummet, Dumas's frozen body shattered when he struck the surface of the swimming pool in Newport Beach.

Beckett felt the platform vibrate beneath his feet, then something hit him in the back of the head. He pitched forward without blacking out entirely, but his muscles didn't want to respond to help him when his legs were lifted from behind and he dropped head-first into the telescope chamber. The weight of his body carried him down past most of the telescope's support structure, bashing a shoulder here and a hip bone there, until he found himself squashed in a heap with most of his torso under the primary mirror. He knew he probably hadn't even damaged any of the equipment. His head continued to spin for a moment before the blood pounding into his skull in his inverted position finally pushed him into the black pit of unconsciousness.

THIRTEEN

When Julie heard the buzzer on the telescope operator's console that announced the closing of the telescope port and the start of precooling, she was busy trying to figure out why the telescope's infrared array on the back of the pressure dome was heating up.

Descartes turned in his seat and looked at Julie. "The spike, you are seeing it?"

"Yes," Julie said, then she frowned. "Wait. The signal's returning to normal."

"Shall I cancel the precool?" Descartes asked.

Julie shook her head, not wanting to knock them off schedule without a solid reason. "No. It looks okay now. How's the telescope?"

Descartes turned back to study the monitors and readouts on his console. "Fine here. Everything was calibrated before we closed the port."

"False alarm, then," Julie said with a relieved sigh.

"Continuing the precool," Descartes said, settling back in his seat. Then he curiously glanced around the cabin. "Where's Beckett?"

Julie looked up. "I haven't seen him since you took him up to see the telescope."

Lisa stood up from behind the IRIS instrument rack. "Do you hear that? I heard a thump a few minutes ago, and now this."

Julie listened, but all she could hear was the hum and hiss of the refrigeration plant pumping liquid nitrogen out of the tanks and into the telescope chamber. But then she heard a tapping sound, and it sounded like it was coming from the telescope.

Yoshi straightened up beside Lisa and smiled. "It's just the chamber cooling down. The Invar support structure has a low thermal expansion coefficient, but the shock absorbers and the walls of the chamber are aluminum. Nothing to worry about."

Julie listened carefully. There seemed to be a pattern to the tapping sound, like Morse code, and she suddenly remembered the most basic message from her girl scout days. SOS. SOS. She jumped up out of her chair and shouted at Descartes. "Cancel the precool!"

"Why?" Descartes asked.

"Just do it! And open the port!" She rushed around the end of the IRIS instrument rack into the narrow passage between the telescope chamber and the restroom, then got down on her knees and yanked on the panel that allowed access to the bottom of the telescope.

"What are you doing?" Yoshi asked.

"Help me!" She tossed the cover panel aside, exposing the heavy release pins that protected the interior of the pressurized aircraft from the low pressure in the chamber at high altitude. While she cranked on one of the pins, Yoshi worked on the other one. Finally, they pulled the hatch free, and a rolling ground fog poured out of the chamber into the passage, chilling her legs. Yoshi switched on a flashlight so they could peer into the telescope cavity, and Julie almost screamed when she saw Ed Beckett staring back at her with his head upside-down.

"About time," Beckett croaked.

After watching the door slide open again over the telescope port, Condor climbed the platform a second time and peered down into the dimly lighted chamber inside the KAO. He frowned, distinctly remembering Beckett's feet sticking up along the edge of the telescope after his fall, but they were no longer in sight. He supposed Beckett's body might have slid farther under the telescope as the muscles in his unconscious body relaxed, but it still seemed odd. He knew Blackthorne was watching him from his safe perch on the high platform at the front of the KAO hangar, so he had to make sure that Beckett was in there, otherwise his boss was going to kill him. And he had no doubt that the crazy real estate developer would fly into enough of a rage to commit murder if he failed once more to kill Beckett.

All he had to do was get a closer look, which wasn't easy since the platform's height was apparently set for mutant telescope technicians over six feet tall. He hauled himself up to where he could balance his waist on the rim of the chamber, his legs dangling outside the fuselage, then he reached forward to place one hand on the telescope support so he could lean down inside.

That was when a buzzer sounded and the chamber door quickly slid shut, knocking him off his perch. The last thing he remembered was banging his head on a big metal strut while he fell down into the darkness.

Julie handed Beckett the bottle of aspirin from the first aid kit. He was seated in the mission director's chair at the left end of the telescope console. "You're sure that's all you want? I think you should lie down."

"I'll be fine," Beckett said, shaking four of the pills into his hand.

"You're only supposed to take two," she said, handing him a bottle of water.

Beckett shook two more pills into his palm, then popped all six into his mouth and swallowed. "This is a serious headache. And I have things to do." He rubbed the back of his neck. "I'm getting too old for this."

"Precool is back on schedule," Descartes said while he watched the falling temperature of the telescope chamber on his console.

Anxious to find the man who had tried to kill him, and to call Detective Daniels with his report, Beckett wobbled to his feet using the seat back for support. His head pounded in time with his heart. He'd have to get his head x-rayed when he was done using it, but he didn't have time for that now.

Julie shook her head. "Where do you think you're going?"

"Out for some air. Too stuffy in here," he said, starting toward the passage that led to the front exit.

Julie took his arm. "I'll go with you so you don't get into any more trouble."

"No, that's not necessary. You've got work to do. I'll be back in a few minutes."

"You're sure?" She looked skeptical when she released him.

"I'll be fine. Really." If someone didn't kill him before he called the police, he thought.

He took a couple of deep breaths on his way to the door, and that helped to clear his head, or perhaps the aspirin was working, he wasn't sure. When he started down the steep stairs, he heard a loud boom, like a truck backfiring, that echoed like thunder in the cavernous space of the hangar, and one of the lights high over his head exploded, showering hot glass down on Beckett and the plane. Hopping off the last step, he dodged under the KAO's wing to avoid most of it, then he saw Tal Blackthorne on his back about fifty feet away with an enormous shotgun at his side. His black suit coat was spread out under his back so that it looked like he had bat wings.

"Stay there a second!" Tal yelled, sitting up while he retrieved the shotgun that had knocked him down.

Beckett didn't wait. The man had a gun, and that was all he needed to know about him. He didn't see any good cover underneath the plane, so he sprinted for the hangar door, hoping to reach his car before Tal could get off another shot. The shotgun was an excellent motivator, so he forgot all about his headache, allowing the adrenaline to take effect, nearly flying across the hangar floor until he slammed through the door and out into the darkness of the parking lot.

He didn't slow as he ran across the empty street, but when he skidded to a halt beside the Rolls, the car rocked with his impact and he saw a digital timer starting a five second countdown on the floor below the passenger side of the dashboard. He knew the timer hadn't been there before, and his legs knew what it was before his brain worked it out. He turned and ran west into the tall grass by the parking lot, heading for the safety of the buildings across the small field, wondering why Tal hadn't yet followed him out of the KAO hangar.

Lightning struck behind him; a brilliant flash followed by a shock wave that knocked him off his feet, slamming him down into the dirt just before he reached the small side road that ran alongside the Navy warehouse building. Scorched chunks of the white car rained down into the grass, quickly starting a small fire, and he was up on his feet again before he realized it, running blindly for cover as he saw Tal step out of the KAO hangar door. Disoriented for a moment by the brightly burning Rolls, Tal didn't spot Beckett immediately, allowing him a head start past the Navy warehouse where a black limousine was parked. Beckett stopped quickly to look in the window, but the key wasn't in the ignition, and the door was locked.

He started sprinting again, his lungs screaming in pain, glancing back to see Tal running for the limousine, the monstrous shotgun swinging in one hand like a heavy spear. Beckett had never seen a shotgun that large, and he didn't want to find out what a blast from it would do to his body. While he ran, his heart beat faster and faster as he hunted for anything he could use as a weapon at close range if Tal gave him the opportunity to use it, but there was nothing, the place was impossibly clean, even along the fence that lined the junkyard to his right where old wind tunnel aircraft models rotted in the open air. He tried the front door of the next building, but it was locked on this Saturday evening. Up ahead loomed one of the massive silver wind tunnel facilities, howling like a hurricane, its deafening force routed by the tunnel walls to thunder over the body of some aircraft they were testing, and the fact that they were using it meant that people were inside, people who would be able to call the police and get him some help.

The wind tunnel became his goal. A boxy center structure with two funnels on each side of it, each one at least one hundred feet tall and surrounded by a spidery support structure of open struts, seemed to be the entrance to the rectangular tunnel ring that occupied three blocks of the research facility. But he didn't know if he would reach it. While the howl of the wind tunnel grew louder at his approach, the roar of the limousine engine grew louder behind him, ready to run him down if he stayed on the road much longer, and his legs were weakening, and his heart was pounding, and he thought his head would explode if the shotgun didn't get to it first.

He stumbled at the curb on Arnold Avenue, almost to the wind tunnel entrance, still trying to suck enough air into his screaming lungs. Rolling on the grass, he saw the limousine slew sideways right behind him and smack the curb, rocking the body hard and slamming Tal's head against the driver's side window. Beckett hoped it would slow him down, but he couldn't count on it. He lurched to his feet, knowing he wouldn't be able to run much longer, his stomach recoiling at the prospect of more physical effort. His clothes were soaked with sweat, and his hands felt clammy, which couldn't be a good thing, but he wasn't going to sit there and get shot after he'd come so far.

The tinted glass door was unlocked. He pushed through into a dimly lighted space. The walls rumbled with the thunder of the captive wind, but the roar seemed to be slowly dying down. A door to a big room filled with tools and aircraft parts on workbenches lay ahead, but the door was locked. The big elevator would be too slow. He blinked the sweat out of his eyes and spotted a staircase going up, and Tal running toward the front door with his shotgun, his suit coat flapping behind his back.

Up the stairs, two at a time, he climbed two flights and reached a locked office door. Back on the stairs, his legs shaking with the effort, listening to the sound of Tal's running below, he went up two more flights and burst into a small lobby outside a glassed-in control room. An overhead monitor showed some kind of fighter jet model, a detailed silver metal form without paint or decorative markings, supported twenty feet above the wind tunnel floor on two upright poles. Trying to catch his breath, Beckett staggered into the control room where two men stood at a large control panel looking out through a thick glass window into the wind tunnel itself where spotlights illuminated the model about forty feet away. The six fans that could produce wind speeds of over two hundred miles per hour were out of view in the darkness on the other side of the big funnel to his left. To his right, the funnel expanded into another dark cavern.

Beckett realized he was trapped. The two men were staring at him as he heard Tal run into the lobby. When Beckett turned to look at Tal, the two men jumped up when they saw Tal's shotgun.

"Call the police," Beckett croaked, unlocking the airlock door that separated the control room from the wind tunnel.

"You can't go in there!" yelled one of the men while the other one grabbed his phone.

Beckett slammed the door behind him, then stared at the wind tunnel hatch on the opposite side of the airlock. It was like a submarine hatch, or a vault door, with a wheel that had to be cranked to withdraw the pins around the rim before it could be opened.

He started cranking.

When the door flew open behind him, he hauled on the wind tunnel hatch and tripped on the knee-knocker ledge as he jumped through into a strong breeze. The howl of the wind had died down considerably, giving him a chance, but he didn't know which way to go. He scrabbled under the hatch to get behind it, then saw the shotgun barrel coming through. Without thinking, he bumped the door against Tal and grabbed the barrel with his right hand, then jumped back when the explosion came, blowing a hole in the wing of the model high above the floor. He kicked under the door and managed to trip Tal as he came through, then used the weight of the door to smash him away from the opening. While Tal was still off-balance, turning with the shotgun, Beckett lurched back into the airlock and slammed the hatch, cranking the wheel to lock it shut while Tal slammed his fists on the other side as if Beckett might reconsider and let him in.

When Beckett burst back into the control room, only one of the men was still there. And they weren't out of danger yet.

"Turn it back on!" Beckett yelled. He'd do it himself if he knew how. "Turn the fans on!"

The man pointed through the observing window. "Are you nuts? There's someone in there!"

Beckett glanced at the man's red photo ID badge, which identified him as Oliver Kelly. "Look, Oliver – " he growled, but he didn't have to say anything else.

Tal appeared on the other side of the observing window with his shotgun raised. Wide-eyed, Oliver ducked under the control console when Tal fired the gun. Beckett heard the thunderous boom through the wall. The powerful shot broke through one layer of the thick glass and starred the second layer.

"Turn it on!" Beckett yelled, hauling Oliver to his feet. "Blow him away!"

Shaking, Oliver slapped three of the six switches that controlled the forty-foot-diameter, six thousand horsepower fans, then twisted the adjacent control knobs. When he and Beckett looked up at the window again, Tal was getting to his feet after being knocked on his back by the shotgun's recoil. The fans were humming back up to speed. Tal's hair and clothing began to flap in the strong breeze as he staggered, raising the shotgun for another blast at the window, trying to remain upright.

"More!" Beckett yelled at Oliver. "This is too slow!"

The wavering shotgun fired again while the wind howled, and Beckett covered his face with his arms to avoid the shower of glass from one corner of the window while the walls trembled with the roaring hurricane wind. When he put his arms down, he saw Oliver lying on his back with blood on his chest, and Tal staggering toward the broken window again to take another shot.

Repeating what he'd seen Oliver do, Beckett slapped the other three fan switches and cranked their control knobs to maximum, ducking under the control console just as Tal's shotgun boomed again, blowing a hole in the ceiling over Beckett's head and showering him with powdery chunks of acoustic tile. The wind howled like a demon, tugging at Beckett's hair and sucking loose papers through the hole in the window like the explosive decompression he'd witnessed on the KAO. Beckett peeked over the console just in time to see Tal stagger sideways, grabbing at the hole in the window to steady himself, a panicked look on his face, letting the shotgun sail away on the wind before he was finally lifted like a leaf to fly away into the darkness.

FOURTEEN

"I can explain," Beckett said, wondering how he could possibly explain hurling Tal Blackthorne through a wind tunnel in a two-hundred-mile-per-hour wind.

"Oh, this should be good," rumbled Detective Daniels. "And you hadn't better be wasting my time after I came all the way up here so early on a Sunday morning, or you won't be seeing daylight for at least thirty years."

Beckett was back at the Santa Clara County Jail in an interrogation room with a mirror on one wall and a long table where he sat on one side and Moses Daniels towered over him on the other. If Daniels wasn't stooped over, Beckett was sure that he'd be rubbing his bald head against the fluorescent lights on the ceiling. He was dressed as Beckett had seen him in Newport Beach, with a stiff white shirt and a blood red tie complementing the dark blue suit on his athletic frame. A county jail official visitor's badge dangled from his shirt pocket. And he didn't look happy.

The Moffett Field military police had turned Beckett over to the Sunnyvale police, and Beckett had spent a restful night in a roomy private cell in the medical ward of the county jail, but when Detective Daniels arrived, he suddenly had priority over the other cops, even though he was from out of town. Beckett didn't understand that, but he thought it might be a good thing. The local cops had not been impressed with his fantastic story in any case. So he tried to fill Daniels in on the rest of the background, having already covered the other details about his investigation into Max Dumas's unusual demise. Although he'd left out the part about Christian Enright stalking him.

"Okay, then what?" Daniels asked. His voice suddenly sounded less demanding.

"Then here we are," Beckett said. "The police arrested me, I might have a concussion, I hurt all over, I'm hungry, and you're here interrogating me."

Daniels shook his head and sat down. He looked tired. "You tell a good story, Beckett."

"I try."

"And it just happens to agree with parts of the story I got from Dr. Ashbrook and some of the others on the KAO crew."

"What about Tal Blackthorne?"

"He's pretty banged up, but he confessed. We have an APB out on Dr. Oberhaus, who seems to have mysteriously vanished. Blackthorne has a good lawyer, he's rich, and he's a respected member of the community, so he's been released on bail for cooperating with the investigation."

Beckett jumped up from his chair. "He's been *what*?"

Daniels motioned for him to sit down. "Take it easy. He's not going any place where I can't find him. And these rich guys always think they can beat us in court. Sometimes they do. But I'm betting that Blackthorne didn't tell us everything, and Oberhaus will cut a deal to keep himself out of prison, assuming we can find the director, of course."

"But he blew a hole in Oliver, that guy at the wind tunnel. Couldn't you keep him behind bars for that?"

Daniels shook his head. "Mr. Kelly is fine. He just got hit with glass from the shotgun blast, and he fainted. The hospital already released him."

Beckett knew Daniels worked in mysterious ways, and at this point he wasn't going to push it by demanding Blackthorne's head. "Hey, did you ever find out who that guy was that I was supposed to have killed at the Friend Lee Motel?"

"Ah, yes, another of your victims. There are so many, I'll have to check my files." Daniels consulted one of the manila folders in the stack he was carrying. "His name was Chris Warden. About your height and weight, age forty, small-time hood working his way up the petty crime ladder. Ironically, he graduated to burglaries in cheap motels just in time to get whacked."

"Who killed him?"

"You did."

Beckett couldn't tell by the detective's expression whether or not he was serious. "I don't remember doing that."

"Amnesia. I've seen it before in serial killers. You can't face up to the dark side of your nature, so you block it out of your mind."

"You sound so rational, I'm starting to believe you."

"It's the badge. Gives me credibility. I can make up all kinds of stuff and get people to buy into it."

"You don't really think I killed this Warden guy, do you?"

Daniels smiled. "No. But I had you going there for a minute, didn't I? Couldn't help myself. The power trip thing is the dark side of *my* nature."

Something was bothering Beckett's exhausted brain, but he had to think a moment before he could dredge the problem to the surface. "What happened to Franz Todlich? Did you find him?"

"We're still looking. But there's an APB out for him, and the locals have his house staked out, so I'm sure he'll turn up soon."

Tal Blackthorne was making good use of the liquor cabinet in the back of the limousine, hoping large quantities of alcohol would help dull the various pains in his battered body. He'd spent ten minutes in the dark stuck to a metal grille that kept flying debris from damaging the enormous wind tunnel fans, and he was happy to be alive after his flying lesson, but he'd been unable to sleep in the prison hospital ward overnight because of the nightmares.

The Russian chauffeur didn't seem to speak much English, but Tal knew Dimitri Akimov had sent the car for him, just as he had sent the high-powered attorney to gain his release from the county jail. He wasn't sure where the chauffeur was taking him to meet the general, but they had already passed through the city of San Francisco and were now well on their way across the Golden Gate Bridge. It was about seven o'clock in the morning, and the city was buried under its usual layer of summer fog. Across the bay to the east, Oakland basked in the sunlight. To the north, the coastal hills of Marin County held back the fog, seemingly aware that Marin residents paid higher property taxes so that they could control the weather. Overhead, the two rusty red towers of the Golden Gate Bridge were wrapped in cotton, but the updrafts kept the fog away from the road. Two hundred and twenty feet below, the swift gray waters of the outgoing tide carried an Asian freighter out to sea, its cargo holds weighted down with stolen computer chips packed in cartons of cigarettes. In the middle of the bay, Alcatraz Island sparkled in the sun, but Tal didn't want to think about prisons right now.

When they reached the middle of the bridge, the limousine slowed even though there was very little traffic. When Tal spotted the massive General Akimov leaning against the railing to look out at the bay like a tourist, he understood that this was to be the meeting place. A good idea, since it was relatively private at this hour, but Tal didn't think his suit coat was heavy enough to protect him from the chilly breeze. With any luck, he wouldn't be out there very long. He sighed and stepped out of the limo.

As the icy fingers of the wind blew straight through the fabric of his suit, Tal crossed his arms across his chest and kept his hands under his armpits while he walked over to stand by the general. Akimov scowled at the water, seemingly oblivious to Tal's approach, as the updrafts whistled through his bushy eyebrows. Tal wondered if the two shrubs above the general's eyes were large enough to keep his forehead warm. Wearing only his usual tailored brown suit, he seemed unaffected by the cold.

"Thanks for sending your attorney," Tal ventured. "I couldn't sleep in the prison hospital."

"Not to worry, my good friend," Akimov boomed. "You'll have plenty of chance for resting with this matter concluded."

"Yeah," Tal said with a half-smile. "Sorry about the way it turned out. I guess you heard the details already."

"I received full report from attorney. And from Oberhaus."

It bothered Tal that the general still wasn't looking at him. The man seemed fascinated by the decaying prison on Alcatraz. "You spoke to Oberhaus? Where is he?"

"He was here ten minutes ago, but he is in safe place now."

"Ah. Better if I don't know so I don't have to lie to the police, eh?"

Akimov nodded slightly. "*Da*. Is true. Have you visited this Alcatraz?"

"No. Can we continue this conversation in the car?" He looked back and discovered that the limo had already left, probably so it wouldn't attract attention.

Akimov ignored the suggestion. "Man named John Paul Scott was only prisoner who survived freezing swim from Alcatraz. Over a mile if swimming is done straight to city. In 1962, boys found Scott on rocks at Fort Point under this bridge. Boys thought Scott was unsuccessful bridge jumper suicide, so they called police, and police returned him to prison. So ironic. Sounds like good Russian story." He laughed briefly, but it was an unpleasant sound, like a bass drum being beaten with a dead cat.

Tal didn't even bother to smile. He was freezing his balls off, and he wanted the general to get to the point so they could get out of there. "Fascinating, general. I wasn't aware that you knew so much about the history of San Francisco."

"I took Alcatraz tour on boat yesterday. Did you see this Clint Eastwood movie, *Escape from Alcatraz*?"

Tal was almost ready to tell Akimov to piss off, but he'd already done enough to make him mad. In fact, he was surprised that the Russian had taken the failure of the project so well. "No. I didn't see it."

"Is good movie. Clint Eastwood is brilliant actor. But tour guide says was all fiction, men in water drowned and swept into sea, impossible to recover. I believe this."

"Yeah, it's pretty cold out here. Even colder in the water, I bet."

"But I am curious man. I am wanting to confirm theory." He turned and looked at Tal for the first time during their conversation, and his stern fatherly gaze made Tal feel a little better.

"And how is that, general?" He tried to keep his voice steady, but his teeth were chattering.

Akimov smiled. "You will experiment."

Tal was shocked. For such a big man, Akimov could really move fast. By the time he figured out what the general was getting at, Akimov had already lobbed him over the railing of the bridge. For the second time in twenty-four hours, he found himself flying.

About halfway down to the deadly cold water, Tal Blackthorne remembered to scream.

After arranging Beckett's release from the county jail, Detective Daniels gave him a ride back to the KAO hangar, parking at a red curb near the door. Across the street, Beckett noted that the remains of the white Rolls-Royce had been cleared away so well that he almost thought he had imagined the explosion. But the blackened dirt in the small field remained as a mute witness to the grass fire.

Daniels climbed out of the rented Malibu and gestured at the smoldering field. "Wherever you go, trouble follows."

"Not to put too fine a point on it, follow me," Beckett said, walking toward the hangar door. He was hoping to catch Julie before the KAO took off on its Shuttle intercept mission at nine o'clock, and it was already eight-thirty. Daniels wanted to talk to the IRIS crew to get more leads on where they might be able to find Todlich or Oberhaus.

The question was answered when Beckett pulled the door open. Todlich had apparently seen him coming, and he was waiting behind the door with a heavy red fire extinguisher, which he threw at Beckett's head. Beckett managed to avoid most of the blow by ducking to one side, but the canister hit his left shoulder with a dull thump and knocked him down. Oblivious to Detective Daniels, Todlich had already picked up a second extinguisher to drop on Beckett's head when Daniels pointed a gun at his face from fifteen feet away.

"Police!" Daniels yelled. "Drop it!"

"That was my plan!" Todlich yelled back, unimpressed by the gun or thinking the detective wouldn't use it, quickly raising the canister for a killing blow.

Daniels fired once, hitting Todlich in the left side. The big man staggered back two steps, then dropped the heavy fire extinguisher on his own head, where it rang like a gong before crashing to the floor. Todlich's back hit the wall of the hallway, and he slid down to a sitting position with his eyes closed.

"I'm really getting tired of this," Beckett said, groaning as he got up on his hands and knees. "I feel like a cat who's supposed to have nine lives, and I'm already working on life number thirteen."

"It's better than being a dead cat," Daniels said, helping Beckett stand up.

"Can't swing a dead cat around here without hitting a murderer," Beckett said, unwilling to lose this word game to a detective, even if he had saved his life and pulled the strings to get him released from jail twice.

"When the cat's away, the mice will play," said the detective, holstering his gun.

Beckett leaned against the open door. "Curiosity killed the cat."

Daniels stooped to check the unconscious Todlich's minor bullet wound. "Dr. Todlich looks like something the cat dragged in."

Beckett had run out of cat sayings. He shrugged, then rubbed his aching shoulder.

"What's the matter?" Daniels asked. "Cat got your tongue?"

Beckett suddenly remembered why he was there. He turned and quickly walked down the hallway into the KAO hangar, but the plane had already been pushed out onto the tarmac to face the taxiway. With the clamshell doors closed, the gleaming white C-141 looked like it had a camouflaged butt. The refrigeration truck was gone and the fuel truck was driving away, but the engines were off and the passenger stairway was still open ahead of the wing. He started toward the stairway, then stopped when he heard voices behind him where people were coming out of the pre-flight briefing room.

When Julie saw Beckett, she dropped her oxygen mask, headset, blanket, and notebooks on the hangar floor and ran toward him. He caught her in his arms, then winced and realized his mistake as his damaged body screamed in response when she hugged him. But he didn't want to let go.

She put her mouth to his ear and whispered one word with her hot breath: "Spaghetti."

"What?"

"A while back, you asked me to find out from Toady what he and Max had for breakfast the morning that Max disappeared. Toady had forgotten about the meeting, so when Max showed up at his office early in the morning, he served leftover spaghetti from dinner the night before."

"Thanks," Beckett said. The information didn't really matter now, but he could tell Daniels that Dumas's last meal with Todlich matched up with the contents of the corpse's stomach at the autopsy.

The rest of the IRIS crew waved as they filed past on their way to the aircraft, and Beckett grimaced at them.

"We have a lot to talk about," Julie said, holding him out at arm's length. "But I have to go right now. The Shuttle's going to deorbit this morning and land in Florida. Dinner tonight?"

"Sounds good to me," Beckett said with a goofy smile, wishing he could stand up straight without screaming. "But you'll have to drive. One of my cars blew up, and the other one has a harpoon in it."

She kissed him and jogged to the KAO, where the others had already boarded and the engines were thundering to life. He felt that he could really get to like this woman.

Just before ten o'clock that morning, the Kuiper Airborne Observatory made an easterly turn over Catalina Island to head for the Gulf of Mexico on an intercept course with the Space Shuttle. Although the KAO was flying at forty-one thousand feet, the air was clear enough so that the flight crew could see all the way down to the ground, and they were able to see the numerous marinas in Newport Bay as they crossed the California coastline.

At that moment, responding to a command from Dr. Julie Ashbrook, the new project manager, Remy Descartes punched the button on his console that raised the spoiler and opened the outer door over the telescope chamber.

As the door slid back, a brief hiss of nitrogen gas shot out of the chamber into the thin air of the stratosphere, accompanied by the small, frozen body of Kermit Busby.

It was the last flight of the Condor.

THE END

For more information, and **to sign up for the newsletter**, please visit https://brucebalfour.com/

Author's Note

Thanks for reading. I have played with time a little bit in this novel. While NASA-Ames Research Center is still operating, it is located at the former Naval Air Station Moffett Field, which was closed and turned over to NASA in 1994.

The NASA Gerard P. Kuiper Airborne Observatory (KAO), a modified Lockheed C-141A Starlifter with a 36-inch infrared telescope mounted in it, was retired in 1995 after 20 years in service as a platform for infrared astronomy. It was the only civilian version of the C-141 and had originally been configured by Lockheed as a demonstrator for a potential civilian passenger jet. The telescope chamber was cooled by liquid nitrogen on the ground so that condensation would not form on the telescope when the chamber door was opened above 41,000 feet (above most of the water vapor in the atmosphere). The first photo below shows the KAO in flight with the door open over the telescope chamber.

About the Author

Bruce Balfour, PhD, is the national bestselling author of *The Forge of Mars* (Ace Books) and its sequel, *The Digital Dead*. You can find the full list of his novels, computer games, and comic books on his website as noted below. He also writes under the pen name of B.J. Balfour, but that's a secret, so don't tell anybody.

Bruce has never been an FBI agent or a serial killer, but he has held a high-level security clearance and has worked with FBI, CIA, DEA, and Secret Service agents in his former life at Sandia National Laboratories (a federal national security laboratory).

Bruce also worked for NASA-Ames Research Center in the 1980s, where he spent part of his time flying on the high-altitude C-141 Kuiper Airborne Observatory (KAO) as computer operator for the Infrared Imagery of Shuttle (IRIS) experiment to intercept the Space Shuttle on re-entry. He does not recall killing anyone with liquid nitrogen while he was there.

Bruce lives north of Phoenix, Arizona with his wife and a fierce Chihuahua named Bug.

For more information, and **to sign up for the newsletter**, please visit https://brucebalfour.com/